# SUNBURNT COUNTRY

AUSTRALIAN SUPERNATURAL - BOOK TWO

NICOLE R. TAYLOR

Sunburnt Country (Australian Supernatural - Book Two) by Nicole R. Taylor

Copyright © 2020-21 by Nicole R. Taylor

All rights reserved.

**This book is written in British/AU English.**

No part of this book may be reproduced in any form or by any electronic or mechanical means, including information storage and retrieval systems, without written permission from the author, except for the use of brief quotations in a book review.

www.nicolertaylorwrites.com

**Cover Design:** Covers by Juan

**Edited by:** Silvia Curry

# AUTHOR NOTE

The author would like to acknowledge the Traditional Custodians of country throughout Australia and their connections to land, sea and community. She pays her deepest respect to the elders past and present and extends that respect to all Aboriginal and Torres Strait Islander peoples today.

All representations of Indigenous Australians are used fictitiously and neither represent persons who live or have died.

For more information on Reconciliation in Australia, please visit:
https://www.reconciliation.org.au/what-is-reconciliation/

*I love a sunburnt country,*
*A land of sweeping plains,*
*Of ragged mountain ranges,*
*Of droughts and flooding rains.*

**'My Country' by Dorothea Mackellar**

# PROLOGUE

Coen lounged underneath the great boab tree, watching the dusting of stars that made up the single long arm of the Milky Way.

A large, grey kangaroo sat beside him, her whiskers twitching as she pawed at the joey in her pouch. Long, spindly legs peeking out the top was the only glimpse Coen had of the baby, but he didn't mind. The joey was warm inside, nestled close to his mother's belly.

Just underneath the Southern Cross constellation was the head of the emu—a dark cloud of stars at the tip of the Milky Way. He stretched all the way across the horizon, his body forming through the dust lanes of the great arm of the galaxy. It was already summer, so the emu had faded with the Earth's rotation, but he would reappear soon enough. The sky spoke to Coen, so he knew.

The kangaroo and the crocodile lived in the Milky Way too, and many other things besides. The whirlwind spirit white fellas called the willy willy, warriors travelling their own paths, and ancient memory sailing through the streams of the Dreaming. Coen knew the dark spaces between were more important to his people than the stars themselves.

As an Indigenous Australian, Coen was connected to the land in more ways than even the supernatural people of Solace.

More than Kyne, who's magic spoke to the earth. More than Eloise, who's elemental ability allowed her to see the threads that bound the physical world to the Dreaming. And Vera, who's arcane witch energy was connected to all things. Wally O'Brien's werewolf was too wild to be tamed, so he wasn't able to see anything. Then there was Hardy, who's vampire nature allowed him to walk in life as the dead—his understanding of the invisible was only learned through time.

Perhaps out of all of them, Drew was the one who could see more than he understood. His dingo spirit walked the paths of the Dreaming, bringing him close to Coen and the *marlu*—an Indigenous word meaning 'kangaroo'. The land called, and so the dingo ran like lightning.

Coen stroked the *marlu's* head as he read the signs in the sky. The emu would soon disappear, the turning of the Earth moving Solace away from the dark core of the galaxy.

The stars held more than stories and spirits from the Dreaming. They carried messages to and fro that spoke of warnings and tidings. White fellas called them omens—*prophecy*—but to Coen, they were always changing, ever moving. Nothing was set in stone until it had happened.

The stars he saw that night...they were flowing through the rivers of the Dreaming as they dipped below the horizon.

"Trouble approaches, *Marlu*," he murmured. "But we knew that. See?" He pointed to the sky and the kangaroo gazed upward. "The emu sets, but he is chased by the lawman. He comes for the swagman's tucker bag as the emu rests at the billabong."

He grinned as he thought of Eloise Hart and her shiny white van. Wally had fixed it, but it had never left Solace.

The *marlu* looked at him, her big brown eyes full of questions.

"Don't worry," Coen told her. "I will watch as I always have. They know what to do."

As summer came, the emu in the sky would land, settling by the billabong that was full of spring rain. He would look after everything that lived there, from the animals to the people, taking the shape of a rare black emu bird. When the wet approached, he would take flight once more.

This, he knew.

# CHAPTER 1

Eloise Hart sat on the step of her motorhome and looked out over Solace.

It was a bright and clear day, the heat of the sun baking the iconic red dirt of the Australian outback, and the sky shone a blue so brilliant, it hurt her eyes.

As she listened to the faint sounds of construction, she could hardly believe it'd been a mere three weeks since her van had broken down on the outskirts of Solace.

Wally, the town mechanic and resident werewolf, had finished replacing the damaged head gasket that morning. Eloise had wasted no time jumping in the cab and driving over to her new plot, keen to get settled. Nestled in a copse of gum trees, she had an elevated view of the town below.

Curling her hands around her cup of tea, her thoughts ran away from her.

Solace was a tiny mining town in outback New

South Wales, a few kilometres south of the Queensland border. It was a 'blink and you'll miss it' kind of place, with few buildings and even fewer residents. The highway cut straight through the middle, bringing the massive road trains—hulking trucks towing three trailers—to the remote parts of the country they were famous for.

The land was rich in silica, which over millions of years, had transformed into glittering opal. It formed in the dried up ancient coral reef and river systems, which was the prehistoric legacy of the dry centre of this part of Australia. The most precious opal of all was black opal, and it was found right there in Solace.

The problem was, opal was difficult to mine and only the bravest and hardiest remained to hunt for the precious treasure hidden deep in the earth. The people who lived in Solace were some of them. They called themselves the Exiles, supernatural outcasts who'd banded together to create a home where they could be open about who they really were.

*The Outpost*, aka the general store, was run by Vera, the Irish witch who supplied food and everything but the kitchen sink to all who needed it. Hardy, the vampire, was the local opal buyer, who cut and polished the precious stone in his workshop in the back. Blue owned the pub at the southern end of the strip, and he was the only human amongst the supernaturals. Wally looked after the garage, serving as the mechanic and supplier of precious fuel—the second most important outback lifeline, the first being water. Drew, the dingo shifter, was the last arrival before Eloise, and he worked at the *Outpost*.

Then there were the fae—a half dozen of them—who lived just outside of town. Finn was their leader and the only one who ventured into Solace. Eloise had never met them, and if she hadn't seen them from a distance, she would've wondered if they existed at all.

Coen was an Indigenous man, mysterious and deeply spiritual. He appeared when he wanted and not a moment before. His best friend was a kangaroo, otherwise known as a *marlu* in the language of his mob. There was no one way to describe who he was and what he could do. Coen was on a walkabout—a spiritual journey through the Dreaming.

Finally, Kyne Brady was the most special of all. To Eloise, he was more than just a romantic fling and the leader of the Exiles. His talents lay in the earth, mining the rare black opal, aided by his supernatural heritage. He was an elemental, just like her, and it was their shared power that helped him lead her out of her lonely, painful life on the road and into a world where she was accepted for who she was—an elemental who could connect with ether, the element that bound everything and everyone together.

Solace was a beautiful and magical place, and Eloise had quickly fallen for everything and everyone —even Finn and his famously sour attitude.

But Solace had a secret.

Underneath the boab tree at the northern end of town was an entrance to an old mineshaft. Through the twisting tunnels dug by opal miners of old, lay an ancient cave which held a dangerous and unknown magical power. The Exiles called it the seal, and that's exactly what it was.

What was trapped underneath it was open for interpretation, but Eloise knew it was bad. When she'd met Andante—the old woman who lived amongst the rivers of the Dreaming—she'd told her about the heart of the ocean and what would happen if the seal was ever opened. The word she'd used was 'calamity'.

Eloise shivered and drank the last of her tea, draining the dregs in her cup. When they'd found out there was a key, that calamity had a real chance of being unleashed, but she'd stopped it. She'd used her elemental powers to make the Dust Dogs—the pack of dingo shifter bikers who wanted to take the seal by force—disappear without a trace.

Shivering again, Eloise dumped her empty cup into the sink and closed the door to her motorhome. The heavy metal ran across the runners with a whizz, then banged shut. The town and seal were both safe for now, but more would come looking for it. And when they did, the Exiles had to be ready.

Walking across the road that led up from Solace, she ventured up the ridge to where Kyne and Drew were busy building.

They were renovating an old dugout that sat on some of Kyne's land behind Solace. It'd once been a mine that buried back into the ridge, but sometime in the last twenty years someone had turned it into a makeshift home.

Most of the houses in Solace were underground—the coolest place to be in the middle of the blistering outback summer. According to Wally, the highest temperature they'd recorded, since someone decided it was best to write these things down, was fifty-two degrees Celsius. It was hot enough to cook a steak on the highway. Well done, too.

Eloise had arrived on the tail end of the wet season, and now the days were beginning to heat up. She hoped the air conditioner Kyne had ordered for her motorhome would be delivered soon. She didn't want to cook like that steak.

Materials and tools littered the clearing outside the dugout, and sawdust showered over Drew as he fired up the circular saw and sliced through a length of wood. What they were building was a mystery, but they'd already made short work of the demolition. Junk lay in a heap to one side where Kyne's ute was parked, a trailer hitched to the tow bar.

"No work on today?" Kyne asked as she lingered in the shade.

"Hardy's out for today," she told them. Her elemental powers had made her a natural at cutting and polishing opal, so she'd become Hardy's new apprentice. "He went to do a sweep of the Dust Dogs camp."

Drew frowned. He turned back to the workbench and began to measure out another piece of wood so he didn't have to say anything.

Eloise glanced at Kyne, who shrugged.

"Probably the best thing to do," the elemental said. "We don't need any more nasty surprises. At least not right away."

She looked at the shifter. "You all right, Drew?"

He glanced over his shoulder and nodded, his blond hair falling into his eyes. Then he went back to measuring.

She couldn't blame him for avoiding the whole thing. The Dust Dogs were responsible for the death of his pack. He was the only survivor but had unknowingly fallen in with the bikers. He'd stolen the key from them when he found out how bad they truly were, but it wasn't until he'd gone back to stop them from coming to Solace that he'd discovered the truth. Eloise hadn't made things easier by allowing him to kill the alpha Roth and disappearing the rest. Drew was now the alpha of a pack who may or may not come back one day...providing they were still in the same world.

*Time*, Eloise thought. *It'd take time for him to come to terms with what'd happened.*

"Can I help with anything?" she asked. "I know

stuff all about building, but I'm an elemental. That counts for something, hey?"

Kyne laughed and shook his head. "It's not the same thing."

"Why not?"

Drew looked over his shoulder again. "Is she really asking?"

Eloise pouted and crossed her arms over her chest. *"Yes, she's really asking."*

"Because hammering a nail is different than making a nail," Kyne told her with a chuckle. "Unless you can use ether to put everything where it needs to go."

Eloise sighed. "That's inconvenient."

"Magic has rules, just like everything else."

"*Lame*," she drawled. Drew laughed and she grinned at him. "Can I see the plans?"

The shifter nodded and tossed her a notebook. Catching it, she ran her gaze over the rudimentary drawings, which were messy and made no sense.

"Well," she declared, turning the book this way and that. "The lack of artistry suggests you need an interior decorator."

Drew glanced at Kyne. "Is she offering?"

"I think so," the elemental replied.

"I can draw," she told them. Looking down the hill into the centre of town, she spotted the rusty windmill and the water tank beside it. "Actually, I've got an idea."

"Here we go," Drew muttered.

But Eloise wasn't listening. Setting the plans back on the workbench, she waved at the men. "I'll see you later."

"Where is she going?" Drew asked.

"Best not to ask," Kyne replied.

"I heard that!" Eloise shouted.

"See you at dinner, then?" the elemental called.

"Nah, yeah, see you there!" She placed a hand on the crown of her hat and ran down the hill, her boots kicking up dust as she went.

Man, did she have an idea.

---

Hardy stood on the rise above the Dust Dogs abandoned camp, watching and waiting.

The shifter pack had settled on the far outskirts of an outback cattle station—Walawala Station—using the remote property line to their advantage. Some of these places were thousands of hectares of open country and rarely walked by the station hands who tended the livestock, but Hardy didn't think it was a coincidence. How they could've gone unnoticed long enough to build a camp this large was an impossibility.

A dozen buildings made up the bulk of the settlement, all of them a patchwork of wood, corrugated iron, and even two rusted caravans. He spotted several water tanks, a rusted-out car, piles of junk, and what looked like discarded machine parts.

The wind stirred, carrying the scent of rust and human habitation towards him. He curled his nose. This wasn't going to be pleasant.

Satisfied that no one was lingering, Hardy made his way down the hill and into the camp.

The place was rough, with many of the buildings ramshackle at best. He hadn't expected a five-star resort, but the Dust Dogs had seemed to have spent more time looking after their motorcycles than their sleeping arrangements. The pristine garage full of tools and equipment was a glaring indicator of the shifters' pride.

Glancing at a portable generator, he wondered if he could bring some of the gear back to Solace but disregarded the idea. The last thing the Exiles needed was to have any link to this place. Eventually someone would come looking for the pack, and the first place they'd ask questions was Solace.

His boots kicked up red dirt as he moved through the camp, peering through windows and opening doors with a bandana wrapped around his hand. Fingerprints were also another thing not worth leaving behind.

Opening the door to the largest building, Hardy stuck his head inside. It stunk of sweat, dried blood, and stale alcohol. Recoiling, he lingered outside in the fresh air.

Yeah, the Dust Dogs weren't big believers in basic hygiene.

Edging his way inside, he looked around, narrowing his eyes at the piles of dirty dishes in the sink. With no one around, the food scraps stuck to the plates had begun to turn, and he didn't dare open the fridge. The power was out, and that made it a recipe for disaster.

His vampire eyes scanned the room, falling on a table in the centre of the kitchen. It was covered in papers and he began to rifle through them.

There were too many questions left unanswered for his liking. How did Roth get his hands on the key? More to the point, how did they know about the seal? They couldn't live out here without some kind of income, so how were they making money? There weren't a lot of prospects in this part of the outback, and he couldn't see them becoming cattle rustlers, even if they were dingo shifters. The expanse of empty land was far too great for it to be profitable.

Picking up an official-looking letter, Hardy's frown deepened.

*Dear Mr. Moody,*

*Further to our conversation regarding the possible permissions of lease, please find enclosed documents outlining the results of our recent geological survey, as is required by state and federal law.*

*With your permission, we would like to set up a*

A mining company was interested in digging near Solace? *EarthBore* was a large-scale operation with several multi-million-dollar open cut mines across the outback. They dug iron ore, not opal. What it could mean for the town, Hardy didn't know, but he knew disturbing the earth so close to the seal couldn't be good.

He rummaged through the papers, finding maps, geological surveys, and copies of mining licenses... including Kyne's. Frowning, Hardy scooped up the documents and shoved them into his bag.

Why the Dust Dogs were interested in mining was beyond him. The letter was addressed to Moody, who was the station owner. As far as Hardy knew, the guy knew nothing about the pack. The main buildings, including the residence, were hundreds of kilometres away across the border.

Searching the rest of Roth's place, Hardy found nothing else of note. The shifters weren't into keeping files or putting valuables in safes, so anything else they had going on died with the alpha or was sent elsewhere when Eloise teleported the pack.

He wouldn't find anything else, but at least they knew *EarthBore* was sniffing around. If the Dust Dogs were working for someone supernatural, or if they were being paid by this McIntyre bloke to edge the Exiles out of Solace ahead of acquisition, they had gone off script when they discovered the seal. Hardy had always wondered if the power emanating from it corrupted the unwary...or the susceptible.

All of this was speculation, of course. They could've been up to anything.

Sighing, Hardy headed back to Solace...and planned to take a long, hot, shower.

## CHAPTER 2

Kyne Brady watched Eloise run down the hill towards Solace, grinning like a fool.

It'd been a long time since he'd felt anything but angry. Sometimes being an elemental wasn't the greatest thing in the world, though the powers he had were quite useful in finding opal.

Human elementals were cast-offs left with their mothers or abandoned as babies—their parentage not born out of love, but curiosity from a supernatural creature who was pure nature. Kyne had gone looking for his father, and when he'd found the elementals, he had learned the lesson of his circumstances the hard way...and hadn't handled it well.

Eloise's recent arrival had turned all that pent-up rage into something a lot more productive. Without her, he'd still be alone on his claim at Black Hole Mine, digging opal and camping under the stars. Two things that didn't sound so bad, but the reality was far from romantic. Mining was dangerous business and the outback wasn't to be trifled with.

*Eloise Hart.*

She blew into town a few weeks ago, her motorhome broken and her spirit damaged.

Turned out, she was like him, though her abilities focused more on the fifth element of ether, otherwise known as spirit. Combined with his talent with earth, they seemed made for a place like Solace. Together, they would work out the rest...including reconciling their pasts with their future.

The morning was hot, the sun already making Kyne sweat as he and Drew continued work on the dugout that was going to be the shifter's new home. He didn't mind the work, but the weather didn't wait for no elemental.

They were cutting timber for new stud walls in the front. They'd planned an enclosed porch that led into the mine. The main house was inside, where it'd be much cooler once the dry season hit in full force. They were still waiting on some materials they needed to seal the rock, but for now, they were building the framework.

The mine itself was a good shape, and Kyne hadn't had to do much reenforcing with his powers. Drew had helped him cut some more open rooms into the ridge, then they'd drilled down from the surface so they could run electrical, ventilation, and plumbing.

So far, so good. The shifter had well and truly proven he was adept with a circular saw.

"*Cooee!*"

The men turned at the sound of Hardy's voice echoing up the hill. The vampire came to join them in the clearing, back from his adventure out at the Dust Dogs camp. Kyne looked him over, wondering what he'd found.

Hardy's wavy brown hair was tied back in its usual man-bun, and a battered satchel with papers sticking out the top was slung over his shoulder. He'd been running across the outback, but he hadn't even cracked a sweat...or loosened a hair. If there was one advantage to being one of the immortal undead, Kyne figured it was that.

"Hey," Kyne said. "Find anything interesting?"

Hardy wrinkled his nose and shrugged. "A week in the sun has made that place ripe, that's for sure."

"They weren't into perfume," Drew drawled, "or disinfectant."

"Not that I'm implying *you* never showered," Hardy said.

"Lucky I had one this morning," the shifter retorted.

Kyne looked at Drew. Like most of the supernaturals in Solace, the dingo had been though a lot in his short life. Like his pack being murdered when he was just a kid, going to live with his abusive grandfather, then falling in with the Dust Dogs only to find they were responsible for his family's deaths. Drew didn't accept things easy, not even kindness, though he seemed to be working on it thanks to Vera.

"You want to hear this?" Hardy asked the shifter. "They're definitely not coming back any time soon."

*If ever*, Kyne thought.

Drew glanced at Hardy before wiping his hands on his jeans. "I reckon I don't want to know the bit that comes after the 'but' you're about to add to that." Nodding towards Solace, he added, "I'm going to see if Vera wants some lunch. I'll be back in an hour."

Hardy didn't wait for the dingo shifter to go far before taking out a pile of papers from his bag. "They had paperwork from a proposed mining site on station property," he said. "Permit applications, maps, correspondence."

"Walawala Station?" Kyne asked. "Why would the Dust Dogs be interested in what they do?"

"They were squatting. Maybe they were concerned they'd get kicked out."

Kyne narrowed his eyes at the vampire. "That's not all you're suspecting, is it?"

He shook his head but didn't elaborate. "I already checked with my contact in the Department of Natural Resources. There's been no movement on the permits for at least a year."

"Queensland government?"

Hardy nodded. "The proposed site is across the border." He rolled out a map across the workbench. It was covered in squiggly lines and numbers outlining the topography of the local area—a geological survey. "Here, on a section of land belonging to the station."

Kyne snorted as his gaze studied the proposed site. "Ten square kilometres..."

"That's one hell of a mine," the vampire muttered. "Industry of that size brings pollution, people—"

"And trouble."

"What would large-scale mining do to the seal?" Hardy asked. "I can imagine, but..." He looked to the elemental. Earth was Kyne's thing, after all.

"Iron ore is mined in open pits," he explained. "At least, in this country. They'll blast the ground morning, noon, and night to get at it." His frown deepened. "We'll feel it here for sure."

"Can anything be done? Magically, I mean."

Kyne shook his head. "If you're asking me to change the composition of a ten-square-kilometre pocket of iron ore, you're shit outta luck, mate."

"It was worth asking." He rolled up the map and slid it back into his bag.

Kyne looked over Solace and wiped his arm across his brow. "It makes me wonder," he murmured. "Is this the next play for the seal? Screw with mine and Eloise's power under the cover of big mining?" If so, that meant someone was watching the Exiles and knew what they could do.

"We can't rule anything out," Hardy told him. "We just have to keep our ears to the ground. Taking on a multi-billion-dollar government-backed industry isn't like facing a pack of dingo shifters."

If it came to it, Kyne wasn't sure it was a battle they could win, even if they tried. There had to be a way to sour the deal before it went ahead.

"Well," the elemental said, "if there's one thing I know about governments and mining, is that they take their sweet time, even for big corp. They'll have to do a thousand environmental tests before they're allowed to even dig a shovelful of dirt. Besides, they need to get a cultural walkthrough before they can even think about testing."

An appointed Ingenious Australian representative conducted a cultural walkthrough to assess the cultural heritage of the land. It was required by state and federal law, and big fines had been slapped on miners before. A few years back, a big mining company had blown up caves that contained priceless paintings and artefacts that dated back tens of thousands of years. The loss to the Indigenous peoples of Australia was unmeasurable.

"Maybe Coen could help," Hardy mused.

Kyne sighed and looked towards the pub. "Maybe. There isn't much we can do but put some feelers out, work out what's going on."

The vampire followed his gaze. They stood on the rise together for a moment, taking in the lay of the town below. Sunlight glinted off metal and the groaning sound of rusted metal turning echoed up the ridge.

Kyne straightened. "Did you see that?"

Hardy chuckled as the windmill, which hadn't moved in over a decade, turned one noisy inch at a time. "Seems Eloise has breathed more life into the town than we first thought. Should we tell her the bore is dry?"

Kyne glanced at the vampire and chuckled. "Is it, though?"

"You tell me... *You're the elemental.*"

---

Eloise looked up at the windmill and sighed. It was rusted, rickety, and likely hadn't moved in about a million years. It stood about eighty metres tall, and the windmill itself looked about three metres wide.

The water table must be huge to need something so large. Eloise wondered why she'd never sensed the water underneath but shook her head. The power seeping from the seal drowned out most things—*no pun intended*—and she was too new to her abilities to understand the difference.

Checking for holes, she walked around the tank and rapped her fist on the corrugated iron. *Bang, bang, bang.* Sounded hollow. She wondered what was inside...

"What's all this noise about?"

Eloise looked up at Vera, the witch who ran the *Outpost*. "Checking for structural defects."

Vera's eyebrows rose and she tucked a strand of flaming red, corkscrew-curled hair behind her ear. "What for?"

She shrugged. "I want to see if it'll hold water."

"That old thing hasn't worked or held anything but dust since before I was here. I don't even think there's any water left in the bore."

"I thought Wally used bore water at the garage," she wondered. "Isn't it from the same source?"

Vera shrugged. "I wouldn't know."

"Has anyone checked?"

"The windmill doesn't even turn."

Eloise frowned. It was clear Vera thought it was a useless endeavour, but she desperately wanted to contribute something to Solace. Polishing opal was one thing...but building something was another.

"What do you think about painting a mural on the tank?" she asked.

The witch raised her eyebrows. "A mural?"

"Yeah, like on all those old grain silos around the country. I've seen heaps of them during my travels. They really bring life to little towns. Tourists, too." Her gaze moved up the windmill, tracing the lines of the metal skeletal structure before settling on the fins of the mill. "It doesn't have to work, but it'd be helpful to have another water source, right?"

"Tourists?" Vera shook her head. "Given what's

sitting underneath us, tourism isn't something we've pursued. We get along just fine without the extra traffic."

Eloise's heart sank. She had a point. The Exiles settled in Solace for a reason beyond the seal—it was a place they could feel safe being open about their unusual lifestyles. Vera could practice her magic wherever she chose. Wally didn't fear his monthly transformations. Drew could shift whenever he felt the urge to run. Hardy didn't have to conceal his speed or strength. Kyne could mine opal with his incredible strike rate in peace, and Coen could definitely come and go with his kangaroo BFF without raising any eyebrows.

More humans meant more secrecy. Blue was the only exception to the rule...*ever*. There'd be no more human sympathisers in Solace.

"Eloise, don't look at me like that," Vera cried. "You've got the whole puppy dog eyes thing going on. Your bottom lip is trembling and everything."

"Oh, I didn't mean..." Eloise flushed and lowered her gaze. "I just wanted to contribute something."

"You've contributed more than anyone," the witch told her. "You saved us from the Dust Dogs."

"That was a fluke guided by Coen. I had no idea what I was doing."

"*Pfft*," Vera huffed. "Of course, it wasn't."

Eloise turned back to the tank, embarrassment getting the better of her. She'd never been able to take a compliment, never knowing if it was coming from a good place or not. She was homeless at sixteen after her powers had driven her out of her home. One touch was all it'd taken to turn her adoptive parents from loving to hateful. And it wasn't just them, it was everyone.

Until she'd learned the truth from Kyne, Eloise had no idea she was an elemental. None at all. So, it wasn't a stretch for her to reject the notion of her saving Solace...because in reality, it'd saved *her*.

Grasping the ladder, Eloise began to climb, the rickety metal clanging against the side of the tank.

"Eloise! Get down!" Vera cried, waving her hands in the air. "That thing is going to fall apart!"

"I'm fine," she called over her shoulder. "I'm an elemental, remember? I can sense the structural integrity through my hands. *She'll be all right.*"

"I don't believe you!"

Eloise wasn't listening. She'd reached the top.

The tank was totally sealed, except for a hinged grate designed for both access and to stop leaves and other trash from getting inside the tank and fouling up the precious water. She leaned over the edge and heaved open the grate, which emitted a sharp whine of complaint.

Eloise peered through the hole, but it was too dark to see anything. It smelled dry and dusty, with no traces of water. Rust flaked off onto her hands and she dusted her palms along her jeans.

A thought crossed her mind when she heard a new voice below.

"What's going on?" Drew asked.

"Eloise wants to get the windmill working again," Vera told him.

"She does?" There was silence for a moment before another quiet question. "Why?"

"She wants to paint a mural on the tank or something."

Eloise looked over the edge at the witch and shifter. "It's empty, but I can't see much. It's too dark."

"What are you doing up there?" Drew asked, shielding his eyes from the sun with his arm. "There's spiders in there, you know."

"*Bull*," Eloise called down. "If there are, they're cooked." She pressed her palm against the corrugated metal. "This thing it hotter than Hades. Those spiders are charcoal!"

"Come down from there," Vera called. "You're giving me palpitations."

But Eloise wasn't done yet. She turned her head, clutching the ladder, and looked up at the windmill. It was three times taller than the tank, its own ladder climbing the rusted iron frame all the way to the rudimentary turbine at the top.

Once upon a time, the spinning fins would've brought water up from the well to the tank—the process helped along by the roaring hot winds that tore across the outback. The windmill had been motionless for decades, the moving parts rusted so badly, they'd seized entirely.

An idea took shape in Eloise's mind, and she leaned over and grasped the nearest iron pole.

"Be careful!" Vera screeched.

"Be quiet for a minute," she called down.

"What *is* she doing?" Drew asked.

Eloise felt the rust break apart underneath her hands and her heart leapt.

*It was working!*

Focusing, she imagined her way along the structure to the very top, where she began working on loosening the gears. Her power flared, warming her from the inside out. Then, something happened.

Slowly but surely, the windmill began to turn.

Eloise laughed and threw her head back. Her hat fell off and fluttered to the ground, making Vera cry out.

"See that?" Eloise called down to them. "It's working!"

The commotion had stirred another of Solace's residents, bringing Wally out of his garage and across the street.

"What in the world is she doing?" the grizzled mechanic asked, joining the others on the ground.

"She wants to paint a mural on the tank," Vera told him.

"Does she now?"

"Is there water in the bore?" Drew asked.

"Hell if I know," Wally told them.

Eloise looked down at the Exiles, beaming. "How you like that, huh? Rust is no match for me!"

Drew laughed and Wally scratched his head. Vera shot her a look of resignation, caving to the fact that the windmill was going to be resurrected, tourists or no tourists.

"Please come down from there," the witch called up to her. "You're making me nervous."

Eloise laughed and climbed back down the ladder. "I told you it was fine."

Vera turned to Wally. "It sounds like a good idea, but...*people*."

"What's wrong with people?" the mechanic asked. "People bring money. As long as they don't stay for longer than a meal at the pub, then it sounds alright to me."

"It makes me nervous," the witch said. "Ever since..." She glanced at Drew.

Eloise snorted and picked up her hat. Dusting it off, she said, "You don't have to help me. I can figure it out on my own. I can use my powers to check for water and loosen some of that rust."

"It's not that," Vera went on. Her cheeks reddened and Eloise did a double take. She'd never seen the witch embarrassed before, let alone lost for words. Vera seemed like the last person on Solace to be afraid of anything.

"I wouldn't worry about the seal," Wally reassured

her. "Kyne's back, Drew's here, and now we have Eloise. There're more eyes on that thing than ever before. If something's going to happen, we'll be ready for it."

"It's just a bit of paint," Drew added. "Can't see the harm."

"Want to help me design it?" Eloise asked her. "I could use some of your flair."

Drew snorted, then immediately ducked as Vera took a swing at him.

"Don't get smart with me, Drew!" she shouted at him. "I know what primary colours are!"

Wally raised his eyebrows and turned to Eloise. "Want to get some lunch?"

"A thousand times, yes," she replied.

"I'm outta here," Drew declared, then darted across the road.

As the men made a move, Eloise lingered with Vera. "I'll be all right," she said to the witch. "If anything happens, it won't be because of a mural."

"I know," Vera replied. "It was just a lot with the Dust Dogs. Threats, severed dingo heads...It was scary there for a moment."

Facing off with a gang of armed and dangerous bikers wasn't Eloise's idea of a fun time either, but Vera had taken the brunt of their violence after Drew. Being wary was to be expected, but Solace needed the right attention. They still had to make some money after all. Opal wouldn't carry the town forever.

Eloise attempted a joke. "So, no dingoes on the mural, then?"

The witch laughed, the tension seeming to leave her. "No, no dingoes please." Pointing to the pub, she added, "You coming?"

"Yeah, for sure."

Eloise looked up at the windmill one last time before following the Exiles across the road. It had to be one special mural, that much was certain.

---

When Eloise walked into the pub, Finn was at the far end of the bar, nursing a bowl of hot chips. The fae winked at her and she grinned.

Despite his sharp attitude and abrasive personality, she kind of liked him. She could only describe his dress sense as 'hippy'—his deep blue dreadlocks and silky shirts were his wardrobe staples. Fae were big believers in telling the truth and vehemently disliked lies. It meant he said things exactly like they were, no matter the consequences...which was good and bad all at the same time.

Eloise sat next to Vera and Wally at their usual table as Blue emerged from the kitchen.

"Eloise got that old windmill turning," Drew said.

Blue's eyebrows rose. "Is that so? I haven't seen that thing turn in decades."

"I want to paint a mural on the tank," Eloise said. "But I won't do anything unless everyone agrees."

"A mural, hey?" Blue mused.

"I thought we could work on a design together. Something to symbolise everyone in Solace." She looked around at everyone. "A kangaroo, some opal, the boab tree—"

"A snake," Finn said with a wicked grin. His fae power was attuned to beast taming, and he often carried a death adder tucked inside his shirt.

"She didn't say how she got it to work," Vera said.

The Exiles turned to look at her and she shrugged. "I used my powers to shift some rust. It seemed to work."

"Well, who's a clever little desert pea," Finn stated. "I knew you had it in you. At least you didn't make it disappear."

Eloise groaned. "Fair call."

"There was water in the tank once," Blue said. "I know because I saw it."

Finn snorted. "I didn't know you were that ancient."

The publican glared at the fae. "Be careful with that mouth of yours or I'll cut you off."

"I'm not an alcoholic," Finn retorted, shoving another chip into his mouth.

"No, you're worse," Drew said as the door opened and Kyne and Hardy walked in.

The fae glared. "Careful, shifter. I still haven't

forgotten the time you hit me in the head with a shovel."

"Too much starch will block you up," Wally warned.

"We've got more to worry about than a constipated fae," Hardy said, pulling up a chair at the table.

"What now?" Vera asked with a groan. "I'm still recovering from *you know what*."

Kyne sat beside Eloise and glanced at Drew, who shrugged.

"Whatever," the dingo said. "I guess I can't avoid it if it's got to do with the town."

Finn snorted, earning himself a warning glare from Vera.

"*EarthBore* is interested in opening up a mine on Walawala Station property," the vampire said. "The Dust Dogs had copies of the surveys and permit applications. Why, I still don't know, but big mining is sniffing around."

"What kind of mine are we talking about?" Blue asked, leaning on the bar.

"Iron ore," Kyne said, laying a hand on Eloise's thigh. "It'll be open cut. They'd be blasting, running large-scale industrial machinery, and trucks at all hours."

"How big is big?" Eloise asked, her thoughts on the seal.

She'd heard about open cut mines. Australia was a huge provider of iron ore and other minerals for overseas export. She hadn't seen it, but she knew there was a mine in Kalgoorlie, Western Australia called the Super Pit. They dug for gold, but it was the same principle. At last count, it was four kilometres long and one and a half kilometres wide. At its deepest point, it hit almost half a kilometre.

"The biggest mine in the country has nothing on the pocket of iron ore sitting out there," Kyne replied. "They're looking at acquiring land in a ten-kilometre radius from the centre of the pocket."

"You could've just said twenty square kilometres," Finn drawled.

"This mine would be worth trillions of dollars," Hardy told them.

"That's if the ore is there," Finn went on. "I've sensed nothing."

"The seal can screw with our abilities," Kyne told him. "It's entirely possible we've missed it."

"We shouldn't worry just yet," Hardy butted in before things deteriorated into an argument. "Permits take time, as does getting proper machinery out to do the ground testing. No one has verified that there is ore."

"This close to the opal fields?" Blue asked. "Is it possible?"

"It's how black opal is formed," Kyne replied. "The iron oxide formed in the old reef from water ways that flowed down from the north. It stands to reason there'd be a deposit that way."

Eloise frowned, knowing so much activity couldn't be good for the seal. Where would the mine traffic go? The only road with decent access north went straight thought Solace. Suddenly, the odd tourist stopping for a photo op at a painted water tank seemed like nothing compared to the infrastructure that'd pop up in the wake of an industrial mine breaking ground.

"Enough about that," Hardy said. "I've got contacts keeping an eye on it. If anything happens, we can figure it out."

"So, what's with the windmill?" Kyne asked, attempting to lighten the mood. "We saw it turning from up on the ridge."

"That's what we were talking about when you came in," Wally told him. "Eloise wants to get it working again and paint a mural on the tank."

The elemental looked at her. "A mural?"

"Why is everyone so surprised?" Eloise asked. "I can draw. I can also dislodge rust with my mind. That's a thing I can do now."

"Is there water in the bore?" Hardy wondered.

"I've lost count of how many times someone has asked that question," Finn quipped.

"It doesn't matter," Eloise said. "I still think we should paint a mural. It'll take our minds off this seal business." She looked to Kyne. He was the town's unofficial leader and had the final say, but she didn't want him to say yes just because they were in the beginning stages of a relationship.

"I don't see why not," the elemental said after a moment's thought. "Though we've still got a lot of work left on Drew's dugout."

"I can do it on my own," Eloise said quickly. "I don't mind."

Hardy grinned and shook his head. "Who could say no to that face?"

"I didn't mean..." She felt her cheeks heat, which was a constant pain in her arse. Having her embarrassment on display made her flush even more. "I just wanted to contribute something."

"You contribute just by being here," Wally told her. "Watching the seal is more than enough."

Eloise lowered her gaze. "That's not what I meant."

"For *za'adei's* sake," Finn declared, cursing in the fae language. "Just let her paint the tin can. She saved the town from those slobbering dingoes. She can do whatever she wants."

Vera snorted. "That's high praise coming from you."

"Glad you think so, *witch*."

Eloise narrowed her eyes, glancing between the pair. There was some kind of ancient beef between them she wasn't privy to, but whatever it was, it wasn't worth her asking unless she wanted to get caught in the crossfire.

Kyne squeezed Eloise's thigh underneath the table, his touch comforting. "Go for it," he told her. "This town could use a little freshening up."

Her heart leapt. "Really?"

"*Really*." He kissed her on the lips and the Exiles let out a *whoop* and clapped.

This time, the flush in Eloise's cheeks wasn't at all unwelcome.

## CHAPTER 3

Five kilometres south of Solace, Vera knelt in the ochre dirt at the base of a scrappy gum tree, sweat dripping down her back. She dug at the roots with her tiny garden spade, cursing and swatting at the flies who were brave enough to circumnavigate her fading magical vanilla repellent.

Summer was nearing and every day seemed hotter than the last. Business was already slowing—the rising temperature kept all but the regular industrial traffic away from the remote outback. Even the few human opal miners who dug on the east side of Solace had called it quits and returned to their families and air-conditioned homes on the coast.

Vera sighed at the thought of white sandy beaches and cool ocean breezes. One day she'd take that holiday she'd been putting off for the last twenty years. Considering she was only thirty, two decades was a hell of a long time to forgo a seaside vacation—and moving from Ireland to Australia didn't count.

Another shovelful of red dirt flew over her shoulder and she shouted, "Yes!"

Vera grinned as she uncovered the prize she'd been searching for. It wasn't buried treasure, but it was the next best thing for a witch obsessed with brewing potions.

"There you are, you little bugger!"

She scooped up the wriggling larvae and dropped it into the plastic container by her feet. It continued to squirm as she added a second beside it.

Witchetty grubs had been a staple in the diets of Indigenous peoples for thousands of years. Their magical properties were curious and something she was attempting to figure out. The grubs were nutritious both raw and cooked, but when combined with other herbs and potions, she'd discovered various healing and increased stamina effects.

The creatures turned into ghost moths, insects that were rather plain to look at but beautiful in their melancholy. These particular moths only lived a week after emerging from their underground cocoons, simply because they didn't have mouths. With no way to feed themselves, their flight was fleeting.

There was a metaphor in that, but Vera was more interested in the larvae than the moth itself. Maybe Eloise could put one in her mural.

"Hello?"

Vera spun, her gaze clashing with the owner of the voice, a male police officer.

"*Bloody hell.*" Her hand flew to her heart and she almost fell on her arse. She hadn't even heard him approach, let alone his car.

*A cop?* Was he looking for the Dust Dogs? Had someone finally noticed? *Stay calm, Vera.*

She looked him over, taking in his brilliant green eyes and perfect teeth. Dusty brown hair poked out from underneath his wide-brimmed navy-blue hat, the front of which was emblazoned with the New South Wales Police insignia. The rest of his uniform, which he wore well, comprised of navy trousers, boots, and a light blue shirt with navy lapels. The name, Clarke, was embossed on his name tag.

There were three silver chevrons on his lapels, but she didn't know what rank they represented, though he must be a little higher than the average constable.

Her gaze flickered to the gun at his side, then to the bottle of water in his hand, and she smiled. He *was* handsome in a clean-cut Aussie bloke kind of way. If that was a way to be.

"I didn't mean to frighten you," the cop said. "I saw you from the road and wanted to check if you were okay. It's a hot day to be out." He held out the water. "Are you thirsty?"

"I'm all right," she said, rising to her feet. Clutching her container of grubs against her chest, she looked him over. "Officer...?"

"Ah, Sergeant Andrew Clarke from Lightning Ridge." He looked at her expectantly.

"Vera Walsh...from Solace."

"Solace?" He craned his neck, trying to see what she had in the container.

"Witchetty grubs," she told him. "And yes, I run the store there. *The Outpost*."

Sergeant Clarke glanced at the container again. "Out gathering stock?"

Vera blinked then laughed. "These? Oh no, they're not for sale. I'm interested in learning about bushcraft. Plants and insects, natural remedies...that kind of thing."

He met her gaze, his sharp eyes taking everything in. His keenness unsettled her, and she wondered if he could see right through her. He *was* trained to catch criminals and keep the peace.

Finally, he said, "What's an Irishwoman doing out in the middle of nowhere, running a general store?"

She shrugged, her brow creasing. "Why not?"

"Oh, I meant nothing by it," he said hurriedly. "It's just curious."

"Well, I don't think so," she said haughtily. "It's as good a place as any. I've got the monopoly on general goods. Business is *booming*."

Sergeant Clarke laughed and tipped the brim of his hat. "I'm sure you do."

"So, what are you doing out here? Lightning Ridge

is a long way from Solace." About 224 kilometres, in fact. "Anything I can help you with?"

His smile widened. He knew she was fishing, but would he bite?

"No, just following up on a police matter," he replied. "Nothing to worry yourself over."

"Okay, well..." Vera looked over to his white and blue police 4WD. "I'm good here. Just digging my grubs." She winced and her cheeks heated. What the hell did she just say?

He chuckled and tipped his hat again. "Great, but would you do me one favour?"

She raised her eyebrows.

He held out the bottle of water. "Take this for my peace of mind, hey?"

"Sure." She reached out and took it gingerly, fluttering her eyelashes for good measure.

"Take care now."

She watched him walk away, her gaze falling to his arse. Tilting her head to the side, she bit her bottom lip. He *was* handsome for a cop. Maybe it was the uniform.

He glanced over his shoulder and caught her staring, his lips curving into a wide grin. "Take care, Miss Walsh."

Vera laughed, her cheeky Irish spirit reigniting, and waved as he climbed into his 4WD.

A handsome cop with a great arse. Who would've thought?

Drew cut the last piece of wood and turned off the circular saw. The blade buzzed and slowed down, coming to a halt.

Handing the cut to Kyne, he grimaced as his muscles twinged.

"Your scars worrying you?" the elemental asked as he added the wood to the frame they'd laid out on the ground.

Drew had taken a beating from the Dust Dogs not too long ago, and with Vera's help, he'd almost healed. All that remained from his scrap was fading yellowish bruises on his left eye and a couple of matching splotches over his body.

The scars were another matter. Vera's powers could heal wounds, but it wasn't a magic eraser. He'd carry the jagged marks of his battle with Roth and the pack for the rest of his life.

"Yeah, nah," he replied. "Just not used to the work yet."

"Here, hold this," Kyne said, gesturing at him.

Drew knelt and held the frame in place as the elemental picked up the nail gun. Air whooshed as the compressor fired nails into the wood. *Thump, thump, thump.*

Kyne surveyed his work and nodded. "That ought to do it."

Together, they lifted the completed stud wall and

fixed it in place on the side of the porch. It was slow work, but the house was already taking shape. At least they didn't have to build walls inside because framing was boring as.

Drew stepped back and picked up his bottle of water. Taking a long draught, he positioned himself in the shade. He still couldn't believe that Kyne was helping him build an underground mine house free of charge. He'd learned the hard way in his life that nothing was for free. No matter how much the Exiles had tried to convince him there was no hidden catch, the dingo just couldn't find a way to reconcile their selflessness.

As Kyne busied himself with sorting through fat rolls of insulation, sheets of plaster board, and boxes of cladding, Drew looked down the hill to where the white shell of Eloise's van glinted in the sun.

"She can't be serious about staying in that van during the summer," he said. "She's mad."

Kyne looked up. "I know, but Eloise is determined. That van is her home."

"You shouldn't be building a house for me," the shifter went on. "If Eloise means that much to you then maybe you should build her one. If you don't, I will."

Kyne raised his eyebrows. "Are you trying to muscle in on my girl?"

Drew shrugged as the elemental grabbed the water bottle out of his hands. "Maybe."

The miner said nothing for a while, his gaze

following Drew's down the hill. "I reckon she'd find it flattering. She's kept herself hidden for so long..."

"I can't imagine her any other way than how she was the other week." How she'd stood up to the Dust Dogs was fearless. In his eyes, Eloise Hart was brave. Braver than he'd ever be.

"I always wondered about you and Vera," Kyne mused.

Drew narrowed his eyes. "It's not like that."

"Isn't it?"

He snorted and looked away, his gaze finding the boxes of cladding. Which part came first on the exterior walls? Cladding, insulation, plaster board? Electrical?

"Why not?" Kyne went on. "Vera's good for you."

"It's not about what's good for me," Drew snapped. "It's different for a shifter."

He'd told Vera things he'd told no one else—about the night his parents were killed. How he'd hidden underneath the burnt-out shell of his house as a kid, his grandfather's heavy-handed idea of raising an emotionally broken dingo shifter. Serious, personal things he'd trusted no one with.

But it wasn't because of any romantic feelings, was it? Vera had taken him in when no one else cared. She helped him, given him a place to sleep and a job at the *Outpost*. Of course he was protective of her.

Kyne turned to him. "How so?"

Drew shook his head. Romance was one thing but

love for a shifter meant forever. One and done. It wasn't an easy thing to find. He cared about Vera, but even if he felt that way, it was clear she didn't. Vera Walsh saw him as a little brother...or at least, a broken thing she could try to fix. He was her 'project'.

"I'm just grateful to be alive," he muttered. "Everyone helped me, not just Vera."

"You're welcome."

"What about you?" he went on. "You can't bunk with Hardy forever. A vampire as a third wheel would be awkward as hell."

Kyne laughed. "You've got a point. I really need to get my own place."

"So why are we building this and not something for you and Eloise? You're cashed up."

The elemental winced. "Things with Eloise...We've only been together for a couple of weeks. I thought it was too soon to ask her to move in with me." *But not too soon to give her a piece of black opal that was worth a couple of thousand dollars.*

Drew scoffed. "Mate, we're supernaturals living in a town sitting on an alleged ancient spirit trapped under a rock. There is no such thing as too soon."

Kyne laughed again and looked down the hill. "You've got a point."

"Ask her. I bet she'll say yes."

The elemental didn't reply. If he was going to ask the million-dollar question, he didn't give it away. He turned back to the dugout where the exterior wall frames were complete and waiting for the next unknown step.

"What's next?" Drew asked.

"Sarking," Kyne replied.

"I don't even know what that is."

"It's a special layer between the interior wall and the cladding that protects the structure from moisture."

The shifter blinked. "I'm glad one of us knows what we're doing."

Kyne chuckled and nodded towards the pile of materials stacked in the tray of his ute. "Give a hand, hey? Once this is up, we can run some wiring for some lights."

Drew glanced over his shoulder, getting in one last glance at the *Outpost*. Vera meant more to him than he cared to admit, but was it romantic?

Unfortunately, he didn't know the difference.

# CHAPTER 4

The sounds of metal clanking on metal echoed out of the garage as Eloise approached. The morning was still, the wind was non-existent, and she could already feel the promise of a blistering summer to come.

Wally was tinkering at his workbench, working on the insides of an old, beaten-up generator. Immediately, she wondered if it was the one that had once hooked up to the hoist on Kyne's mine—the one she'd accidentally destroyed.

Lingering in the shade, she knocked on the roller door and the old mechanic looked up.

"Eloise," he said, smiling brightly. "To what do I owe the honour?"

"You never gave me that invoice for the repairs on my van," she told him.

He waved a grease-stained hand at her. "Don't worry about it. She'll be right."

Her smile faded. "But—"

"You saved us. It's the least I can do."

Her cheeks heated and she shook her head. "I can't not pay you for your work. The part—"

"Was my pleasure."

"*Wally.*"

"I don't want to get into a barney with you about it," he told her. "I won't take any money and that's final."

"It's thousands of dollars' worth of work!"

"I had nothing else to do."

She pinched the bridge of her nose to stop herself from crying. "I don't know what to say."

Wally laughed and wiped his hands on an old stained rag. "You don't have to say a thing."

"You're making me feel bad for what I'm about to ask..." she began.

"Which is?"

"I was wondering if you could help me with something."

"With the windmill?"

She nodded. "I'm not quite sure what I'm looking for. The tank is old and rusty. If there are holes, they'll need to be patched."

"Ah." He held up a finger. "I've got some welding equipment. I reckon I can rustle up some scrap, too. Have to get inside maybe..."

"Don't get too excited." She nodded out the door. "Would you come and look with me?"

"Sure, let me just find my hat." He wandered

around the garage for a moment, searching. "Ah, there it is." He pulled out a beaten, wide-brimmed brown hat out from underneath some machine parts and slapped it on his head. "Lead the way."

They went outside and walked across the dirt track to the windmill.

"So, how are you about settling in Solace?" Wally asked. "Your new spot any good?"

"It's a good a place as any," she replied.

"I worry about you, though," he went on. "Summer is going to come early this year. I can smell it."

"You can smell it?"

He grinned. "Wolves have good noses."

She laughed as they stopped before the rusty water tank. "Why would you be worried about me?"

"Summer in that van? You'll cook."

She frowned, knowing he was probably right. "Maybe Vera will let me cool off in one of her freezers."

Wally shook his head. "Or that boy should get off his rear and build you a house."

Eloise lowered her gaze, suddenly overcome with a bout of shyness. 'That boy' was Kyne, and he was currently helping Drew build a dugout up on the ridge. He'd already done so much for her, including gifting her an expensive piece of black opal...that was more than enough.

"So, what do you think?" she declared, tapping the outside of the tank. "Is she salvageable?"

Wally chuckled and they walked around the

tank. He rapped his knuckles against the side, rubbed at some dense patches of rust, and *ummed* and *ahhed* a great deal. "Looks decent. Have to get inside and check in there though. If you want it to hold water, it'd probably be best to get a new tank installed inside. One of those special plastic contraptions."

"So, it'll be like corrugated cladding?"

The werewolf nodded. "It'd keep to the heritage of the town. Couldn't see a big ugly plastic thing sitting here, mural or not."

Eloise looked up at the tank and totally agreed. "There sure is a lot of history here, supernatural or not."

Wally's eyes brightened. "Have you been to see the settler's cemetery?"

"Not yet."

"It's interesting," he went on. "Some headstones are worn, but a few have inscriptions you can still read. Solace was founded in the early 1850s, so there's a lot of men who died in mine collapses."

"Yeah, you mentioned. People came looking for gold."

The werewolf nodded. "Gold is big business these days, but back then, it was another world. One big strike could set a miner and his family up for life and then some. The biggest nugget ever found was in the Golden Triangle down in Victoria. They called it the 'Welcome Stranger'."

"I bet it was welcome," Eloise said with a laugh. "How big was it?"

"Just shy of one hundred kilos. Worth about four million bucks today."

She raised her eyebrows. "*Holy cow.*"

"Nothing ever found like it since."

"Kyne said they found gold here," she went on, "but not enough for it to be viable."

Wally nodded. "Apparently, the miners back then only found fine traces of alluvial gold. That's gold dust washed down the ancient riverbeds. When they dug down, they found opal instead. Eventually the high cost, low strike rate, weather, and the remoteness drove everyone away."

Eloise glanced at the boab tree. The seal lay underneath lonely, forgotten, and forbidding. Who knew what would've happened if the people back then had uncovered it, though someone had at some stage. The old tunnels Coen had led her through were testament to the discovery.

"Wally?" she asked, looking back at the mechanic.

"Hmm?"

"Who discovered the seal? I mean, a miner made the tunnel, but the cave its in is natural."

"All of us, in our own way," Wally told her. "We all felt there was something different about this place...we could feel the magic. Especially Finn and the fae. They need magic to survive."

"They do?"

"Oh yes," Wally replied. "Magic is like oxygen to them. Our world isn't as seeped in it like their own."

"When did everyone arrive?"

"Well, Blue was here first. Then I came, followed by Hardy, then Finn and the fae, Kyne, Vera, Drew, and then finally, you."

"What about Coen?"

"It's hard to say. I think he's always been here, but it wasn't until we found the seal that he made himself known."

Eloise frowned. There was a lot more to Solace's origin story than she'd first realised. Everyone had their tale, and they were all embroiled with the seal. Why the Exiles were here—whether by some prophetic design or chance—was unclear. All that mattered was their guardianship and their relationship to each other.

"You know nothing else about the seal?" Eloise asked. "Like who put it there?"

"Nothing," Wally replied. "Coen told us we should protect it, but we'd already decided that. It wasn't until you came and met that mysterious Andante sheila, that we knew more."

*The heart of the ocean...* Eloise frowned, her thoughts going back to the windmill. Bore water was deep, and in this case, likely ancient. Maybe she shouldn't worry about getting it to work. Maybe painting it was enough.

"First things first," Wally declared. "We have to

prepare this surface for painting. That means removing the rust and putting down some sealant." He sighed. "Not looking forward to that job."

"Maybe I can help speed up the process." Eloise pressed her palms against the tank and focused.

The sound of an approaching car had Wally tugging on her shirt. "We've got visitors. Maybe later, eh?"

Stepping back, Eloise waited with Wally as the car came into view at the southern end of town, zooming up the highway and shimmering through a glassy mirage. The sun glinted off the windscreen, then she spotted the big black aerial mounted on the bull bar of the now clearly visible 4WD.

Eloise tensed as she saw the white and navy-blue checks with the word 'police' written across the side and over the bonnet. The New South Wales Police emblem was on the passenger door, looking all official and menacing.

"Police?" She glanced at Wally. "Do you think they're here because of the Dust Dogs?"

"Dunno." The mechanic narrowed his eyes as the 4WD pulled into a park outside the *Outpost*. "Don't worry. They can't prove anything, and even if they did, it'd be laughed out of court."

Eloise snorted. Trying to prove she made an entire pack of bikers disappear into thin air would ruin anyone's career in law enforcement pretty quickly. Still, the attention a case like that would bring to Solace would be a bag of trouble. She could imagine the wave of UFO hunters, supernatural conspiracy theorists, and TV crews descending on the town like moths to a flame.

A man with cropped dark hair climbed out of the 4WD and put on a blue hat. His uniform was crisp, and his sunglasses glinted in the sun as he scanned the street.

Eloise quickly looked away, guilt heating her cheeks. Why did she always feel like she was about to be arrested every time she saw a cop, even though she was innocent? But she *was* guilty, and Drew... God, Drew had killed Roth.

"We can get a generator hooked up to a pump and see if there's water down there," Wally said, not fussed about the police officer. "Do it the old-fashioned way."

"I'm not sure we should," Eloise said, still distracted by their unexpected visitor. "I mean, after what Andante had told me about *the thing*. I wonder if the water table is connected to it."

"I draw bore water at the garage. I've had no problems."

"Yeah, but that's a different bore, isn't it?"

Wally nodded. "You're right. Maybe we should take it slow. Get a little water up first and then Vera could test it."

"She can do that?"

"Sure. If it's *that way* inclined, she has the tools to detect any interference."

The code words made her chuckle and Eloise smiled. "Okay, I feel better about that. I wouldn't want my first contribution to Solace to wake a sleeping giant."

Wally winced and wiped his brow. "Strewth, I hope it isn't a bloody giant."

"Me too..." Eloise looked across the road to the *Outpost* where the police officer was opening the door. "Me too."

<hr>

Vera pulled the trigger on her pricing gun, the plastic clicking. She swiped it across the barcode of a can of soup, sighed, and then repeated the process.

Click, swipe, shelve. Click, swipe, shelve.

*Open a store, they said...* she thought. *It'll be fun, they said.*

A fluorescent tube buzzed above her, the speakers blared some random playlist she'd connected to her battered mobile phone, and the air-conditioning hummed.

Sometimes she enjoyed Solace's slow pace—the quiet, the isolation, the magic flowing through the land—but lately, things felt unsettled. Almost like the seal was waking up, which was absurd.

She shook her head and priced another can of soup. It was just her imagination running away with her again—it happened every year around this time. It was just her memory playing tricks on her again.

The front door buzzed, and her head shot up. Perfect timing.

"Hello? Anyone here?"

Vera rounded the end of the aisle and hesitated when she saw Sergeant Clarke standing by the counter. He held his hat in his hand and for the first time, she could see him clearly.

He smiled when his gaze met hers. "Miss Walsh."

"Vera," she said, trying not to let her gaze fall. She couldn't check him out when he was likely there to ask questions she didn't want to answer. "Miss Walsh makes me sound like a primary school teacher."

"Sure, Vera it is, then." He stuck a thumb out, pointing at the boarded-up window. "What happened there?"

"Oh, it was a stray bird," she lied smoothly. "Smashed right into it. Haven't got around to fixing it just yet. It's a pain to get anything done around here."

Clarke frowned. "Must've been one hell of a bird."

"God rest its soul." She crossed herself and smiled. "What can I do for you, sergeant? I don't know why you'd want to come all the way out here. Nothing ever happens in Solace."

"I'm looking for someone," he replied. "Craig Roth. Big bloke. You know him?"

Vera tensed, her smile fading. For a moment she thought about touching Clarke so she could conjure a vision but decided against it. Firstly, it'd look weird if she randomly touched him and went all vague mid-interrogation. Secondly, she wasn't sure she wanted to know about the guy she was crushing on. He *was* a cop.

Before she could plan a reply, Clarke went on, "Ah, I see you know the guy."

She nodded. "He's come in here a couple of times. Can't say I want his business. His, uh...*reputation* proceeds him."

"I'm not surprised. Mr. Roth has made quite the name for himself right across the opal fields."

Vera bit her bottom lip and glanced at the window. "Are you looking for him?"

Clarke nodded. "He had a squat not far from here, but no one's there." He looked confused by it, though he didn't say anything more. "When was the last time you saw him in here?"

"Not for a couple of months," she said truthfully this time. The alpha hadn't technically been *inside* her store, only outside. "A couple of his bikie mates were in a couple of weeks ago."

"Really? What did they want?"

"Tomato sauce." Vera screwed up her nose, remembering how they'd threatened her over Drew, intimated Eloise, and smashed her stock.

Clarke's brow furrowed. "Tomato sauce?"

"I figured they were having a barbecue." She sighed and picked up the pricing gun. "Look, I don't ask questions when men like that come into my store.

If they were doing something dodgy, I'd report it. I don't put up with that kind of business here. Zero tolerance. Have to have it in this world of men us women find ourselves indentured in. Grumpy miners are one thing, bikies are another. I refuse to put up with their shit."

"I assume you have a firearm under the counter?"

She grinned, held up her pricing gun, and snapped the trigger. "Want to see my permit?"

"I don't doubt you have one," Clarke said with a chuckle. "For that and the handgun under the counter."

"Shotgun," she corrected. *Damn, he didn't let up easy.* "Give me a little credit, sergeant."

His gaze lowered to the price sticker. "How much am I worth?"

Vera snorted. Was he flirting with her? Swiping the pricing gun over his chest, the sticker clung to his shirt. "Three ninety-nine."

"Is that all?"

"What do you want with Roth, anyway?" she asked, narrowing her eyes. "Should I be on the lookout for an attempted armed robbery or something?"

"No, nothing like that," Clarke told her with a shake of his head. "There's a warrant out for his arrest. Skipped out on a court date. If you see him, call triple zero."

"And you'll come sirens blazing all the way from

Lightning Ridge?" Even at top speed, it'd take him at least forty-five minutes to get to Solace.

"Distance is an occupational hazard." The sergeant shrugged. "You work here on your own?"

"Mostly," she replied. "I have someone who works two days a week, so at least I have some time off."

"To dig witchetty grubs?"

She flushed. "Is this an interrogation?"

"Ah…" He smoothed his palms over his uniform. "Off the record."

"That's something journalists say." She waggled her finger at him. "Anything I say to you may be used against me in a court of law."

He smiled sheepishly at her. "Damn, you're good."

"The best, apparently."

"I don't mean to be pushy. I'm just intrigued why a young, beautiful, Irishwoman would want to open a business all the way out here in outback Australia. It's a long way from home."

"Home is relative," she stated, her heart doing a double beat at the thought of Clarke finding her beautiful. "It doesn't matter where someone was born. People can make a home wherever they are."

"So, if I may ask, why did you leave Ireland?"

Vera tensed, the sergeant's questions brining up memories she'd rather forget. She'd do anything to see her family again, but they were beyond her reach. Not even magic could conjure their spirits.

Clarke sensed her unease and took a step back.

"I'm sorry. I didn't mean to pry. I'll just..." He turned to the fridge and opened it. Taking out a bottle of soft drink, he set it on the counter. "How much do I owe you?" He fumbled for his wallet in the back pocket of his trousers.

She knew he was just trying to smooth things over so he could maintain a good reputation with Solace. It was part of being a cop in the outback. He was only as good as the trust he held with the locals.

Her gaze fell to the price sticker on his shirt. "Four ninety-nine."

Clarke's eyebrows rose. "Four ninety-nine?"

"It's the outback," she told him with a grin. "I've got the monopoly on soft drinks for a two-hundred-kilometre radius."

"I could go to the pub," he said, rising to the challenge.

"Be my guest...but you'll be back."

"Don't be too confident."

"I don't need confidence," she said with a grin. "All Blue's got is watered down carbonated cordial." She pointed to the drink in his hand. "That's the real deal right there."

"Damn," Clarke said, opening his wallet and peeling out a pink five dollar note. "You *are* good. I can see why you opened a shop out here."

She took the money from him and smiled sweetly. "There hasn't been one cent coins in this country since 1992. I'll have to round it up to an even five."

"Of course, you do." Clarke put on his hat. "If you see Roth, would you give me a call?"

Vera nodded. "Yes, officer."

"Andy," he told her, backing towards the door. "You can call me Andy."

She snorted and watched him leave. It was the best view of him, if she said so herself.

"Oh," he said, sticking his head back through the door. "I know a guy who could get that window fixed for you. Can I give him your number?"

Vera laughed and shrugged. "Sure. He better be willing to negotiate."

"I'll give the guy fair warning." Clarke grinned and let the door close before he strode across the verandah to his 4WD.

*Call me Andy.* Vera crossed her arms and watched him drive away, her head in two places. The cops were looking for Roth, and she was crushing on Sergeant Andy Clarke.

*Damn it,* she thought, turning back to the aisle. *Damn it all to hell and back.*

## CHAPTER 5

The Exiles sat around their usual table that night at the pub, drinking as the sun set in a blaze of orange and red through the windows.

Eloise sat beside Kyne, Hardy lounged on her other side, and Wally and Drew were opposite. Blue was fussing behind the bar, pouring a jug of beer. Finn wasn't there that night but was likely with the other fae doing whatever fae did in the middle of nowhere.

They were currently discussing Eloise's van with great enthusiasm while she complained about Wally's lack of invoice, but one voice was missing. Vera was late.

The witch seemed frazzled when she finally came in, which seemed out of sorts compared to her usual fiery spark. Her hair was tangled and her eyes looked a little red.

Eloise sat up straight and shot the witch a worried

look. Vera just shrugged and sat beside Drew, who moved his chair aside to give her room.

"You're late," the shifter grumbled.

Vera looked around the table. "What are you arguing about?"

"Wally won't invoice me for the van repairs," Eloise told her.

"Bloody right, I won't," the mechanic grumbled.

"Let me reimburse you for the part at least," she complained.

"If someone's offering you something for free take it," Vera said.

"Free stuff usually comes with a catch," Drew stated, then jerked as the witch kicked him beneath the table. "Ow! What was that for?"

"Who was the cop we saw going into the *Outpost* today?" Wally asked, conveniently changing the subject. "Eloise and I were over at the windmill when we saw him pull up."

Vera tensed and her cheeks flushed. Eloise tilted her head to the side, wondering if that was what had her so frazzled, but her friend shook her head.

"Sergeant Andrew Clarke," Vera replied to the group. "Came all the way out here from Lightning Ridge."

"A sergeant?" Hardy asked. "What did he want?"

"He was looking for Roth," the witch told them. "Apparently, he missed a court date. Got himself an arrest warrant for the trouble."

Drew paled and drained his beer.

"There's zero evidence, for one," Hardy said. "I made sure to cover our tracks at their camp."

"And I was the one who made the whole pack disappear," Eloise added.

"I was the one who blew his brains out," the shifter muttered.

"I was the one who let you," she said. "We're in this together."

Hardy nodded. "All of us."

"Us Exiles are family," Vera told the dingo. "What happens to one, happens to all."

"I feel sick," Drew said, shoving to his feet. He strode out of the pub, looking green.

Eloise glanced at Kyne, who shook his head. "He'll be all right."

"I wouldn't go after him right now," Hardy said. "I can hear him chucking up outside."

"What'd that copper say about the window?" Blue asked.

"He wanted to know what happened," Vera replied. "I told him it was a bird. He seemed to buy it. Even offered to find a glazier for me."

"Strewth," Wally declared. "Looks like you've got yourself an admirer, Vera."

"I'll say," Blue added. "He came in here and told me you said I only sold watered down carbonated cordial."

"That's because you do." Vera laughed, but Eloise noticed the usual light in her eyes was a little dull.

"Did you get a vision?" Kyne asked her.

Vera shook her head. "I didn't want to draw suspicion. It's not exactly a subtle science."

The door opened and Drew staggered back in, wiping his mouth with the back of his hand. "I'm okay," he said as he sat back down. "I just need to shift soon."

Kyne's eyebrows rose. "I didn't know it made you that sick."

"The longer I leave it, the more my gut revolts. Trust me, you don't wanna know."

"What did you tell Clarke?" Hardy asked Blue, swiftly changing the subject.

"Nothing," the publican replied. "The Dust Dogs never came in here. Knew they wouldn't get anywhere with me. According to the police, I haven't laid eyes on the bloke for months."

Kyne snorted. "And he bought it?"

"I don't have superpowers like you lot, but I can spin a yarn when I need to."

"I saw him yesterday as well," Vera said. "I was out digging for witchetty grubs just off the highway and he pulled over. I reckon he was paying the Dust Dogs' camp a visit."

Kyne looked her over. "He spoke to you?"

"Yeah," she said with a shrug. "Wanted to see if I needed any help."

Eloise frowned, but it was likely innocent on Clarke's behalf. The seal and Andante's warning had her questioning every little out-of-place happening in Solace, and from the look on the other Exiles' faces, so were they.

"Don't look at me like that," the witch complained. "He was just doing his duty. He's human."

"How do you know?" Drew asked sullenly.

"I'm a witch." Vera pouted. "That's how I know."

"If this Sergeant Clarke is sniffing around, then it's likely we'll all receive a visit," Hardy said, drawing attention away from Vera. "We have to get our stories straight."

"Not that he can prove anything anyway," Wally stated.

"Sure, but we don't want to draw attention," Kyne told them. "We've got enough going on without the police investigating us, too."

"None of us have seen Roth for months," Wally said. "And that's the truth. Let's just forget about the standoff."

"And I haven't seen him at all," Eloise stated.

"What do I tell him?" Drew asked, his voice quieter than usual. "I ran with them for months..." He coughed and reached for his beer.

"As much of the truth as possible," Hardy said. "The best lies are ninety-nine percent true."

Vera laid a hand on the dingo's arm. "Tell him you were homeless and they took you in, but you left when you realised what kind of men they were. You came here, and we helped you. You weren't in deep, so it was easy to disappear. Everything else is irrelevant."

"Shooting Roth at point-blank range isn't exactly irrelevant," Drew muttered.

Eloise tensed, her brow creasing. She was beginning to regret letting the shifter kill the alpha. He was trying to get justice for his family, but the toll on his state of mind was far greater than Roth not being around to hurt anyone else.

"Drew, you have to keep it to yourself," Vera said, leaning towards him. "Just while Clarke is around."

"I know," he muttered. "*I know.*"

Eloise watched their silent exchange, her gaze following the witch's touch on his arm and the way Drew edged closer. Was there something going on there? Vera seemed to notice and pulled back, rubbing her hands up and down her arms.

"What about Finn?" Eloise asked. "Someone has to give the fae a heads-up."

"I'll go see him later," Hardy replied. "He'll listen to me."

"It's probably best he keeps himself scarce for a few days," Vera drawled. "God knows he likes to draw attention to himself."

Kyne shifted beside Eloise, and she looked up at his troubled expression. "I agree."

"Food's up," Blue said, putting an end to their conversation. "Someone give me a hand in the kitchen."

"I will," Vera blurted. She was out of her chair before anyone could blink.

"Is she all right?" Eloise murmured in Kyne's ear.

"Yeah," he whispered, "she's fine."

Somehow, Eloise wasn't sure that was entirely true.

---

Outside, the night was warm.

Eloise looked up at the stars as Kyne stood beside her, her belly full of Blue's outstanding cooking. The silver points shone so brightly, their light broke through the artificial orange of the bulbs outside the pub. She didn't think she'd ever get tired of how beautiful this country was. Away from human habitation, the outback was as stunning as it was dangerous.

"Want to go for a walk?" Kyne asked.

"Sure."

They wandered across the yard, their boots crunching on the ochre gravel. The muted sounds of music and voices echoed from the pub behind them, but everything else was still. Eloise shivered, knowing that other things besides animals, reptiles, and insects roamed the darkness. It was eerie, but they were safe within the bounds of Solace—the light and magic kept the wandering spirits away.

"Vera seemed a little off," Eloise began as they

walked along the side of the highway. "You said she was fine, but..."

"It wasn't proper to say anything at dinner," Kyne said. "A cop poking around is one thing, but it's coming up to the anniversary of her family's death. I don't blame her for feeling a little off-kilter."

Her heart skipped a beat. "Her entire family?"

"Yeah. Her coven was murdered back in Ireland. That's why she moved here."

"Murdered?" she whispered, horrified. "I knew she'd lost people, but everyone? *Murdered?*"

"That's a story she should tell you," Kyne said. "If she chooses."

"Of course." Eloise nodded, making a note to check in on the witch.

They passed Hardy's shop, crossed the side road, and went by the darkened *Outpost*. The boarded-up window was the last remaining sign that the Dust Dogs had ever been there.

"Can we go up to the cemetery?" Eloise asked. "I haven't seen it yet."

Kyne looked up at the moon. It was a little over half full, but bright enough to see past the three light posts that lit Solace's highway.

"Sure," he said. "Should be okay."

The settler's cemetery sat on a small square block a hundred metres north of the windmill.

A historical marker—an obelisk with a bronze plaque—was placed out front by the road, and just beyond were the headstones. Some were crumbling, others were faded, though a few were still legible, just like Wally had told her.

A half-rotting white picket fence surrounded the plot, though it'd done nothing to keep out the scrappy plants of the outback. Spinifex grass had crept in, and they had to be careful walking between the gravesites or they'd be skewered alive.

Eloise turned to the closest headstone, a cracked piece of white marble, and read the inscription.

*Edward Hardy*
*1835-59*
*Died searching for his fortune*
*Aged 24 years*
*May God rest his soul*

She looked up at Kyne. "Hardy?"

"No relation to our friendly town vampire," he told her. "I've already asked."

"How old is he anyway?"

Kyne scratched his head. "You know what... He's never told me."

Eloise sighed and walked around the rest of the cemetery. Kyne was right. Everyone had their story, and it was their choice to tell it if they wanted.

The rest of the legible headstones told much the same tale as poor Edward Hardy's—mine collapse or mining accident. The outback had claimed so many young men who were desperate to escape poverty and find their fortunes. It wasn't just here, though. Similar stories were written all through Australia's gold rush history. Opal was yet another rush that was even more of a gamble.

"How are you feeling about your powers?" Kyne asked, drawing her attention back to the present. "What you did to the Dust Dogs...that was pretty out there."

"Even for you?"

He nodded. "Even for me."

She shrugged. "I'm okay, I guess. I feel a little stronger every day. Now I understand what I've been feeling, I can figure it out."

"You're a natural."

Smiling, she gazed at the lonely cemetery and the darkness of the outback beyond. She was the sum of all her experiences. Her path had been long, but it'd led her here. Her dreams had foretold it in a strange way, but there was still one piece missing—the black mountain. Whatever it meant, she didn't know.

Wondering if she'd change any of it, Eloise shook her head. Regretting the past would eat her up inside. Things were good, and for the first time in her life, she could picture a future, regardless of her silly dreams.

"What are you thinking?" Kyne murmured.

"Just about life and the long, winding road that led me here."

He waited, giving her space to tell him if she wanted.

"My life was lonely for a long time," she began. "I was lost for a lot of my formative years. Years I was supposed to spend growing as a person...but instead, I hid. That kind of stuff leaves a mark I'll probably carry for the rest of my life. I still feel weird about touching people, but that'll change. It'll take time to adjust." Like the river that ebbed and flowed with the currents of time and space. The river she was able to draw from with her elemental power.

Kyne grinned at her, his eyes sparkling.

Eloise hesitated. "What?"

"That's probably the wisest thing I've ever heard you say...and you've said some wise things since I've met you."

She blinked. "You think I'm wise?"

"Why wouldn't you be?" He took her hand in his. "You've travelled far and wide, been through some tough times, looked after yourself when no one else would, stood up against an armed bikie gang, got lost in the outback..."

She smirked and tugged on his hand. "And handed you your arse."

He laughed and shook his head. "Don't remind me. That wasn't one of my finest moments."

"We were both cast out by our birth parents," she told him. "Though my adopted parents...that was my fault." She sighed and looked up at the stars.

"It was an accident."

Eloise didn't reply. Maybe one day when she knew what she was doing with her powers, she could go back and try to fix what she'd done.

"We're all a work in progress," she finally said.

He was silent for a moment, his brow furrowed. "Can I ask you something?"

She nodded.

"Are we together?" he asked. "One hundred percent?"

Eloise frowned. "What kind of question is that?"

"Well, we haven't really spoken about it. Everything happened all at once with you getting lost, the seal, the dingoes... We haven't really slowed down until now."

She bit her bottom lip. Her inexperience with people and relationships had come back to bite her on the rear end. *Again.*

"I didn't know we had to..." she muttered hesitantly.

"I guess not, but this is kind of new to me, too."

"You've never—" She looked him over. Kyne was handsome, put together, kind, and had a stable income...even though he made his cash underground. How had he not had a relationship?

"Ah..." He looked sheepish. "I've had girlfriends before, but never anything serious."

Suddenly, Eloise felt jealousy punch her in the gut. When he'd kissed her the other week, it'd been her first time. Knowing he'd been with other women... She hissed and ran her hands over her face. This relationship business was tough.

"I didn't mean..." he began backpedaling *hard*. "I just wanted... I only want you, Eloise. Just you."

"Well, in that case, I only want you, too. Is that okay?"

"Is it okay?" Kyne laughed, relief making his shoulders sag. "Bloody hell, of course it's okay."

Her cheeks were hot. "Can we not have this conversation again?"

"*Deal.*"

They wandered back out to the road and lingered by the obelisk.

"When Drew and I were working on the house," Kyne began, "he said something that made me think about things with Black Hole Mine and Solace. I own a big chunk of land and have the permits..." he trailed off like he was uncertain about telling her.

"You want to develop it?" she asked, not seeing the big deal. "Is there opal there?"

"No, I bought it to help safeguard the town," he replied. "It wasn't about the money. With my powers back, it won't be so hard finding a new vein of opal on my lease. I knew there was more than one source when I first went out there. With the ridge, I was thinking of the future."

Eloise nodded. "I know the feeling. I feel like I have one now. A goal to work towards." Not that she was sure what that goal looked like.

"Then..." He took a deep breath. "You can't stay in your van through summer. Even with air conditioning, it'll be unbearable *and* dangerous. I can't have it."

She blinked, taken aback by the sudden change in topic. "My van is my home. I'll handle it."

"I want to build you a house," the elemental went on. "I mean... I want to build *us* a house."

Her smile faded. "What about Drew?"

"Most of the hard work is done already," he replied. "It helps to be an earth elemental. Just gotta wire the electrical when the solar panels and batteries come. And paint. We're doing the plumbing tomorrow. It'll be totally off-grid once it's done. No bills, powered by the sun. Perfection. Well, we might have to plumb into the town's water, but that's no big deal."

Eloise watched him as he prattled on about Drew's dugout, her heart beating a million miles an hour. Kyne wanted to build them a house to live in together. He was really serious about her. It'd only been a few weeks and her life had changed one hundred percent.

She turned, resting her hand on the fence. Taking a deep breath, she lowered her gaze.

"Eloise?"

"It's fast," she managed to say. "Really fast."

"I know, but I'm serious. I know how I feel about you. We're sitting on an ancient power that could destroy us all. I don't want to wait before I say it."

Her bottom lip trembled, and her throat tightened as a hurricane of unknown emotions flooded through her. She struggled with her words, not knowing what to say. Yes? No? *Maybe?*

"I'll build it for me, then," Kyne blurted. "You can stay there if you want to. I'll build you a place where you can park your van." When she looked up at him, he held up his hands. "Totally optional. It'll be there when you want a change of scenery. Anyway, I'm tired of rooming with Hardy. Vampire's barely sleep, you know. He's always waking me up at odd hours doing vampire-y things."

"Okay..." she managed to squeak. Who knew what 'vampire-y' things entailed?

"I'll get the best air conditioning money can buy."

Her fear began to thaw and a smile crept onto her lips. "I do like air conditioning."

"Well, then." Kyne grinned and got down on one knee. Taking her hands, he asked, "Eloise Hart? Will you stay with me this summer?"

Laughing, she nodded. "Sure will."

## CHAPTER 6

Two nights later, Vera left her dugout and ventured into the outback.

It was a clear and warm evening. The air was electric, as if it sensed she was about to call upon her magic. Tonight was for memory...and for ritual.

Grit worked its way underneath her sandalled feet, digging between her toes as she walked. She followed a faint path through the scrub behind the *Outpost* and wound through bushes, ducked under trees, leaving the lights of Solace behind her.

Her bag was heavy on her arm, the cream calico full to bursting with the tools she needed. Potions, offerings, and her athame—a silver ritual dagger. The blade wasn't something the covens used until modern times, but it would serve its purpose.

That was the thing about witches—they used what they needed and made do with the things they had. It was the witch, or warlock, and the magic they welded that mattered. Everything else was an extension bent to their will or a connection to the forces they wanted to summon or create.

Emerging into a clearing deep in the scrub, she set down her bag and began to take out all the things she'd brought along. Her ritual required certain offerings to the elements, all of which would connect with her magic when the time was right.

To the earth, she offered a small bag of crystals—quartz, fluorite, and smoky onyx.

To the air, she placed a silver bowl full of found feathers. Some were from eagles and hawks, while others bore the bright colours of outback budgerigars and parrots.

To the water, she gave a collection of seashells—limpets, periwinkles, turban shells, and whelks—that she'd gathered from various beaches.

To the fire, she lit a fabric-wrapped torch, the flame catching on the kerosene-soaked material with a whoosh. Beneath it, she spiked a stick of lit incense into the ground, the scent of cinnamon catching on the newly conjured breeze.

Vera knelt before her offerings and looked to the sky as her magic stirred.

*They were listening.*

"I remember those I have lost and offer them solace in the next life," she murmured, holding out her hands. "To the Nightshades who bind the dark. To the Crescents who lead us towards the light. For the

Earthstones who shelter us, and the Brinewolds who carry us home." Her magic swelled, purple light gathering in her palms. "I am Vera Brinewold of the water on high, daughter of Claire Brinewold and Matthew Nightshade. I remember those I have lost. Their magic was taken from them, and if I am the last of my coven, I remain to guide them home. Though I am far away, I will never forget."

She lowered her head and closed her eyes, remembering. Her mind swelled with magic as her ritual gathered force, sending her spiralling into a nightmare she'd become all too familiar with.

A girl of ten, returning home from school to find the withered husks of her family...her coven. Drained of magic, *of life*. Mummified corpses laying about the house, the walls scarred and scorched by magic. They'd fought, but what use was it against those starved and crazed creatures?

*The fae did it*, a dark voice whispered in her ear. *They fed on their magic.*

A chill spread through her bones. A power of shadows and death. A warning.

Vera gasped and her eyes snapped open. The torch flame flickered as a gust of wind buffeted her, and she tucked her hair behind her ears.

Looking around the clearing, she watched the darkness, but nothing stirred. The breeze fell flat again and warmth returned to her chilled fingertips.

*That was strange.*

With her ritual complete, Vera decided it wasn't best to linger. She'd usually spend a few hours out here, meditating and watching the stars, but not tonight. Things felt different this year. Was it the seal? Perhaps. The magic she felt emanating from it had changed after Eloise's arrival and the Dust Dog's attempt at taking control of Solace.

Whatever it was, Vera wasn't about to tempt fate. More would come, that much they knew for certain.

She gathered her offerings and doused the torch, plunging the clearing into shadow. Returning to the trail, she began the walk back home.

What was that voice? Her father was from the Nightshade coven, who was bound to the dark. A part of her suspected it was the legacy of his power manifesting through her blood, but that didn't sound right. If she was to inherit any of his talents, she would have done so from birth. The only thing she had of him was the hue of her magic. *Purple Nightshade.*

She was so lost in thought that she didn't sense a figure standing on the trail ahead. A shadow loomed out of the darkness, and Vera raised her athame with a yelp.

Silver eyes flashed in the moonlight and she cursed. "Finn! *Bloody hell.* I almost stabbed you!"

"With that little thing?" the fae asked with a raised eyebrow.

"Didn't Hardy tell you to stay away from Solace?"

Finn shrugged. "He said something about police."

His nonchalance was really grinding her gears. Didn't he *care?*

"Of all the days to annoy me, today isn't the best one," she hissed.

"I don't want to upset you, Vera."

She snorted. "That'd be a first. Forgive me if I don't believe you."

"I'm Unseelie, so that brings a certain level of abrasive arrogance," he drawled. "But this time, I'm being sincere."

"Then why are you lingering out here like a perverted creeper?" she demanded.

Finn ground his teeth for a long moment. "I wanted to tell you I'm sorry," he managed to say, "for what my people did to your coven."

Vera froze. Finn had never told her once that he was sorry for anything. He'd never spoken with this level of seriousness, either. Was it a fae trick? She knew they were known for being duplicitous and had a penchant for illusion magic. As far as she knew, they revelled in it.

"I was trapped here," he told her. "I was here when the portals to my world closed. I couldn't return."

Vera hesitated and looked him over. She'd always thought Finn was exiled recently. Sent from his world to hers to live out the rest of his life starved of magic. Whatever he'd done to warrant it, she hadn't cared to know. Now, he admitted he was here all along.

"But the portals were closed a thousand years ago," she murmured cautiously.

Finn kicked the toe of his boot in the dirt. "Don't ask me what I did all that time because I hardly remember."

She swallowed hard, her thoughts on her family. "Did you take any magic to survive?"

He frowned and lowered his gaze. "I took from nature, which was worse to my people. I'll never be able to go home."

"Why were you here in the first place?"

"It hardly matters now," he replied. "Anyone who cared is dead and gone."

"It couldn't have been nothing," she said. "You're still here, so it matters to you."

Finn smirked, his silver eyes flashing, and Vera knew she'd lost the one spark of heart the fae had ever shown her.

"We might have one day a year we call a truce to our verbal sparring," he said, "but we aren't close enough for me to tell you *that* story."

Vera sighed and looked towards Solace. "Whatever. I'm going home."

Finn whistled as she walked away.

"Don't stray too far from the path," he called out. "The shadows are watching."

Vera stopped in her tracks, her heart leaping. Did he know what she'd felt during her ritual? She turned, opening her mouth to retort, but Finn was already gone.

Her gaze went to the darkness and she shivered as goosebumps prickled over her arms. Suddenly, she didn't feel so alone.

Trembling, Vera hightailed it back to Solace, not daring to look back.

Drew's dingo eyes worked best at night.

He watched Vera walk down the path into the scrub, his sharp gaze following her every move. She held a heavy bag over one arm and her shoulders sagged.

She was sad.

He crouched in the shadows, wondering if he should follow or wait. Things lurked in the night he didn't want her to come face to face with.

Before he'd come to Solace, Drew had seen lights hovering in the pitch black of the outback. The moon and stars could only light so much with their dim silvery glow, so when twin yellowish orbs bobbed across the scrub, flickering in and out of focus, he took notice.

Later, Vera had told him they were called 'Min Min lights'.

"She honours her mob," Coen said, appearing out of thin air. "It's not for us to see."

Drew looked up at the Indigenous man. There were a few things he wanted to say, but words were beyond him in his current shape.

Coen always seemed to appear when Drew was a dingo, never when he was a man. It made things awfully one-sided, though he could see far more than he had ever managed as a human. Coen had an aura that was different from the other Exiles.

Everyone had a certain smell and presence that he could detect, though Coen was the only person he could 'see'. Colour followed him in the night, like the glistening galaxies and nebulas in the sky. If it was part of his supernatural gift, Drew wasn't sure. Everything Coen was, was a mystery—one that wasn't for him to know, apparently.

Drew sniffed the air, looking for the kangaroo that usually accompanied Coen's appearances.

"*Marlu* is away." Coen grinned and rubbed his belly. "Resting."

He tilted his head to the side, hoping he didn't mean he'd had the thing for dinner.

"She has a joey," the Indigenous man explained. "A boy."

Drew wagged his tail. At least someone was happy around here. Everyone else seemed to have some kind of turmoil they were constantly working through.

"You care for Vera, but she'll be all right," Coen said. "She needs to make her own peace. Her journey is best travelled inside." He thumped his fist over his heart. "Within darkness, there is light...and a path."

Drew whimpered softly and looked towards the trail. Vera had disappeared from sight. Finally, he stood and looked up at Coen before he turned towards Solace.

He'd wait for her in the shadows near the *Outpost*. Just to make sure she got home safe.

She'd never know he was there.

***

Kyne grunted as he lifted the first slab of solar tiles into place on the verandah roof. They slid onto the terracotta tiles easily, clipping together to create one seamless row. He stood on the ladder, leaning over as he fixed them into place. Easiest solar install ever.

Drew had been out running all night, so Kyne took the opportunity to get some work done on his own. Not that he didn't mind the help, he just got things finished up quicker.

Next, he drilled into the tile, creating an outlet for the wiring.

"Cooee!" a voice called. "Hello up there!"

Kyne turned, glancing down at Sergeant Clarke. The cop was a young bloke, maybe in his mid-thirties. He'd certainly done well for himself in the force for his age, that was for sure.

Kyne brandished the drill and raised his eyebrows. "Sergeant. Clarke, was it?"

"You've been expecting me, I see..." Clarke trailed off, nudging the elemental for his name.

"Kyne Brady. Vera told me she saw you out on the highway," he said, climbing down the ladder. He set the drill down, then picked up his hat and shoved it on his head. "If you're checking up on the build, I can go get the permits for you. Got them in the glovebox of my ute just there. It's all above board."

"I don't doubt it," Clarke said. "But I'm not here about permits."

Kyne looked him over. "Nah, I didn't think a sergeant would stoop to checking up on council regulations this far out from the Ridge."

"Craig Roth. You know him?"

Kyne snorted. "Of course I know him. The man has a reputation."

"Well, I'm keen to talk to the guy. You seen him?"

"Not for a couple of months, I guess. Him and his bikie mates don't come to town all that often. Vera refuses to do business with them if she can help it. The rest of the town is the same. We're an upstanding lot here, sergeant."

"You wouldn't want to do something about that, would you?"

"If you're insinuating something, sergeant, forget about it." Kyne laughed and shook his head. "I've got too much going on to think about that. I've got a house to build and opal to mine. That takes up all my time."

"You mine opal?"

Kyne nodded. "For the last ten years."

"If I might ask, why aren't you out there now? All the miner's I know from the Ridge are obsessed with chasing the stuff. Grind right down to their last dollar."

"I don't doubt it," he replied. "It's a rare bit of stone." He shrugged and wiped his hands on his jeans. "I was on a good bit of ground for a while, but I pulled out all the veins. Got some good stuff, so I'm having a break before I try again."

"And building a house is a break?"

He laughed. "Beats being underground this close to summer."

The sound of a heavy body bashing through the bush caused them to turn their heads, and a moment later, Drew came barrelling into the yard.

"Sorry I'm late, I—" He clamped his mouth shut as he laid eyes on Clarke.

"I don't believe we've met. I'm Sergeant Andrew Clarke." The cop held out his hand.

"Drew," he said, glancing down at Clarke's proffered hand, though the shifter didn't take it.

Clarke grimaced and pulled back. "I was just having a look at the dugout. Got some nice work here."

Drew narrowed his eyes and glanced at Kyne. "Thanks."

"Listen, I won't keep you blokes, but I will ask..."

Clarke turned to Drew. "I'm on the lookout for Craig Roth. A warrant is out for his arrest. Have you seen him at all?"

Drew shrugged. "What'd he do?"

"Nothing serious," Clarke replied. "Just skipped a court date."

"A warrant, hey?" Kyne asked, drawing the cop's attention away from Drew.

"People don't show, we have to bring 'em in. Times are tough in the outback." He shifted his gaze onto Drew again. "How do you know him?"

"Roth?" Drew shrugged. "He was the unwelcome wagon when I first came to town. I'm not into bikie gang crap, so I came to live here. Work at the *Outpost*."

"Ah, so you run the shop the days Vera is off," Clarke mused. "Good to know."

"Is that all, sergeant?" Kyne asked. "We've got a lot of work to get finished before it gets too hot."

"Yeah." Clarke nodded and gave Drew a curious look. "If you see Roth, give the guy a wide berth and call triple zero."

"Sure," Kyne said. "Will do."

They watched Sergeant Clarke walk towards the road and get into his shiny police 4WD, waiting until he was out of earshot before moving again.

"How'd I do?" Drew asked.

Kyne sighed and watched Clarke drive off. "Could've been better."

"He seemed *familiar* with Vera," the shifter

murmured. "Talked about her like she was something to eat."

"I didn't notice."

Drew grunted and kicked a stone across the yard. "I can smell stuff being a dingo."

Kyne turned and curled his nose. "I really don't want to know."

"He was wearing cologne. Nice stuff, too."

"He'll be back and when he does, he'll ask questions about you," the elemental warned. "Forget about how he smells."

"Shit," Drew muttered. "My head's all screwed up after shifting."

"Don't worry about it. We've got your back." He turned to Drew and narrowed his eyes. "Why do you care what the bloke smells like? Are you jealous?"

"No," the dingo blurted. "*Am not.*"

Kyne shook his head and shoved Drew playfully. "Yeah right, pull the other one."

The shifter scowled. "I'm just looking out for her. I owe her."

"If you say so," Kyne said, picking up the drill. "Let's get back to work. Summer's coming, and I've got another house to build."

Drew's eyes widened. "Eloise said yes?"

"Eloise said *maybe*." He grinned. "She's one in a million. I'll take any crumb I can get."

## CHAPTER 7

Eloise wandered down the hill towards the highway, the morning sun already coaxing a fine layer of sweat across her forehead.

She'd had a couple of days to dwell on Kyne's proposal, but she still wasn't sure what to do. She couldn't use him for air conditioning, could she? No, she wasn't *that* shallow...wasn't she?

Frowning, Eloise pushed open the door to Hardy's workshop. She'd have to give him an answer before he was done building Drew's place.

"Nothing?" Hardy said. He looked up as she walked in and pointed to the mobile phone in his hand. "I thought there would be some movement by now. These big mining corps never sit still for long. They always play employment numbers to the government." He scowled as whoever was on the other end spoke. "Yeah, well, keep me posted. I'll swing by next time I'm in the city." He grinned and let out a small hiss, glancing at Eloise. "Be careful. I just might."

Eloise sat in her usual chair and pretended not to listen. She got the feeling his contact at the Queensland Department of Natural Resources was a woman—one who Hardy seemed to enjoy the company of a great deal.

Eloise coughed nervously. She hoped it wasn't a 'meal' type of deal.

"You're early," the vampire said.

"Was that your *contact* in the government?" she asked, busying herself setting up the grinder.

Hardy nodded. "Yeah. Still no movement on those *EarthBore* permits."

"That's good, right?"

"For now."

Eloise grimaced and double-checked the belts on the grinders. She was glad she wasn't on her own when it came to thwarting a big mining company. How would they manage it, anyway?

"I hear Kyne asked you to move in with him," Hardy stated.

Her eyes widened and she turned to the bag of rough opal she'd been working through the previous day. "Yeah. To a house he wants to build for us."

"So? Most women would jump at the chance."

"Yeah, but I'm not *most women*."

"No, you're definitely not."

Her cheeks heated, an annoying habit she was

developing around the men in this town, and she sighed. "Clarke hasn't been to see you yet?"

"Not yet," Hardy replied, "but it's only a matter of time. Things work slow out here, so who knows when he'll decide to show up."

"Can you..." She waved her hands over her eyes. "Do that thing?"

His lips quirked. "What thing?"

"*Hardy*. Kyne told me that you could...*influence* people."

"Compel?" He raised his eyebrows. "I could, but that's a rabbit hole I wouldn't want to go down. I could throw him off the scent, but there's an entire police force behind him. Reports, prosecutors, *evidence*. It's not as easy as it sounds." She bit her bottom lip, and the vampire laughed. "I can't do it to other supernaturals, just so you know."

"Oh, good. That's reassuring."

He studied her for a moment. "How are things going with that windmill?"

"Slow. Wally's going to help me see if there's water in the bore."

"Are you going to use your powers?"

She blinked. "I thought about it, but I'm not sure how..."

"I'd use them sparingly."

"Why?"

"We're open about ourselves with each other, but we still live in a world dominated by humans," Hardy told her. "Being inconspicuous isn't just about not drawing unwanted attention to the seal. We shouldn't rely on our abilities or become too relaxed using them."

Eloise shook her head and picked through the opal, feeling out the next piece she wanted to cut with her powers. She was getting better at tuning into her elemental side, but sometimes it felt like a double-edged sword. The whole 'with great power, comes great responsibility' thing. Maybe Hardy was right about not relying too heavily on them. Vera had the same attitude about her magic and she could do so much more.

"Someone out there knows about Solace and the fact the Dust Dogs had the key," Hardy mused. "More supernaturals will come, and that's just a fact we have to live with. We can't make it easy for them. If they don't know who we are and what we can do, then the better off we'll be."

"You're right." Eloise grimaced. Her thoughts went back to her arrival in Solace, the dreams and seeing them come to life when she was lost. "I wonder if the black mountain is a clue."

This got Hardy's attention. "The mountain in your dreams?"

"Yeah. It's the only part of them that hasn't shown itself." She shrugged. "Coen didn't seem fussed about it, so... I dunno, maybe it's nothing."

"Or maybe it's everything," the vampire mused.

"Maybe…" Everything had been connected so far. Eloise looked up, her gaze fixing on the array of machinery along the back wall of the workshop. "The police will go back out there, won't they? They wouldn't leave an abandoned bikie squat alone, especially since they're looking for Roth."

Hardy nodded. "A criminal gang that just up and moves is a red flag. The police will do forensics but their motorcycles are gone, and that's something that works in our favour."

"What'll happen if they don't stop looking?"

"Then we'll have to give them a reason," Hardy told her.

"What? Make one up?"

The vampire grunted and turned back to his work. "Wouldn't be the first time I've had to plant evidence."

"Do I want to know?" Eloise stared at him, wondering about his life before Solace. How old was he? Vampires were immortal. At the thought of Hardy being hundreds of years old, she paled.

"I heard that," he said, his voice muffled.

"Heard what?"

"Your heart skipping a beat."

She swallowed hard. "Sorry?"

He turned and grinned at her. "You have nothing to fear from me, Eloise. It's been a long time since I was new. The things that drive a vampire in the early days no longer give me any satisfaction." His expression turned wistful and his smile widened. "Not unbidden anyway."

Eloise shot him a wry look and picked up the bag of opal. *Tell that to your mistress in the Department of Natural Resources*, she thought. *On the other hand, maybe she likes it.*

She set down the opal and took a deep breath. Maybe she *should* ask.

"What is it?"

Eloise turned and couldn't help the flush in her cheeks. "How... The sun."

"That's not what you really wanted to ask, but I answer both," the vampire replied. "I can tolerate the sun because of magic. I have a spell woven around me that stops me from bursting into flames. As for the other thing..." He shrugged. "Well, you don't want to go looking in my fridge."

Eloise raised her eyebrows and snorted. Blood bags. She definitely didn't want to know how he got them.

"Thank you," she said. "My ignorance is embarrassing."

Hardy chuckled. "Not at all. It's not every day someone meets a vampire and lives to tell the tale."

"And what makes you different?"

Hardy's smile faded a little. "That's a long story." Then he turned back to his work, forcing an abrupt end to their conversation.

Eloise let out a shaky breath and picked up a promising piece of raw opal. That was that, then.

---

Vera's head was throbbing.

She pinched the bridge of her nose and willed the ache to go away, but that only seemed to make her brain pulse even harder.

Getting up off the couch, she went into the kitchen and rustled around in the cupboards. There was a good recipe she knew for a headache cure but wasn't sure if it would do much. This felt magical, almost like a bad hangover from using too much power.

Had she really used that much in her ritual last night? No, she hadn't...she'd barely touched her magic at all.

Taking a small plastic Ziplock bag out of the cupboard, Vera tipped the contents into a mortar. The dried grass had been cut into small lengths, ready to be ground.

This particular variety of native lemongrass had similar properties to aspirin and had been used by native peoples for generations. Perhaps with a bit of magic, and a few other ingredients she'd been trialling, it'd help rid her of the throb in her temples.

As she crushed the grass, the pestle released a pungent scent of warm lemon. The plants here weren't like the ones she knew from back home in Ireland, but they had proven to be more potent than anything she'd used before. Who knew simple lemongrass would be more effective than feverfew?

A knock at the front door broke through her thoughts and she set down the pestle. Who could that be?

Pushing through the beaded curtain at the end of the hall, she climbed the stairs, her magic humming. When she opened the door, she was surprised to see a familiar face. "Eloise!"

"Hey," the elemental said. "I'm not interrupting, am I?"

"No, not at all." Vera stepped aside. "Do you want to come in?"

"Sure." Eloise edged past her and walked down the stairs. "I wanted to come and see how you were doing. Kyne told me about... Well, just that it was..."

Vera knew she was trying to be tactful about it, but she shrugged. "It was a long time ago. You don't have to be gentle with me."

Eloise paused in the hall. "Maybe, but it's polite."

The witch smiled and pointed through the beaded curtain. "I'm just finishing up on something in the kitchen. Go through." She followed the elemental through the curtain and into the kitchen.

Eloise's gaze ran over the mess on the countertop. "What are you making?"

"I've got this rotten headache," Vera replied,

picking up the pestle. "I'm trying a new mixture, but it needs some tweaking."

"Maybe you should take some ibuprofen?" Eloise suggested. "Just for now."

Vera sighed. "Maybe you're right."

"Do you have any? I've got some in my van if you want me to go get it. It'll only take a minute."

"No, no, that's okay. I've got some in the bathroom." Vera gasped abruptly and waved her hands. "Where are my manners? Do you want a cup of tea?" She took out a canister and opened the lid. "I've got this beautiful black tea infused with vanilla and cinnamon. Here. Smell it." She thrust the tea at Eloise, who dutifully sniffed.

"Oh," the elemental declared, "that does smell good."

"I'll make you a cup. You'll love me for it." She took out two teacups from the cupboard. "I know you like tea because I've seen it in your van."

"From when you and Drew broke in, you mean?"

Vera's head flew up. "I, ah…"

Eloise laughed and waved her hand dismissively. "Just kidding. I forgave you both for that ages ago."

Vera rolled her eyes. "Hilarious!"

"Give me that and go take something for that headache." Eloise took the tin out of her hands. "Shoo!"

"Make me one, too?"

The elemental's smile brightened. "Of course!"

Vera ducked into the bathroom and opened the medicine cabinet that sat behind the mirror. Taking out some ibuprofen, she chased down a couple of white tablets with a handful of water.

*They sucked their magic out.*

Vera gasped at the sound of an eerie voice in her ear and slammed the cabinet shut. Looking around the bathroom, her heart thundered in her chest, but no one was there. She could hear Eloise in the kitchen as she fussed with the kettle and the plop of water as a drop fell from the shower head in front of her.

Vera shook her head and smoothed down her hair. It was just her imagination. She was tired, her head ached, and bad memories were always thicker this time of year. That's all.

Jutting out her chin in defiance, Vera went back out to the kitchen.

"Everything okay?" Eloise asked.

Vera took one of the teacups and nodded. "Yeah. Almost knocked half the contents of the bathroom on the floor." She coughed hastily. "Let's sit in the lounge."

She settled on the couch while Eloise took the armchair. Cradling the teacup in her hands, she blew softly on the boiling liquid.

"I guess you want to know about my family," Vera began.

Eloise shrugged. "Kind of, but I thought it would be too cheeky to ask outright. I didn't know witches existed, so I'm curious... I don't know how it all works."

"Well, my coven was called the Brinewold," Vera told her. "We lived by the ocean in the north of Ireland. It's not all sandy beaches like here. I'm talking rocky shores, sheer cliffs, wind that'll take the skin off your face, and extreme rough swells. We told stories about the kelpie and puffins." She grinned. "Man, I loved the puffins."

"Puffins?" Eloise asked.

"Little birds with big orange beaks that turn grey in the winter. Cute as hell," Vera replied. "They love the cliffs, you know." Eloise just blinked, so she kept going with her story. "My mother was a Brinewold, but my father was from a different coven, the Nightshades. They were..." She frowned. "Not so good, but my dad was different. He was estranged from them, and when he married my ma, he became one of the Brinewolds. I get the colour of my magic from him. There are a lot of little covens, but there are five main lines of witchcraft to go with each of the elements, and five major covens to match."

"You were one of the five?"

"Yeah. There's the Brinewolds, Nightshades, Crescents, Earthstones, and Zephyrs."

"The five elements," Eloise murmured. "What happened to your coven?"

"Their, uh..." *Their magic was sucked out.* "A group of fae drained their magic."

"The entire coven?" Eloise seemed to pale, her words rasping in her throat. "It was fae?"

"There was a time where the fae used to freely roam between our world and theirs," Vera went on hastily. "Then the portals were closed. It was a whole thing with a dark witch and magic draining, taking over the world... You know how it goes. Well, when the way was shut, it was done without notice. Witches were trapped on their side and fae were trapped here. It wasn't so bad for the witches, but the fae..." She sighed.

"They can't thrive away from magic," Eloise murmured. "That's why Finn and the other fae live near the seal, right?"

Vera nodded. "Cut off from their world and their lifeline, they became withered, crazed husks. The witches called them the 'craglorn', which means 'the lost and lonely'. For a thousand years, they hunted anything with magic..." She trailed off as an image of her parents flashed in her mind's eye. *Withered husks.*

Thankfully, Eloise seemed to get the gist of it. "Vera, I'm so sorry..."

"Ironically, the portals were reopened not long after the Brinewolds were—" She coughed loudly. "But it's difficult to forget."

"So that's why you and Finn are at odds?"

"Yeah," Vera replied, thinking about what he'd admitted to her last night. "Though it's not his fault. He wasn't the one who took them from me. It's just..."

"There's bad blood on both sides."

Vera nodded. "That's one way of putting it."

"Is that why you came to Australia?"

The witch sat up and began to fuss with the empty teacups. "I needed a fresh start. A new adventure. The memories... Witch politics are suffocating. I'm the last of the Brinewolds and the last descendant of the Nighshades that still has access to their legacy. If the covens had it their way, I'd be married off and made into a baby incubator to preserve their precious magic. Fire and water. *What a mix.*" She snorted. Perhaps if she went to the Crescents, their matriarch might help her, but Ireland was the problem, not the covens. It held too many memories she'd rather forget.

"How's your headache?"

Thankful for the change in topic, Vera pressed a palm to her forehead. "You know what? It actually feels much better."

Eloise grinned. "Good."

"So... How is that mural design coming along?"

"I haven't had much time to think about it," the elemental replied. "I've been busy cutting opal and trying to figure out how to get that windmill working again."

"Hmm," Vera mused. "Wally mentioned something about a generator."

"Yeah... I'm worried about tapping into the bore," Eloise admitted with a frown. "Now that I know about the seal and the whole 'heart of the ocean' thing, I wonder—"

"If the water table is connected to it?" Vera thought

about it for a moment. "Maybe, but water was being brought up from that bore for a long time before the windmill stopped working. I see nothing to worry about. Is it important for it to work?"

Eloise shrugged. "Not really, I guess."

"Then we can repair the tank, *just in case*, and paint the mural."

"We? You've changed your mind, then?"

"I guess so," she murmured, thinking about Finn. "What harm could a little paint do?"

Eloise grinned and straightened up. "I was hoping you'd say that. Do you want to help with the design?"

Vera's heart swelled and she nodded. "I've got an old sketchbook we can use." She scrambled off the couch. "Hang on, I'll go grab it."

She really liked having Eloise around. Female company was a rare thing to behold in the male-dominated outback. It wasn't every day a woman shoehorned herself into the mining industry or moved away from the city to a place like Solace.

"Hey," she said, lingering in the doorway. "How do you feel about witchetty grubs?"

Eloise made a face. "I don't know?"

"Wanna try one?

"Uh... Maybe?"

Vera laughed, feeling better than she had in days. Maybe was good enough for her.

## CHAPTER 8

Blue stared at Finn with raised eyebrows.

The fae was slumped against the bar, stuffing his face with a bowl of hot chips and tomato sauce like a drunk nursing a bottle of hard spirits.

"Do I want to know what's got you down in the dumps?" the publican asked.

Finn snorted and held up a chip, rotating it as he gazed at it. "Be thankful I'm only addicted to deep fried potato, not alcohol."

"Hardy asked you to stay away from Solace," Blue told him. "While that cop is sniffing around—"

"I don't care."

"Everyone else cares. Why don't you?"

The fae narrowed his eyes. *"Nobody puts Baby in a corner."*

Blue sighed and glanced at the door. It'd been a day since Sergeant Clarke had been in to question him about Roth. The guy had seemed satisfied with his answers, though that wasn't all he'd been asked about.

'*Vera Walsh,*' Clarke had said. '*She there in that shop all on her own?*'

Blue had been behind a bar most of his life, so if he had a supernatural power—which, being one hundred percent human, he didn't—it'd be reading people. Their demeanour, their intentions, what kind of drunk they were...that kind of thing. So, he knew right off the bat that Sergeant Andrew Clarke had a sparkle in his eye when it came to the local witch.

It wouldn't do anyone any good to bring it up. Besides, if there was anything romantic going on there, it was up to Vera to decide what she wanted. She was an intelligent, capable woman who could decide what to do with her personal life.

If things went sideways and she got her heart broken, then there was an entire town of powerful people who'd defend her honour until the cows came home. Except maybe Finn.

"I know what night it was last night," he said to the fae. "This isn't stress eating, is it?"

"I don't stress eat," Finn retorted. "I eat for pleasure. We don't cook potato like this where I come from."

"How do you?"

"Boil. Bake." He screwed up his nose as he thought. "That's about it."

"I'm surprised you have potatoes there."

Finn snorted. "They're not quite the same. They're

more like sweet potatoes for one. And they are more red than orange. Nothing like these white, starchy things. *Qua'zah*. Boil them in oil? *Amazing*."

Blue shook his head. Potatoes from another world wasn't what he wanted to know. "You didn't go out and watch Vera last night, did you?"

Finn narrowed his eyes. "So what if I did?"

"It's insensitive, for one."

The fae opened his mouth to reply but was cut off by the door opening. Unfortunately, it wasn't a Solace local, but Sergeant Clarke.

Blue sighed and took the tea towel off his shoulder. "G'day, sergeant. Stopping by for a drink? Kitchen's open, too."

Clarke took off his hat, his gaze going straight to Finn. "Not a social call, I'm afraid."

"Still after that Roth fella?" Blue shook his head. "Nothing's changed since the other day. Ain't seen no hide nor hair of the bloke. Been quiet."

Clarke was still looking at Finn, his lips pursed. It was unclear if he was trying to stop himself from laughing or not. "And you are?"

On a normal day, the fae stood out like a sore thumb. At first glance, it seemed like he'd be more at home in a hippy commune than an outback mining town. His idea of masculinity—with his silky shirt, deep blue dreadlocks, and pretty features—was the opposite of the dusty, rugged men who frequented places like Solace.

"Finn."

"Finn...?" Clarke raised his eyebrows.

"Oreah'anza."

"That's an interesting name. What's the origin?"

"A land far, far away," the fae drawled.

Blue coughed loudly and leaned against the bar. "Can I get you anything, sergeant?"

"No, thank you," he replied, still looking at Finn. "Tell me... Do you know anything about Craig Roth?"

"Do I know anything about *Craig Roth?*" Finn drawled, leaning towards the sergeant. "You got a crush on him? I can see why. You'd go together like—"

"We haven't seen him since the other day," Blue interrupted. "Nothing's changed."

"I hope the bastard's fallen off a cliff someplace," Finn stated. "It'd do us all a favour."

Clarke stared at the fae, his gaze taking in everything. "And what would you know about that?"

"I wish I'd shoved him off, but you're barking up the wrong boab, *Andy*."

The sergeant's expression faltered and Blue glanced between the men. Did Finn know something he didn't?

"You'll have to forgive Finn," he said hurriedly. "His mouth runs off on its own. There's a reason he lives out in the middle of woop woop."

"I'm beginning to see that," Clarke replied.

Finn snorted. "And here I was thinking it was just the potatoes." He held up a chip. "*Qua'zah.*"

Blue scowled and turned back to Clarke. "Anything else I can help you with?"

The sergeant shook his head. "It doesn't matter. I can come back another time." He nodded and walked back across the room.

The moment the door shut behind Clarke, Blue turned to the fae and glared. "*Finn*," he hissed, "are you bloody mad?"

"Relax, old man. They've got nothing on us."

"That's not the point!" He slammed his fist on the bar. "We don't need people watching Solace, least of all the law."

"My Unseelie blood is strong," he drawled. "It makes me truthful *and* uncaring. He's lucky I left my snake at home."

That was the wrong thing to say. Blue's anger rose hot and hard and he snapped, "Get out of here. Get out, and don't come back until it's safe. Your *Unseelie blood* will get us all in trouble."

Finn stood and snatched the bowl off the bar. He went to walk away, but turned, his expression cold. Snatching up the bottle of tomato sauce, he held it against his chest and sneered at the publican. Then he strode across the room and shoved out the door.

"Bloody hell, Finn," Blue murmured. "What the hell's got into you?"

Vera sat behind the counter at the *Outpost*, her mind wandering.

She was staring at the rack of cheap sunglasses by the door, studying the reflection in a pair of garish blue lenses. Her hands curled around a hot cup of tea, the chamomile-scented steam wafting around her nose.

The memories of her parents had risen again during the night. Her dreams were alive, but she could barely remember the visions, only that they were there. It usually meant something when Vera dreamed like that. If it was foresight, a warning, a message, or just the echoes of her ritual, there was no way to tell. Life had to play out as intended, and her actions could scarcely change things where her coven was concerned. The future was unwritten, and the past was long gone.

Vera set down her cup and sighed. Flexing her fingers, she calmed a few stray sparks of magic. She couldn't shake the feeling that something was in the air. Maybe it was the changing seasons...

The door opened and the bell rang, causing her heart to skip a beat. Vera looked up as a tall woman strode in, her long, earthy, floral dress trailing behind her.

For a long moment Vera stared at the woman, who seemed so familiar, yet changed by the inevitable passage of time.

Waist-length auburn hair, iridescent hazel eyes, flawless yet freckled skin, perfect blushed lips, tall and willowy... The woman was everything Vera had wished she 'd been blessed with as a gangly teen. As for herself, her figure was less than symmetrical and her fiery red hair frizzed at the slightest hint of humidity. Magic helped tame her curls now, but back then, it was a sight too horrifying to describe.

*Why was she the only one to survive? She was too ugly even for the craglorn.* The old barbs came back to haunt her, and Vera wished the woman standing inside her shop was nothing more than an illusion.

"Vera?" the woman exclaimed in a thick Irish accent, her eyes widening. "Is that you? *Mo bandia*, you finally grew into your curves."

"Rosheen?" Vera tried not to scowl as she felt a familiar wave of magic emanate from the woman.

"Don't look at me like that," she said with a wide smile. "I'm not a ghost, Vera Walsh, though I was beginning to think *you* were."

Vera blinked, her daze broken, and she rounded the counter. "What are you doing here?"

"Well hello to you, too!" The woman opened her arms wide. "Give me hug!"

Vera embraced Rosheen, the sight of her friend sending a strange reverberation through her psyche. It'd been years since she'd left Ireland, and in all that time she'd seen no one from her past. No one at all.

"That's more like it," Rosheen said as she drew back. "Do you know what I've been through looking for you?" She clucked her tongue and looked around the *Outpost*. "Working in a supermarket in the middle of nowhere? No wonder I couldn't find you!"

"This is *my* supermarket," Vera told her.

"What? You own the place?"

She nodded. "It's all mine."

"Well, it seems we have a great deal to catch up on. How long has it been?"

Vera counted in her head. "Ten years, give or take." She'd taken off as soon as she was legally allowed, which was at eighteen.

"More like twelve, but who's counting?" Apparently, Rosheen was.

Vera ignored her. "You came all this way to see me?"

"Of course, I did. I've been looking for you for a long time."

"Why?"

"*Why?* We were like sisters," Rosheen scoffed. "Then you just up and left without a word. The coven was devastated."

Vera snorted. "I bet they were."

"Ack," the witch declared. "We weren't no Brinewolds, but the *Gealach Fola* embraced you all the same." *Gealach Fola* was Irish Gaelic for 'blood moon'. The coven took their name seriously, and it was something that had never sat well with Vera.

"They're just sad I couldn't be married off to mix Brinewold-Nightshade blood with theirs."

Rosheen rolled her eyes. "It wasn't like *that*. We

took you in after your parents died. We were your *family*."

"Is that why you came all this way? To remind me of all the things I supposedly owe?" Ten years was a long time. Vera was hardly the same person, so who knew what Rosheen was into these days. "I never asked for anything."

"No, you didn't, did you?" She pursed her lips and flicked her hair over her shoulder. "Forget about it. I didn't come all this way just to open old wounds."

Vera eyed Rosheen with a healthy dose of skepticism. The *Gealach Fola* did nothing 'just because'. If anyone bothered to ask her opinion, she'd say they were power hungry social climbers. Elitism was the worst, especially when it came to magic. She could only hope her one-time friend was above all that.

Vera suspected the seal had something to do with Rosheen's arrival, but she chose to disregard the notion. The witch was many things, but a threat to Solace wasn't one of them.

"Did something happen?" Vera asked her. "With the coven, I mean."

Rosheen shook her head. "No, nothing like that. I've just been thinking about life a lot recently. Unfinished business, missed chances... I think I'm going through a mid-life crisis."

"Mid-life crisis? You're only a year older than I am."

"A belated quarter-life crisis, then," the witch said with a musical laugh. She breathed deeply and held out her hands. "This place has a strange taste to it, don't you think?"

"If you're going to stay, then you have to know…" Vera trailed off, wondering just how much she should say about Solace's residents, but there was no use hiding the fact that they were magical. Rosheen would pick it the moment she crossed paths with… *Oh no.*

Suddenly Vera hoped Finn and the fae were serious about staying away from town. She could tolerate them being here, even after what happened to her family, but would Rosheen?

"Know what?" the witch asked, tilting her head to the side.

"Other supernaturals live here. It isn't just me."

Rosheen's smile widened. "Now I'm beginning to see why you chose the place. It's a haven."

Vera opened her mouth to reply, but sunlight glinting off metal drew her attention outside. Clarke's 4WD had just pulled into a spot outside Hardy's shop and her heart skipped a beat.

Things were getting complicated. The police seemed to be in for the long haul, her crush on Clarke was becoming a real thing, and now Rosheen was here, bringing baggage from Vera's past—a past she'd rather forget. What was she going to do?

*Nothing,* a small voice told her. *Let him go. It's too complicated. He'll never understand.*

"What are you staring at?"

"Nothing," Vera replied, her gaze superglued to Clarke as he got out of his 4WD.

Rosheen came to stand beside her. "*Dia duit a stór,*" the witch exclaimed in Gaelic. "Who is *that?*"

"No one," Vera muttered. "No one at all."

## CHAPTER 9

Hardy peered at the piece of opal through his magnified jewellers loupe and tilted the stone back and forth.

The cool light from his lamp caught the specks of colour as they flashed in a flame of reds, purples, and blues. The magnifying glass allowed him to see the finer details and get even closer than his vampire sight allowed.

He studied the teardrop cut and polish, looking for imperfections, but found little to be disappointed with. An expert wouldn't see the things he could and wouldn't find a flaw when they inspected the gem. It really was a spectacular piece.

Eloise was a natural, though it helped that she was an elemental. Maybe it was an unfair advantage, but business was business after all.

The buzzer on the front door let out an electronic screech and Hardy set down his tools. A moment later, he stood in the showroom—which was just a fancy word for a few glass display cases, a couple of padded chairs, and some posters on the walls.

Sergeant Clarke jumped and his heart hammered. "Crikey, you scared me."

Hardy smiled, taking in the stature of the police officer for the first time. "My apologies."

If the vampire was being honest, there was nothing remarkable about the sergeant. He was the clean-cut type, with freshly pressed trousers, buttoned-up shirt, and shiny badge. On first glance, Clarke seemed the type to do things by the book, even if it was to his detriment.

"I was wondering when I'd see you," the vampire said. "I'm surprised it took you so long."

Clarke looked around the shop, his gaze taking in the display cases. "Word travels fast."

"When a town consists of less than ten people, it only takes five minutes and a night at the local pub."

The sergeant smiled politely. "It seems I need no introduction, but I'll give you one anyway. Sergeant Andrew Clarke." He held out his hand.

Hardy shook it, squeezing a little harder than he ought to. "Hardy."

Clarke winced but didn't let go. "First name or last?"

"Just Hardy. I'm like Beyoncé," he said with a chuckle. "I only have one name."

He let go of Hardy's hand. "Officially, I don't think that's allowed."

"Frederick Marmaduke Hardy," the vampire said with a sigh. "Unfortunately, my parents were old-fashioned. It was like they lived in the eighteenth century or something." He grimaced and made a show of looking over the sergeant's shoulder. "Please don't tell anyone. It'll ruin my street cred."

Clarke grinned and took off his hat. "Your secret is safe with me." He looked around the showroom, taking in the opal on display. "Tell me, why set up shop all the way out here? Surely there's more business to be had in the Ridge?"

"There's some rich ground here abouts, and I was here first." Hardy leaned against the counter and fixed his gaze on Clarke's. "Don't tell anyone." The sergeant's pupils dilated slightly, and the vampire grinned as the small compulsion took hold. "You're from Lighting Ridge. You know how cutthroat the opal business is. Word gets out, the town booms to its detriment, leases are bought like wildfire, ratters come scurrying out of the woodwork and trash mines in their zest for common thievery. You know how it goes."

"Unfortunately, I do."

Hardy snorted. "That's the Ridge for you. Good people, but where there's big money to be made, trouble surely follows."

"You're not worried about leaving all this on

display?" Clarke gestured to the glass cases and the opal inside.

"Not at all," Hardy told him. "I've got a state-of-the-art alarm system." A system that included a vampire with super strength, super hearing, and a thirst for teaching thieves a lesson...but he couldn't say *that* out loud.

"Fair enough." Clarke set his hat on the counter. "So, you already know I'm asking around about Craig Roth."

"Straight to business. *I like it.*"

"Well, from a lawman to a businessman, do you know him?"

"Of course I know of Roth. Him and his gang of bikers...what are they called?" He waved his hand. "Dirt Devils, Devil whatevers..."

"Dust Dogs," Clarke said.

Hardy shrugged. "Anyway, when a bikie gang sets up shop near a small town like Solace, people take notice. Miners tend to get protective over their claims, so they come in here and talk."

"They never come in here causing trouble? Attempt to break in?"

"Like I said," Hardy said with a grin, "state-of-the-art alarm system."

"When was the last time you saw Roth?"

"Roth?" He shrugged again. "Dunno. His hangers-on come into town occasionally to get supplies at the

*Outpost*. Vera's too nice with them if you ask me. The rest of us ran them out a long time ago."

"Ran them out?"

"I've been in business a long time, sergeant. After a while, you can pick the troublemakers. It's best to cut them off as soon as possible. So, we decided as a town to deny them service. We're honest folk out here and don't need that sort messing up the peace and quiet."

"And Vera? Have they harassed her at all?"

Hardy picked up on the missing beat of Clarke's heart at the mention of the witch. "If they have, she can take care of herself."

"The window of the *Outpost* is broken. They have anything to do with it?"

"I hear that was a bird," Hardy replied.

Clarke frowned, clearly not one hundred percent convinced that a stray parrot could cause that much damage. "The bikies cause any other trouble lately?"

"Not that I know of. I haven't seen Roth or any of his hangers-on for months. I'm mostly in my workshop, so I see little. Sounds to me like they decided they were done here. Skipped over state lines."

"State lines don't matter," Clarke told him.

"Anyway, not my problem. As long as they're gone, they can't bother us. I worry for Vera there alone, but she knows how to handle herself."

Sergeant Clarke sighed and wiped his hands on his trousers. "Seems that way."

"So, if I see Roth or any of the other Dust Dogs, just call you?" Hardy prodded.

"It would be greatly appreciated. The sooner we find him, the sooner I'll be out of your hair."

"What if you don't?"

Clarke met Hardy's gaze, his eyes giving nothing away. "I'll tackle that if it comes to it, not a moment before, Mr. Hardy." The vampire chuckled as the sergeant picked up his hat. The kid had gumption, that was for sure. "Have a good one, eh?"

Hardy stared after the sergeant, studying his gait and the thrumming of his heartbeat. The sound cut off as the door closed and the vampire shook his head.

Clarke had the hots for Vera. What an unsuspected turn of events.

He turned back to his workshop, his thoughts wandering. Clarke seemed the type who wouldn't give up easily. That could be both good and bad for Solace and the seal. He hadn't considered a threat coming from a human element, but if his long life had taught him anything, it was to expect the unexpected.

*Always.*

---

Eloise stood beside the water tank and watched Sergeant Clarke go into Hardy's shop. Her brow furrowed. It seemed he was leaving no stone unturned in his hunt for Roth. He must have a performance review coming up.

Eloise sighed, knowing she was next in line for question time. She was the kind of person who felt guilty for not having both hands on the steering wheel when passing a police car on the street, so there was no telling what would happen when Clarke put the screws on her. She hoped she wouldn't crack under the pressure. As Solace's newest Exile, that'd be the worst.

Her gaze flickered briefly to the silver rental car outside the *Outpost*. At least someone was having a productive day.

"There's a couple of points of light in here," Wally shouted from inside the water tank. "*Strewth*, that's loud."

"Don't shout," she called out. "You'll burst your eardrums."

Wally had wheeled out a dirt-encrusted generator and a box of tools so he could have a look at the old electric pump at the base of the windmill. When they'd opened the box, they'd found an enormous spider's nest, complete with matching giant spider.

Needless to say, she'd asked him to be the one to get inside the tank. He might be in his sixties, but his werewolf genes made him feel as spritely as a thirty-year-old man—especially when a full moon was approaching.

"I reckon we can fix this up real good," he called out. "Weld a few patches. Might need a pressure washer to get this grime off the inside. It's like a dank dust bowl in here."

"Maybe we should just worry about the surface," she said. "It sounds like too much trouble. Let's just do the mural. It can be aesthetic only."

"Hang on now," Wally shouted. "Don't give up so easy! Let me just see..."

Eloise sighed and angled herself into the shade. Tipping the brim of her hat low, she looked towards Hardy's shop and the bright white and blue 4WD parked out the front.

Andante had said to watch out for others who'd come for the seal, but she'd assumed they'd be supernatural. But what if they were human? She thought about Hardy and what he'd told her about vampiric compulsion. *Maybe...*

She shook her head as she caught sight of Clarke coming out of the opal shop. He spotted her and lifted a hand. Her next sigh deepened as she waved back. She was doing a lot of unfortunate breathing exercises lately, perhaps her lung capacity was growing.

Like the rest of the locals, he didn't bother looking for oncoming traffic as he crossed the highway.

He was wearing a pair of aviator sunglasses, which only added to his lawman mystique, and his uniform was a little too crisp and clean for the amount of red dirt around. She'd quickly learned that there was no keeping the stuff out of her van or off her clothes, so for him to be so spotless made her do a double take.

He took his job seriously, right down to the dress code.

"G'day, I'm Sergeant Andrew Clarke." He reached out a hand towards her and she froze, her gaze fixed on his outstretched fingers.

She was getting a handle on her powers, but what if she accidentally scrambled Clarke's brain and made him hate her? She'd end up in a cell over in Lightning Ridge and the Exiles would be in a giant pile of—

"I-I'm sorry," she stammered. "I have... I have anxiety issues. I..."

"Ah, never mind," he said with a smile. "Don't worry about it. It's all good, Miss...?"

"Hart," she told him. "Eloise Hart."

He looked up at the windmill. "What's going on here?"

"I'm trying to figure out how to get this thing working. Apparently, it's been rusted for a million years."

"Is there any water left in the bore?"

She shrugged. "Yet another thing on the figuring out list."

"You want to try your power?" Wally called out from inside the tank, his voice echoing off metal.

Eloise rapped her knuckles on the side of the tank. "Sergeant Clarke is here," she blurted. "You want to come out and say hello?"

"Power?" Clarke raised his eyebrows so high, they popped up over the top of his aviators.

"I have a way with tools," Eloise told him, hoping her cheeks weren't red. She tapped her toe against the generator. "Have to living on the road."

"You live on the road?" he echoed as Wally climbed the ladder inside the tank.

"I have a motorhome. A 2005 Fiat Ducato. I was doing the Big Lap when I busted a head gasket just outside of town."

Clarke grimaced. "Bad luck. You get it fixed?"

"Yeah. Wally helped me out." She nodded up at the werewolf, whose head appeared out of the hole at the top of the water tank.

"Sergeant!" Wally called, looking flustered. "I'll be down in a mo."

"Take your time," he replied before turning back to Eloise. "So, you got your engine fixed and you haven't moved on yet?"

Eloise shrugged. "It took a couple of weeks and I made some friends here. I figured it wouldn't hurt to stick around a while longer."

"No family to go home to? No job?"

She blanched at the direct questions. "Ah, no family. I was adopted as a baby, and I'm not on good terms with my parents. I'm doing some work with Hardy at the opal shop. I saw you come out of there just now."

Clarke watched her closely, his gaze burning through the lenses of his sunglasses. "You seem to have found yourself in a town full of some interesting people, Miss Hart."

"It's the outback," she said, trying to be absent about it. "I figured it was part and parcel of the place. You know, people have to be a little eccentric to want to live in a remote place chasing opal. There are certainly easier ways to make money."

"There certainly is."

Wally had climbed out of the tank, and his boots were firmly back on solid ground. He approached the sergeant without hesitation.

"Wally O'Brien's the name. I suppose you want to hear what we know about Craig Roth and his gang of bikies," he said, wiping his rust-stained hands on his jeans. "Well, I can save you some time. We do honest business with honest people here, sergeant. I've got no time for men like Craig Roth, and he knows better than to show his face around here. It's called denial of service."

"And he never gave you grief over it?" Clarke asked. "Made threats and followed through with them?"

"Never," Wally replied.

"That seem strange to you?"

"No. I bet he had bigger fish to fry than the scraps we have out here."

Clarke glanced at Eloise. "You ever see 'em?"

She shook her head, knowing full well what'd happened to Roth and the Dust Dogs. Who knew where they were right now? The alpha was one hundred percent dead, but the rest of them were either lost in a Middle Eastern desert or sunning it up in a nearby resort. The jury was still out on what reality it was happening in, though.

"I've only been here about five weeks or so," Eloise told the sergeant. "I've heard about them but haven't seen them. I'm kind of glad I haven't had the pleasure."

"All right then," he said, offering a reluctant smile. "I won't take up any more of your time." He looked up at the windmill. "Good luck with your project, Miss Hart."

The Exiles watched him walk back across the road in silence, not speaking until he'd gotten into his 4WD and driven away.

"That went better than I thought it would," Eloise remarked. "I always feel guilty around cops."

"You do?" Wally asked with raised eyebrows. "A sweet thing like you?"

"I am the master of illogical conclusions." She turned to the tank. "What was it like in there?"

"Dirty. I think something's been living in there."

Her expression fell. "Like what?"

The mechanic shrugged. "Don't know. More than spiders, I'd say."

"How did it get in there? The grate was closed."

"Magic."

Eloise shivered. "As long as it's not one of those creepy shadow people, it's all good."

"I don't know about that," Wally told her.

"Stop creeping me out." He had to be having her on.

The old werewolf chuckled and nudged the generator with the toe of his boot. "Wanna try the pump?"

"We've come this far." She sighed, wondering if they were tempting fate. "It's just water, right?"

"Water is the lifeblood of the outback. A little more never hurts."

# CHAPTER 10

"Wow, your place is really something."

Rosheen looked around the underground house Vera called home, her lack of enthusiasm thinly veiled behind a sweet smile.

"It's called a dugout," Vera explained. "It's made out of an old opal mine."

"Really? How *resourceful*."

Growing up, Rosheen had always been passive-aggressive towards anything she disliked. At first, Vera had thought she was just trying to be nice...until she'd witnessed one too many ambushes on other students at school to keep brushing it off. Rosheen was a mean girl, and old habits died hard.

"It isn't exactly a misty forest, but it's the best place to be when the dry season hits," Vera said. "Not all magic thrives in damp environments."

"Yes, but," Rosheen looked at the rocky ceiling, "couldn't there be a little sunlight?"

"I like it."

Rosheen set her suitcase beside the couch and made a face that looked *somewhat* like a smile. "As long as you are happy, Vera, that's all that matters."

Vera *was* happy, but her friend's approval suddenly meant something to her. Rosheen was her only link to her old life *and* the Irish witches. Ancestry meant something, even if it'd become muddied by status and power.

Rosheen ran her fingers over a bunch of drying plants hanging in the corner of the room. "What are all these?"

"They're all native plants and herbs," Vera replied, brightening. Finally, something they could bond over. "I'm making a study of them. There are some plants here that have some amazing properties. I'm brewing teas and potions. Balms, too."

"Really? You go out and pick them?" She shuddered. "With all the snakes and spiders?"

"Yes. The outback isn't *that* dangerous. Aussies like to take the piss out of foreigners, that's all."

"Venomous snakes are hardly something to joke about."

Vera felt herself blush and scowled. "It doesn't matter. Common sense is all you need. Anyway..." She dusted her hands on her shorts and smiled. "Are you hungry? We usually meet at the pub for dinner."

"Who's we?"

"All the townspeople," Vera told her. "The other supernaturals."

Rosheen raised her eyebrows. "So soon? Well, I better freshen up first. It's a long drive out here and I feel *rumpled*."

Vera grimaced as the witch flipped her perfect hair over her shoulders. If that was rumpled, then she wasn't looking forwards to feeling inadequate when Rosheen put effort into it.

"Do you want me to wait?"

"It's that place by that enormous gum tree, right?" she asked. "I'm sure I can find it."

Vera nodded. "Well, come down when you're ready."

Rosheen paused. "You're going like that?"

Vera looked down at her khaki peasant blouse, denim shorts, Blundstone boots, and shrugged. "Sure. Solace isn't a five-star kind of place. Casual is as dressy as it gets around here."

Rosheen glanced at her suitcase. "Okay. I won't take long. Just a quick shower, then I'll come and find you."

Leaving the witch to freshen up, Vera hurried out of her dugout. She bolted down the highway and across the yard in front of Blue's pub, kicking up a cloud of red dust in her frenzied wake.

She was kind of relieved that she wasn't waiting for Rosheen. It'd give her time to see if Finn was hanging around. A witch and a fae coming face-to-face was one meeting she wasn't keen on happening. She was gracious about his presence in Solace, but Rosheen wouldn't be so enthusiastic about maintaining peaceful relations. A lightning strike on a tinderbox had more subtlety than an angry *Gealach Fola* witch.

Pushing into the pub, Vera sighed in relief when she saw Finn wasn't amongst the other Exiles. They were sitting at their usual table, nursing dinks, but the fae's seat by the bar was empty.

Vera slid into a chair beside Eloise, ignoring the frown Drew aimed at her. "Where's Finn?"

"Staying clear while Clarke's sniffing around," Hardy replied.

"*Good.*"

"Clarke came in again today," Blue told her. "Finn was here and didn't make a good impression."

"Are you serious?" Vera's heart twisted. "What did he say?"

"Exactly what you expect," the publican replied with a sigh.

"Clarke came to see me straight after," Hardy added.

"Then me and Eloise," Wally said.

"He's collected the whole set now," Kyne remarked. "Unless he wants to have another round with Finn, we can't see any reason he'd come back. It's clear he won't find Roth or any clues to his whereabouts here."

Vera felt her stomach roll. She snatched Hardy's beer and gulped down the rest of the contents, the cool liquid doing nothing to settle her nausea but everything to blur the edges of her mind.

The Exiles stared at her, but her thoughts were going a million miles an hour.

Things were going great. She was happy. She was content. She'd made peace with the death of her family. She was simply Vera. Not Vera Brinewold. Not Vera *Gealach Fola*. She was Vera Walsh. *Just Vera.*

And they were wrong about Clarke. *Andy.* A spark in her heart told her he'd be paying another visit to Solace before long. God, how long was Rosheen planning to stay?

"Are you all right?" Eloise asked, leaning towards her.

"There's more than Clarke to worry about," Vera blurted. "It seems my past has come a-knocking, so please keep talk about the Dust Dogs and the seal at zero. *Please.*"

Kyne eyed her for a moment. "Your past?"

Vera's throat tightened.

"The silver car I saw," Eloise began.

She nodded. "Rosheen."

"Who's Rosheen?" Drew asked.

"After my family died, I was taken in by a coven called the *Gealach Fola*," she explained, glancing at the door. "Rosheen was my age, and we were like sisters, I suppose."

"You suppose?" Kyne asked.

"I wasn't exactly a poster child of proper magical

behaviour," Vera muttered. "I left as soon as I was old enough...and I kind of never told anyone. This is the first time I've seen her in twelve years."

"And she just happened to find you all the way out here?" Drew asked. "That's convenient."

"I know, I—"

"We have to be careful," Hardy interrupted. "Others are coming for the seal."

"Hang on," Eloise said, speaking up. "We know nothing for sure. Let's give her a chance. Not everything is a threat around here."

The door opened at that moment, cutting off the Exiles discussion.

Rosheen glided in, the setting sun casting a burning, magical light behind her—the perfect entrance—and she looked around the pub, her smile flickering slightly as she beheld the battered, slapped together finery of the outback.

She was wearing a short, mint-green floral dress, her long toned legs on full display. Her black heeled boots certainly helped shape her calves, much to Vera's jealousy. The witch shook her head, her long, flowing hair shimmering like threads of burnt gold in the fading sunlight.

The men stared at her like she was a mirage, and it wasn't until Eloise kicked Kyne underneath the table that they snapped out of it.

"This is Rosheen," Vera said dully.

"Well, hello," the witch said brightly, knowing exactly the effect she had on the opposite sex.

"Let me introduce you," Vera said, waving her forwards. "Wally owns the garage. He's a werewolf. Drew is a shifter."

"Really?" Rosheen smiled at him. "What shapes are you?"

"Shapes?" Drew asked with a scowl. "There's meant to be more than one?"

"He's a dingo," Vera said quickly.

"A dingo..." The witch looked him over. "*Interesting.*"

Vera tugged on her arm and continued the introductions. "This is Kyne and Eloise. They're elementals."

Rosheen stared at them, her magic flaring before she declared, "You're not exactly *real* elementals, are you?"

Eloise's smile faded and Kyne narrowed his eyes at the witch. "My powers certainly feel elemental enough," he said.

"She's talking about the elementals from the fae world," Vera blurted. "They don't have any humanity."

"We're well aware of our human element," Kyne drawled, his gaze moving back to Rosheen. "But thanks for the reminder."

Vera coughed loudly. "This is Blue. He owns the pub, but he's human."

The burly publican waved. "There's gotta be at least one token human amongst this lot, right?"

Rosheen laughed and shook his hand.

"Hardy here has the opal shop. He's a—"

"Vampire," Rosheen said as she took his hand.

Hardy grinned up at her and offered her the chair next to his. "Have a seat. So, how long are you staying?"

"Oh, I hadn't really thought about it," the witch replied, smiling sweetly at the vampire. "A few days, I hope. Vera and I have so much to catch up on, and I want to know what her life is like. Magic outside of Ireland is proving to be interesting, to say the least."

"How so?" Drew asked, leaning back in his chair.

"Well, look at all of you," Rosheen declared. "I've never seen so many supernatural people in the one place at the one time. I've certainly never met a vampire before," her gaze fixed on Drew, "or a dingo shifter."

"I'm not that special, sweetheart," the shifter drawled.

Hardy shot Drew a warning glare and turned to Rosheen. "Can I get you anything to drink?"

"Oh, I'd love something," the witch exclaimed, unaware of all the feathers she'd ruffled. "What's on offer?"

The vampire grinned. "Come with me and we'll see what Blue hides underneath that bar of his."

As they moved across the room and Hardy dazzled

Rosheen with his vampiric charm, Kyne tugged on Vera's arm.

"Don't worry," she said as the other Exiles began to mutter and watch the new arrival behind the bar. "I won't tell her about all the things."

"Good," he replied, "though that's not all I'm worried about."

"I'm fine."

"You don't seem yourself," he murmured. "Your ritual—"

Vera shook her head. "It was fine," she lied. "Went off without a hitch."

"You went home early."

She raised her eyebrows. "How do you know?"

"I went by in the morning to check on you. After everything with the Dust Dogs, I thought it was better to be safe than sorry."

Vera sighed and looked over at Rosheen as she shamelessly flirted with Hardy.

"I'm still here, Vera," Kyne murmured. "Just because Eloise and I are together now, doesn't mean we have to stop being close."

"I know. It's just... Rosheen represents everything I left behind in Ireland, but it isn't her fault."

"Neither is her *stellar personality*," Drew drawled, giving away that he'd been eavesdropping.

"*Drew*," she hissed.

"What's for dinner?" Rosheen asked as she returned to the table holding the solitary bottle of decent red wine in the whole of Solace. "I'm dying to know."

Drew snorted, earning himself a kick under the table from Vera.

"It's just simple pub food, darlin'," Blue told her. "But I'm sure I can whip something up you'll like."

"Oh, don't go to any trouble on my account," Rosheen said. "I'll have whatever Vera's having."

Vera grimaced, knowing the witch wasn't going to like her current diet, which was less plant-based than it was when she lived with the *Gealach Fola*.

"Vegetarian," she said to Blue, knowing his kitchen was full of meat. Soy-based products weren't something that was easily accessible in remote places. She ought to know, she ran the supermarket. "Anything vegetarian."

"Brilliant!" Rosheen declared. "*I can't wait.*"

---

Eloise lay in her bed, staring at the roof of her van. She studied the shadows playing across the fan set into the body of the motorhome, her gaze tracing the outlines of the gum leaves as they moved. Outside, the copse of gum trees rustled in the slight breeze, the scent of warming eucalyptus wafting through the open windows.

Early morning sunlight streamed through the gaps in the curtains, and Kyne stirred in bed beside her. It was still strange to have someone near her as she slept, the fear of her touch forcing her to keep everyone away. Until now, that was.

Eloise gazed at him, the curve of his muscles rather pleasing to the eye. How did she get so lucky?

"Are you staring at me?" Kyne asked without opening his eyes.

"Yes."

His lips quirked. "You know, for being wedged in a van, this mattress is pretty comfortable."

"It's memory foam," she said proudly.

Kyne opened his eyes and laughed. "It's much better than Hardy's couch."

At the mention of the vampire, Eloise was reminded of Hardy's shameless flirting with Rosheen the night before. Not that she cared if he was interested in the witch, but there was something about her that rubbed Eloise the wrong way. A *feeling* she couldn't quite put her finger on.

Kyne's hand found her thigh under the sheet. "What are you thinking about?"

"Last night," she replied.

"Rosheen. She's an interesting sort."

Eloise snorted. "You were perving on her."

"I reckon she puts a little magic in it," the miner said a little too quickly for her liking. "Or, at least, picked a moment that had maximum effect."

Kyne was right. Rosheen seemed like a special sort of person. She was aware of her beauty in an annoying kind of way. All she ever seemed to do was put her foot in her mouth, but with one flick of her perfect hair, all was forgiven. If it wasn't magic, it was pure law of sexual attraction.

Eloise was painfully aware of it, and one glance at Vera confirmed the witch felt the same. Come to think of it, Vera hadn't seemed like herself at all last night. She was withdrawn and quiet—two things she definitely wasn't.

"She spoke down to Vera, don't you think?" Eloise asked, sitting up. She reached into the overhead cupboard and took out a clean T-shirt and pair of denim shorts.

Kyne shrugged. "Vera can handle herself. I doubt she'd let anyone, let alone someone like Rosheen, walk all over her."

Eloise frowned as she rustled around for a pair of socks. She wasn't sure about that, but maybe it was simply because she didn't know the witch as well as the others. Not yet anyway.

She didn't want to dwell on other women, especially ones her boyfriend had checked out, so she promptly changed the subject. "Are you working on the dugout today?"

"Yeah," Kyne replied, rubbing his sleepy eyes. "I'm fixing up the electrical. Wiring and shit."

"Cool." She slid out of bed and began to wriggle into her clothes. "I'm going to go for a walk before it gets too hot. I'll be hunched over cutting opal all day."

The miner sat up, his dark hair sticking out in messy clumps. "You're leaving me alone in your van?"

Her gaze dipped to his bare chest. *Damn.* "Yeah. Just make sure you lock it on the way out." She held up her keys as she shoved her feet into her boots. "And if you're thinking of driving like you stole it, think again."

He laughed and reached out for her, his hand wrapping around her arm. Tugging her against the bed, he pressed a kiss to her lips. "I'll see you at dinner?"

She nodded and ran her hand through his mussed hair. "It's a hot date."

Kyne tugged her back as she went to step away. "I forgot to ask. Did you and Wally get any water out of that bore yesterday?"

Eloise shook her head. "The generator didn't have enough guts in it to pump anything but air."

"You didn't try your powers?"

"I didn't think it was appropriate, considering Sergeant Clarke had just finished his tour of the town."

"Another day, then."

She smiled and nodded, planting a kiss on his forehead. "Don't work too hard."

Outside, the day was already heating up.

Eloise put her hat on and began to walk down the hill towards town, letting her power loose. Practice made perfect, and she was spending as much time as she could trying to tell the difference between normal and elemental.

As she set foot on the trail, she spotted a flash of colour through the scrub and her magic pulsed. It'd reacted to something...or someone.

Eloise swallowed hard and continued down the path, then ducked between the scrappy gums and dodged the spiky spinifex grass. She emerged near the enormous boab at the northern end of Solace and spotted Rosheen lingering. The entrance to the seal lay hidden at the base of the tree and the witch was dangerously close to stepping on the hatch.

Deciding to swallow her apprehension, Eloise walked towards her, wondering how to distract her before she figured out what was buried underneath the town. Now she was beginning to understand how the other Exiles had felt when she'd first arrived. It explained a lot actually.

Rosheen was gazing up at the boab, her eyes misty as if she were looking at something far away. The witch hadn't sensed her approach, though if she did, she made no move to announce it.

Eloise took another step closer. "Rosheen?"

She blinked and glanced at the elemental. "Oh, hello."

"Are you all right?" Eloise was unsure about asking, not knowing what witches liked to do.

"There's a strange smell in the air," Rosheen said. "It's different from the forests back home." She breathed deeply. "It's ancient, but... I can't quite put my finger on it."

Eloise wondered if she was picking up on the magic coming from the seal, just as she had when she'd first arrived. She tucked a loose strand of hair behind her ear and shrugged. "I wouldn't know. I'm still learning how to tell the difference between normal and supernatural."

Rosheen turned to stare at her. "How so?"

"I know I was born like this, but I didn't understand that I was an elemental until recently," Eloise explained. "I guess I'm playing catch up."

Her eyebrows rose. "So, you never knew about magic?"

She shook her head.

"Then this town..." Rosheen looked around. "It must have been an eyeopener."

"Vera was the first witch I had ever met," Eloise told her. "Meeting another is strange, yet fascinating. I don't know what to expect."

"You're the first elemental I've ever met, too," Rosheen told her. The witch's expression softened. "I'm sorry if I was rude last night. Witches tend to get embroiled in their own business and forget that there's a whole supernatural world outside of Ireland...most of which seems to live in this little place." She said 'little' with a lit that rubbed Eloise the wrong way.

"It has its moments," the elemental said. "But it's peaceful despite the remoteness. I don't think I'd manage my powers if it wasn't for that."

"Yes, being close to nature is the key to creatures like us..." Rosheen trailed off and looked Eloise over.

"So, uh..." She nervously tucked an invisible strand of hair behind her ear for something to distract her shaking hands. The witch was stunning—like supermodel stunning—and it was kind of intimidating. "You knew Vera?"

"Yes. She came to live with my family after her coven died." Rosheen sighed and glanced at the boab. "It was a trying time for all of us. Our world was so unpredictable. It was a shame that the portals opened soon after. A few weeks between life and death." She turned to look at Eloise again, but this time the elemental felt another kind of magic in the air.

Rosheen reached a hand out towards her and she jerked back, but the witch kept coming. She grabbed Eloise's bare arm and the moment their skin touched, a vision flashed before her eyes like someone was flicking through channels on a television at lightning speed.

Darkness. The kadaitcha. The boab. *Marlu.*

Eloise wrenched herself away and glared at Rosheen, who was standing before her with a blank expression on her face.

"What do you think you're doing?" she snapped.

The witch blinked and shook her hand as if a bolt of static electricity had zapped her. "Oh my goodness," she exclaimed breathlessly. "I... *Oh my.*"

Eloise held her arms over her chest, her heart

beating a wild rhythm in her chest. "You're lucky I didn't fry your brain," she hissed.

"I suppose I am." The witch sighed and smoothed her hands over her dress. "Well, I have to get going. I promised to help Vera in her little shop this morning. That shifter is on his day off. He's building a house or *something*."

"Drew," Eloise corrected her. "His name is Drew."

"That's it," Rosheen stated. "*Drew*."

Eloise didn't know what to say, let alone do. She stared at the witch in open-mouthed shock. She couldn't be serious right now.

"Well, have a nice day then," Rosheen said.

"U-uh, yeah... S-sure," she stammered.

It wasn't until the witch had walked away that Eloise realised she hadn't apologised.

# CHAPTER 11

Vera turned on the lights inside the *Outpost* and sighed as the artificial tubes clicked and buzzed as they came to life.

To say last night had gone badly was an understatement. Rosheen had unknowingly dug herself a hole so large, she may as well start a new career as an opal miner. The only saving grace was that Finn had done what was asked of him for a change and stayed away from Solace.

Still, despite Rosheen's tumultuous debut, Vera was still torn over her friend's arrival. Half of her felt guilty about leaving the coven without a word, while the other wanted the witch to bugger off and never come back.

It was official, Vera Walsh was a terrible person.

Standing behind the counter, she turned on the till and waited for the EFTPOS machine to power up.

She'd have to ask Rosheen how long she intended to stay...and get a solid answer out of her.

Just as Vera was mulling over the ethics surrounding wiping the memories of a member of her ex-coven, the bell rang as the door opened, letting in the witch of the hour.

"How was your walk?" she asked, looking up from the till.

Rosheen wiped her brow and turned the stand full of postcards. "There really isn't much to see, is there?" She picked up a card, flipped it over, then put it back.

"I don't know what you were expecting, but it's the outback," Vera retorted. "Space, heat, and dust are the three major tourist attractions. The plus side is opening at ten-thirty and no one batting an eyelid."

"I think I may have upset your friend."

She raised her eyebrows at the abrupt admission. "Which one?" *Because there was a few.*

"That cute little elemental with the blonde hair."

"Eloise?"

Rosheen clicked her fingers. "Yeah, that's her name. I didn't realise she was new to her powers. I mean, how could she *not* know? Magic isn't exactly subtle."

Her stomach rolled, the nausea threatening to dislodge her breakfast. "What did you do?"

"I just wanted a little vision," the witch replied with a shrug.

Vera's mouth fell open. "You *touched* her?"

"Just for a moment. Not that I saw anything that

made sense anyway. Kangaroos are cute and all, but what does that have to do with anything?"

"You can't just go around forcing your power on people," Vera fumed. "Especially not on other supernaturals. It's rude. Besides, Eloise has an elemental affinity with ether that she barely knows how to control. She could've done some serious damage."

"So she said, but it's fine, Vera. I'm not the same witch I was all those years ago. I've grown up."

Vera begged to differ but didn't mention it out loud. "Whatever. You just don't go poking around in other people's business like that." It was a little hypocritical of her to chastise Rosheen after she'd done the exact same thing, but she'd done it to protect the seal, not for shits and giggles or some mean-girl scheme.

"Why is it so dark in here?" Rosheen suddenly declared. "All this artificial light really washes you out."

Vera rolled her eyes. "Gee, thanks."

The witch turned to the boarded-up window. "Why is this broken? All you have to do is wave your hands around a little." She raised her arms and before Vera could open her mouth, Rosheen's magic flared and the board flew off the window, dirt and sand swirled on the side of the road, and glass formed in a puff of blood-red magic.

"Rosheen!" Vera screeched.

"Calm down," the witch said as the glass rippled and finally settled into place.

"Someone could have seen!" she cried, rushing over to the window and looking out at the highway. "I had it handled."

"Handled by a repairman who would've charged you triple for being a woman in a man's world." Rosheen rolled her eyes and pouted. "I did you a favour and besides...no one saw because *no one's here.* Not one person!"

A flash of light reflected off metal as a car drove up the highway and Vera turned to glare at Rosheen. "You were saying?"

She shrugged and smiled sweetly. "*Oops.*"

Vera's heart lurched as she saw the police 4WD pull up out front. It was Sergeant Andrew Clarke. *Oh no.*

"Oh my," Rosheen said. "Would you look at *that*?"

The bell rang as Clarke came into the shop. "G'day."

"My ovaries just exploded," Rosheen swooned. "He says g'day. *G'day.*"

Clarke took off his hat and held it in front of him, his fingers worrying the brim. "I'm sorry to interrupt," he said, glancing at Rosheen.

"No, not at all," Vera told him, glaring at the witch. "This is my *friend* Rosheen. She's visiting from Ireland."

"Delighted," she purred as Clarke looked her over. "Say g'day again."

"G'day?" He had an annoying magical-assisted *twinkle* in his eye that had Vera wanting to blast Rosheen across the supermarket but instead, she coughed loudly. "So, what brings you back to Solace, sergeant?"

"Ah," he blinked, "you actually."

"Me?"

"Yes, uh…" He looked at the window Rosheen had just fixed. "I see you got that window seen to. Did Jack call you?"

Vera frowned. "Jack?"

"The glazier…" Clarke shook his head. "You know what? Never mind. I was wondering if you were free for lunch today."

Vera's cheeks flushed, and she opened her mouth to reply before Rosheen did, but the shop door opened, the bell ringing furiously. Drew barged in, adding to the supernatural pile on, and she pursed her lips. The day hadn't even begun and there was already more chaos than she would've liked. Maybe she should start drinking coffee again.

The shifter came to an abrupt halt and narrowed his eyes at the sergeant.

"Drew," Clarke said with a sharp nod.

"We've answered your questions," he snarled, balling his fists. "Quit bothering us already."

"What questions?" Rosheen asked.

Vera shot a warning glare at Drew. "He's not asking any questions."

"Yes, he was. He was inviting her to lunch," Rosheen purred, a sly grin curving her perfect lips. She grabbed Vera's shoulders and pushed her forwards a step. "She'd love to."

Clarke smiled like he'd won the lotto. "I'll come back at twelve, then?"

Vera nodded and tucked her fiery curls behind her ear. "I'll wait out the front for you."

The sergeant glanced at their two onlookers and backed away towards the door. "I'll see you then."

"Can't wait."

The sergeant grinned and pushed open the door with his shoulder and Vera watched him walk all the way to his 4WD, ignoring the two supernaturals festering behind her.

Once Clarke had driven away, Drew leaned against the counter and pouted. "For a cop, he's not very assertive, is he?"

"That's a big word," Vera drawled, turning around. "I didn't know you understood more than one syllable at a time."

"She still has some of her fire after all," Rosheen murmured. "What. A. *Hottie.*"

Vera wasn't listening. "What's your problem, Drew?"

"He's fishing for evidence," the shifter said. "Clearly he doesn't buy what we've been selling."

Her mouth fell open in shock. "You did not just say that to me!"

He shrugged. "Say what?"

"Andy wants to take me to lunch because he *likes me*, not because he thinks he has some kind of perverted ownership over me just because I was nice to him!"

Drew raised his eyebrows and snorted. "You're calling him *Andy?*"

"You never listen, Drew!" she shouted. "After everything, you still don't get it!"

"What story?" Rosheen asked, batting her eyelashes.

"There's no story," Vera blurted. "It's his job to patrol places like this."

"Patrol my arse," Drew muttered.

"A police sergeant?" Rosheen wondered. "I seriously doubt this pimple is on his radar. It took me *hours* to drive here, and I never saw a house or a car or a single soul!" She let out a little squeal. "Oh, this is fabulous! He's got a crush on you, Vera! What are you going to wear? *I have just the thing.*"

"You're seriously going?" Drew asked angrily. "Who's going to look after the *Outpost*? Because I'm not."

"I will!" Rosheen declared. "How hard can it be? It's not like there'll be any customers."

Drew ignored her. "A date with a pig? *Vera.*"

"Did you just call Andy a pig?" Vera cried. "Don't be such a child!"

"Give her a break." Rosheen pushed Drew back with her palm. The shifter cursed as she zapped him with a spark of red magic. "If Vera wants to go to lunch with the hot cop, then she can go to lunch with the hot cop. You're not her boyfriend, Drew."

"D-did you just shock me with magic?" he demanded, his cheeks turning red.

The witch turned and stared at him. "Yes. Yes, I did. You want to know why? Because a witch is not anyone's property, shifter. *Especially* not a Brinewold witch. If you understood how powerful Vera really is, you wouldn't be treating her like a fragile little flower. She could blow your head clean off your shoulders!"

Drew's eyes narrowed, but he didn't try to argue the point any further.

"Anyway, it's none of your business what I do," Vera told him, *and* Rosheen for good measure. "If I want to go out with Andy, then I'll go out with him. I don't need anyone's permission. I'm a gown woman."

Drew ground his teeth, flashing a look at Rosheen. There were things he wanted to say, but while the witch was there, he couldn't berate Vera.

*Good*, she thought. *The last thing I want is a lecture about keeping secrets.* It was difficult enough keeping up with who knew what about who around here now that Rosheen was in the mix.

Rosheen clapped her hands together. "Oh, I have

just the dress," she cried. "Let me go get it. You'll love it, Vera. It'll bring out the sparks in your hair."

She didn't wait for Vera to reply and rushed out of the *Outpost*, leaving her and Drew alone.

"Vera," he murmured. "A cop? After everything that happened with the Dust Dogs?"

"I'm not arguing with you about this anymore," she hissed. "I understand what's at stake. I'd never betray Solace, but I won't sacrifice my happiness." Her heart twisted as she thought about her family and all the things that'd happened between then and now. "Not anymore."

Drew snorted. "Well, I hope you know what you're doing, because if it comes down to it, I'll do whatever it takes."

Vera felt her magic rise and balled her fists to stop it from surfacing.

"Get out," she whispered.

Drew obliged without complaint, storming out of the *Outpost* and disappearing.

She stared at the window Rosheen had repaired and sighed. She wasn't going to let him or the witch's pushiness ruin her date with Clarke. This was her time.

*Finally.*

Drew stormed back up the hill to the dugout, empty-handed.

Vera was going on a date with a cop. A cop who was asking about the shifter Drew had killed. Was he the only one who saw the problem with that?

As he strode back to the clearing out front of the dugout, Kyne glanced at him before turning back to the mess of wiring he was attempting to wrangle.

"Almost done with these panels," he said. "Until I can get someone from the power company to come out and hook the place up, the batteries will hold plenty. When the rains come, you'll need the extra juice, but this'll be good for now."

Drew was only half listening as the elemental ducked out from underneath the verandah. Rosheen was a bad influence. She'd never fit in here.

Kyne looked around frowning. "Where's lunch?"

"Forgot it," the shifter mumbled sullenly.

"You forgot it?" the elemental complained. "That was the only thing you had to get."

"Vera's going on a date with the cop," he said.

"What?" Kyne asked. "Are you serious?"

"He was down there when I went in. Rosheen just shoved Vera at him like she was something to eat." His scowl deepened. "I don't like her."

"Who's looking after the *Outpost*?"

"Not me. I was kicked out *again*. Rosheen said she'd do it."

Kyne cursed. "And the place will be on fire or worse

before Vera gets back." He dusted off his hands and began to pack up his tools.

"What are you doing?" Drew demanded. "We haven't finished."

"I know Vera vouched for her, but I'm not letting Rosheen take care of that shop on her own."

Drew sat on a fallen log and snorted. At least someone seemed to hold the same opinion of the newest arrival as he did.

"Is she really that powerful?" he asked, stopping Kyne in his tracks.

"I guess." The elemental set down his toolbox. "Vera doesn't rely on her magic, so I get why you don't know. She's not into flaunting her differences."

"I know that," he said. "But is she?"

"She doesn't talk about her past much," Kyne told him, "and I don't blame her for wanting to leave it behind, but she once told me that her coven was one of the five most powerful in Ireland."

"Brinewold," Drew said. "That's what Rosheen said she was."

"Representatives of water," the miner said with a nod. He sat next to Drew and turned his gaze towards the horizon. "Her father was a Nightshade. Fire."

"Fire and water?"

Kyne chuckled. "I always thought it explained a hell of a lot." He dusted his hands on his jeans. "Anyway, two powerful covens with opposite elements, both manifesting in Vera. When you think about it, that probably makes for some explosive magic, huh?"

Drew grunted, his thoughts playing over the elements. Water gave life, but it could also be terrible—tempests, tsunamis, storms. Fire was much the same. It cleansed and made way for renewal, but it burned hot and without remorse. Water quenched fire, but if there wasn't enough of it... He shook his head, confused. No matter how it worked, it was clear to him now—Vera was a magical force of nature.

"If she's that powerful, then she probably knows something about Rosheen that we don't," Drew muttered. He wasn't entirely convinced, but he knew the harder he pushed Vera, the worse her retribution would become. He wasn't keen on finding out what came after potatoes on her list of ammunition.

"You're probably right," Kyne said. "If Vera wants to leave Rosheen in charge, then that's her business. As for Clarke..." He sighed and looked down the hill towards the Outpost. "Maybe that's her own business as well."

Drew raised his eyebrows. "You're not worried he'll find out what we're doing here?"

"Yeah, of course I worry about the seal and what happened with Roth, but it is what it is. We have to stay alert, but not to the point that we're fighting amongst ourselves."

Drew scuffed the toe of his boot in the ochre dirt, his inner dingo stirring. He'd have to shift soon, but that was the last thing he wanted to do. He didn't trust Rosheen or Clarke as far as he could throw them.

But the more he thought about it, the more he wondered if Kyne was right. Vera was more than capable of handling herself.

"If worse comes to worse, Hardy will compel Clarke," Kyne went on.

"That mind control thing?"

He nodded. "He doesn't like it, but if times are tough, I suppose he will." The miner stood and picked up his toolbox, putting it into the tray of his ute. "Anyway, I'm going to head down to Blue's since you forgot lunch. You coming?"

Drew sighed. "Yeah. In a few."

Kyne narrowed his eyes slightly but didn't press. "Righto."

The shifter sat on the log, watching as Kyne disappeared down the hill, his thoughts troubled, which was nothing new. No matter wherever he went, he always seemed at odds with the world. Either that or his naïve ignorance and tendency to let his temper take control got in the way.

But one thing was for sure...he didn't know Vera as well as he thought he did.

# CHAPTER 12

era sat on the bench outside the *Outpost*, lingering in the shade of the verandah.

She had to admit that the dress Rosheen had made her wear was rather pretty. It wrapped around her waist and reached just above her knees, and the mint green floral fabric was cool against her skin. Plus, it matched her brown gladiator sandals and fiery hair. Her fingers were laden with her usual silver rings, and a shard of raw, clear quartz crystal hung on a long chain around her neck, the jagged point resting between her breasts.

Her shiny silver aviator sunglasses slipped down her nose as she anxiously waited for Clarke to arrive. Shoving them back into place, she sighed. Nerves had her stomach rolling for the first time in years.

*Get a grip*, she thought. *You've faced spirits and monsters without breaking a sweat. Now is not the time to be contemplating running back inside for a last-minute nervous poo.*

Before she exploded, she caught sight of Clarke's 4WD soaring down the highway from the north. It slowed as he reached the town limits, then sailed around in an arc as he zoomed into a parking spot in front of her.

When he got out of the car, she frowned. He was in his police uniform, which didn't bode well. The Queensland border was to the north...and the Dust Dogs camp.

Noticing her gaze, he said, "I would've changed, but I'm on the clock."

"So, you're taking a woman on a date while you're supposed to be working?"

His lips quirked. "Well, I am in charge, Miss Walsh."

She stood and smoothed her hands over her dress. "If you say so, sergeant."

"You look gorgeous, by the way."

Her cheeks flushed and she shook out her hair. "Thank you."

"Have you got a little time?" he went on. "I thought we could go for a picnic someplace quiet."

Vera looked around Solace. It was already 'pretty quiet', but she was hyperaware that Rosheen was staring at them through the window. Then there was Drew and the other Exiles. They were a family, but the rumour mill still worked just as well here as anywhere else in the world.

"Sure," she said, knowing if she was going to be safe with anyone, it was a police sergeant. Not that it was a problem, but there was a first for everything. "I'd love to."

Clarke smiled and held out his hand to help her down off the verandah. For a moment, Vera hesitated. Should she try for a vision or would it be too intrusive on a first date? Maybe she should play it safe.

Closing off her magic, she took his hand and jumped down onto the side of the road.

"Let me get the door for you." He held onto her hand for a moment longer than he needed to, his smile widening. Finally, he let got and opened the passenger side door of his 4WD so she could climb in.

Vera slid into the seat, her gaze running over the CB radio and internal computer. There were so many buttons and lights, she couldn't tell if she was in a car or a spaceship.

Clarke jumped into the driver's seat and she turned to him. "What is all this stuff for?"

"Standard highway patrol gear," he explained as he put on his seatbelt. "All our cars out here are fully loaded with the radar, comms, and computer. You should see the gear in the back." He nodded over his shoulder. "It's a survivalist's dream."

"If we break down, then I'm in the right car, I suppose," she mused. "So, where are we going?" She envisioned a short ride to the nearest dusty roadhouse and wondered if she should've brought along a couple of sandwiches and a six pack.

"A little way to the south. I have some food in the esky in the back," he said. "That bloke at the pub helped me out."

"Blue?" Vera asked, raising her eyebrows. "Really?"

"Sure." Clarke shrugged and did a U-turn, the 4WD manoeuvring smoothly across the highway. "He said he knew what you liked, so I left it to him...but I'm not sure what he gave me."

"I guess it'll be a surprise for the both of us."

Clarke floored it, and the 4WD quickly came up to highway speed. They soared out of Solace, leaving the town and all of its supernatural chaos behind.

As the feeling of magic bleeding from the seal eased, Vera's mind cleared. She breathed deeply, the scent of Clarke's aftershave filling her nose. It smelled like spice and wood, reminding her of something she'd forgotten but couldn't quite remember. *Frustration more like it,* she thought.

"I wanted to apologise about this morning," she blurted. "Drew—"

"I get it," Clarke interrupted. "Small, close-knit town. Where there're cops, there's trouble."

"Drew's not a bad guy, he's just..." she trailed off, wondering why she was still protecting him after all they'd been through. Drew was a grown man who needed to take responsibility for his own actions. He wasn't part of the Dust Dogs anti-human pack anymore. He was an Exile, and she was definitely not a beta.

But that's it, wasn't it? Drew *was* an alpha.

"Protective," Clarke finished for her.

"Huh?"

"He's protective of you," the sergeant added. "Like an older brother... *I hope.*"

Vera laughed, some weight lifting off her shoulders. "Yes, like a *younger* brother, actually."

"Have you known him long?"

"A couple of months," she replied.

He said nothing, but Vera sensed the police procedural cogs turning in his mind.

About twenty minutes outside of Solace, Clarke pulled off the highway and into the scrub. Parking the car in the shade of a scrappy gum tree, he turned off the engine.

Vera peered out the window with a frown, wondering what was so special about this place. It didn't look any different than the rest of the scrub that covered this part of the outback.

Trees that were beaten low by the unforgiving winds, *check.*

Armed and dangerous spikey spinifex, *check.*

Dust, dirt, and the promise of snakes, *check.*

What had she gotten herself into?

"Here we are," Clarke declared, unhooking his seatbelt. "I think this is the spot."

Not wanting to be impolite, Vera got out of the car and followed him around to the back.

The sergeant opened the back of the 4WD and slid a green and white esky towards him. Opening the top, he took out a reusable shopping bag from the cooler before handing Vera a chilled bottle of wine. He threw a red and black checked blanket over his shoulder, then shut the boot. It closed with a dull bang and the indicators flashed orange as Clarke rattled his keys in his hand.

"Where to now?" she asked, reading the label on the wine. It was one of Blue's fancy bottles—a red pinot noir vintage from the Yarra Valley.

"Through here." Clarke led her past the thicket of trees, holding back a low-hanging branch laden with eucalyptus leaves so she could pass.

Vera ducked, stepping past him, and when she saw what was waiting just beyond the curtain of foliage, her heart leapt.

The clearing was full of wildflowers. Yellow, daisy-like blooms dotted small greyish green shrubs, while a dusting of red and black Sturt's desert peas sprung up from the red sand.

The colours were beautifully bold and stark, and Vera found her eyes welling with tears. The crisp blue of the sky, the rich ochre of the sand, the yellows and reds of the wildflowers, and the myriad of greens running through the foliage of the trees and shrubs.

All of it was amazing to her. Life found a way, even in the harshest of environments.

"I remembered you liked native plants," Clarke said behind her. "So, I asked around."

"It's beautiful." She dabbed at her eyes before turning around. "Bloody perfect." Blending over, she held one of the butter-coloured flowers between her fingers. "This yellow one is *senecio magnificus*," she told him. "This is a native variety, but they grow all around the world in one form or another."

"I didn't know that. It looks like a daisy to me."

Vera knelt beside the elongated red and black blooms. "And Sturt's desert pea."

"Now that one I know," Clarke declared proudly.

She laughed and rose, breathing in the sweet earthy scent of the spring wildflowers.

He busied himself by setting out the blanket under the shade of a gnarled gum, then unpacked the food from the bag. Inside, with a pair of disposable plastic cups, was a selection of sandwiches, chocolate and coconut covered lamingtons, and a tub of fruit salad with a can of whipped cream. Blue had totally come through with the goods.

Vera sat on one edge of the blanket and took the cups, filling them both with red wine.

"Lamingtons?" Clarke asked, sitting beside her.

"They're amazing," she replied. "One of the best things about Australia."

"What are the other things?"

"Hmm...let me think." She made a show of pondering before she added, "Tim Tams, Caramello Koalas, Cherry Ripes, Twisties...Oh! And BBQ Shapes!"

Clarke chuckled and shook his head. "Those are all food and lollies."

"So? Have you got a problem with chocolate, Sergeant Clarke?"

"Not at all." He picked up a lamington and bit half of it in one go. "Definitely not." Crumbs tumbled down the front of his crisp blue police shirt and she laughed.

They divided up the sandwiches and ate, enjoying the silence of the little copse of wildflowers from the shade.

"So, did you always want to be a police officer?" she asked.

"Yes and no," Clarke replied. "My dad was a cop in the big smoke. Sydney. After fifteen years on the force, he got shot during a routine stop on the M1. Pulled a bloke over for speeding and when he went to question the driver, the guy pulled a gun."

Vera's heart dropped. "Oh... I'm sorry."

"He was okay," he went on, "physically, but I don't think he's ever gotten over the psychological mess it left behind."

"I expect having a gun pulled on you is the last thing anyone would expect walking up to a car like that. The randomness of it..." she trailed off, her thoughts troubled.

"That's it, but no one can predict the future or control what other people do, even the police." He shrugged. "He didn't want me to join the force, but I suppose I'm stubborn like that."

"As long as you're happy," she told him. "You seem to have made something out of it, *sergeant*."

He chuckled. "What about you? Was running a business something you always wanted to do?"

Vera frowned. She couldn't exactly tell him about the *Gealach Fola's* plans to breed her magic into their bloodline, could she? Besides, any dreams she had died along with her coven and in the wake of all that tragedy, all she could think about was leaving.

Finally, she settled on, "I kind of...fell into it."

"You seem to have made something out of it, too," he said, reaching out to refill her almost empty cup.

In that moment, her magic broke through her suppression and lashed out, zapping Clarke with a crack of static. He yelped as a vision pierced her mind —a single frame laced with doubt.

Vera pulled her hand back, the cup slipping from her fingers. Red wine spilled across her legs and onto the blanket.

She wiped her palm across her shins, the gesture only making the spill worse. "*Shit*. I'm so sorry."

"Don't worry about it," Clarke told her. He took out some serviettes from the bag and dabbed at her legs. "It's just a bit of wine."

"It's red," she said with a moan. "It'll never come

out of your blanket." She clucked her tongue. "*Shit on it.*"

"It's just an old blanket. I can get another one." He chuckled and rose onto his knees, helping her wipe the rest of the sticky wine off her legs.

Leaning close, Clarke's gaze moved from her legs, to her eyes, to her mouth, then to her eyes again. He was an inch away from kissing her—really, it was a perfect kiss moment—but all she could see was the vision her magic had dragged out of the forefront of his mind. It was just a flash, but it was more than enough to piss her off.

The beginnings of a police file...with her name on it. There was probably one on each of the Exiles as part of the Roth investigation. But him bringing her here, playing on her heart? *Asshole.*

Vera's gaze narrowed. "I get the feeling you're trying to trick me into saying something I'll later rely on...*in court.*"

Clarke sat back and his brow creased. "Vera—"

"I'm not stupid, Sergeant Clarke."

"Fine, you got me." He sighed heavily and screwed the cap back onto the bottle of wine. "You really don't know anything?"

She lowered her gaze, trying to mask her disappointment. "If I knew something, I'd tell you. I'm honest like that."

He sighed and pinched the bridge of his nose. "I

really like you, Vera, I do, but I can't help feeling like there's something you're leaving out."

*Yeah, I'm a witch protecting a magical seal and covering up the supernatural murder of Craig Roth.*

"Everyone has secrets, *Andy*," she stated. "What I'm not telling you is *personal*. It has nothing to do with those bikers."

"What happened to you in Ireland?"

Vera smirked. "Now you're asking the right questions. They should make you a detective."

Clarke shook his head. "Vera—"

"You're not going to let it go, are you?"

"I've seen my fair share of eccentric, small-town behaviour, but Solace... That place is next level."

"It's refreshing to know that all I'm good for is information," she drawled, tossing her empty cup into the bag. "Why do all men think charming a woman is foolproof? It's patronising and sexist as hell."

"I'm sorry," he said hastily. "I may have had a secondary motivation for today, but I asked you out because I like you, Vera."

"If we weren't in the middle of nowhere, I'd walk out on you." She stood and crossed her arms over her chest. "I'd like to go home now."

Clarke nodded glumly and cleared the remains of their lunch while Vera went and sat in the 4WD.

Her magic simmered and she flexed her fingers, bolts of purple sparking on her fingertips. *Just once...*

she thought. *Just once I would like a man to love me for me. Was that too much to ask?*

*Yes*, the voice whispered in her ear. *He'll never understand.*

When Clarke got into the car, she balled her hands into tight fists, closing off her magic once more...and they never spoke a word all the way back to Solace.

<br>

Eloise barged into the opal workshop, her anger causing the lights to flicker.

"Settle down," Hardy complained, looking up from the opal he was polishing. "You'll make the power go out."

"Sorry," she muttered, tossing her hat onto the table.

The vampire sighed and swirled his chair around. "Okay, out with it. What's got you all hot and bothered?"

"*Rosheen*," Eloise declared. "She was hanging around the boab, so I went to see what she was doing and...*she grabbed me.*"

"What did she see?"

Her annoyance spiked even more. "You're not going to ask if I fried her brain?"

Hardy laughed. "You'd be more animated if you'd done that."

Eloise rolled her eyes. "I'm not quite sure what she

saw. I think it was *Marlu* and something about the kadaitcha." She sat in her usual chair and ran her hands over her face. "I don't like her. She reminds me of a high school mean-girl."

"She certainly has no filter," Hardy remarked. "But I don't know her well enough to consider her mean. Not yet, at least."

"You're kidding, right?" Eloise shook her head. "Actually, scratch that. I can see why men like her. She's a bloody supermodel powered by magic."

"You are rather pretty yourself, Eloise," the vampire told her.

"Pretty? *Ugh.*" She rolled her eyes again. In her experience, men used *pretty* when they didn't want to commit. "The point is, she was at the boab like she sensed something."

"No doubt." Hardy grimaced. "Of course, we need to remain vigilant, and Rosheen is still an unknown variable, but she's a witch. She's going to sense something."

"She didn't even *apologise.*"

"Is this genuine concern for Solace or jealousy?"

Eloise screwed up her face and wished she *had* fried Rosheen's brain...just a little. How could she be jealous when she had Kyne?

"I don't want to talk about it anymore," she stated, turning to her work. These men were *impossible.*

Aware Hardy was still staring at her with his strange, unblinking vampire eyes, Eloise picked up the opal she was working on and turned on the grinder. If he saw something more than she did, it was a mystery. Actually, Hardy was a pretty mysterious guy. Sometimes she wondered why she trusted him so much when he gave so little information about himself.

The vampire didn't press for more and she relaxed as the sound of the polisher fired up behind her. Losing herself in the colour of the black opal was bound to calm her down.

And lost she was.

When the electronic bell on the shop door buzzed, it made her heart leap. Before Hardy could get up, Vera appeared in the workshop, her cheeks red and her eyes full of fire. She was wearing a minty green floral dress and strappy sandals. The look suited her, but it was rather dressy compared to her usual bohemian uniform.

"What's got you all dressed up?" Hardy asked.

Her shoulders sagged. "I just went out with Clarke."

Eloise raised her eyebrows. "Really? On a date?"

"From the look on your face, I'm assuming it didn't go so well," Hardy said, leaning back in his chair.

"No, it *stunk*," the witch told him as she pulled up a chair. "He had an ulterior motive, though he claimed it was a *secondary* motivation. *Whatever.*"

"Roth?" the vampire asked.

The witch rolled her eyes, but Eloise caught the

fleeting stab of heartbreak that flashed through her eyes. Vera really liked the guy, which made it all the worse.

"What a tool," the elemental declared. "Stuff him. If he can't see how amazing you are, then he can go jump."

The witch's expression brightened a little, and she let out a strained laugh. "And I'll be the one giving him a shove off the edge."

"That's the spirit!"

"Who's looking after the *Outpost*?" Hardy asked, his amused gaze moving between them. "Drew?"

Vera shook her head. "Rosheen, actually."

The vampire snorted. "Are you sure she hasn't burned the place down yet?"

"It's debatable, but I'm not ready to go back yet," Vera replied. "Rosheen will have a field day when she hears things didn't go so well, and I'm not sure what to tell her."

"You're really bowing down to Rosheen as the alpha witch?" Hardy asked, unblinking. "It's a little pathetic."

"Hardy!" Eloise cried. "*What the fu—*"

Vera raised her eyebrows, clearly pissed off. "I'm ready to go now."

The vampire grinned. "Well, that was fast."

"Let me walk you out," Eloise said, shooting Hardy a glare. He was going to cop an earful when she got back.

Outside, the two women lingered in the shade cast by the shop. The day was dry and dusty, and the sun had charged the surrounding air to the point it hummed with radiant heat.

Eloise pulled her hair off the back of her neck, combing it forwards over her shoulder. In the distance, she could hear an electric nail gun echo down the ridge. *Pisht, thud. Pisht, thud.* Kyne and Drew were hard at work.

"I'm sorry about what Rosheen did to you this morning," Vera told her. "I don't think she realised you're still figuring out your powers."

Eloise was debating that, but it didn't seem an appropriate time to bring it up. "Are you okay?" she asked instead. "I mean...with Rosheen being here, you haven't been yourself and now Clarke..."

Vera sighed and looked towards the *Outpost*. "She's... Rosheen is..." Her next sigh was deeper. "She represents a piece of my past I'd rather leave behind."

The elemental nodded. "I get it. I have a past like that, too."

"I still don't know what to tell her."

"About Clarke?" She thought for a moment. "Just tell her he was trying to get into your good books so he could get a foothold in the town. Police like to do that sort of thing. You don't have to say anything about the Dust Dogs, and there's no reason he'd come back to ask more questions. It's just enough of the truth without lying about it."

Vera hesitated. "I guess..."

When she didn't make a move, Eloise waited, lingering in the shade as the witch composed herself.

"I really liked him," Vera finally murmured, lowering her gaze. "I thought he—" She snorted. "Listen to me. I sound like a schoolgirl whose crush just humiliated her."

Eloise smiled and pulled her friend in for a hug. This time, her power remained where it was supposed to as she comforted the witch. "That's why they call them crushes," she said. "He's a fool."

"Thanks, Eloise," Vera said, drawing back. "You're a good friend."

"If you need moral support, I'm always here."

"Thanks." She took a deep breath. "Wish me luck."

"Luck." She smiled as Vera crossed the road. The witch would be okay, given some time. Vera was the strongest person she knew.

Inside, Eloise strode across the workshop and kicked Hardy's chair to get his attention. "What the hell was that?"

The vampire shrugged. "Someone needed to reignite her fire."

## CHAPTER 13

Rosheen walked up and down the aisles at the *Outpost*, surveying all Vera Walsh had built.

Picking up a packet of instant noodles, she snorted. Trading a comfortable life of magic with a full coven for *this*? It was insulting. Abandoning the *Gealach Fola* was unheard of. Still, Vera wasn't bound to them and was free to come and go as she wished...for now, at least.

Returning to the front of the store, she began to try on all the sunglasses on the rack by the front counter, peering at her reflection in the tiny mirror glued to the plastic display.

When Rosheen had first arrived in Solace, she'd felt a vibration in the air the moment her feet touched the ground. It was only for a second before it was gone again, as if something had reached out to see who she was—a greeting of sorts.

Then there was the concentration of supernaturals.

She'd never met half-breed elementals before, let alone a vampire. That dingo shifter obviously had some sort of feelings for Vera—though he was trying to hide it—and that werewolf was basically geriatric. He'd be no trouble at all.

Rosheen mulled over that enormous tree at the northern end of town as she set down the sunglasses and began sifting through the magazines. There was something strange about it. A lingering reverberation that felt ancient, but was it still active? She didn't know what to make of it yet.

One thing was for sure, this land was old and more ancient than even Ireland. That had to mean something, especially to a witch like Vera. Why else would she think moving to this dust bowl in the middle of nowhere was a good idea?

Sitting behind the counter with a copy of *TV Week* magazine, Rosheen decided she wasn't leaving Solace until she found out what was going on. If she could convince Vera to return to Ireland at the end of it, then she'd be the toast of the coven. The *Gealach Fola* would earn their place in the new hierarchy and then some.

The witch was almost through reading about the latest gossip on Australian TV when Vera shuffled into the shop.

Rosheen leaned forwards, pressing her elbows on the countertop. "*So...*how was it?"

Vera frowned and worried her bottom lip with her teeth.

Rosheen straightened. "Oh no, I don't like that look on your face." Heartbreak she could work with.

Vera shrugged. "Turned out he wasn't so much interested in me as he was getting into the town's good graces."

"Forget about him," the witch stated. "He'd never understand anyway. The moment you tell a human you're a witch, it's either acceptance or denial...and we both know acceptance has a one percent strike rate."

Vera's expression tightened and her vision shifted over Rosheen's shoulder before she tensed as if she was listening to something. *Curious.*

"Vera?"

The witch blinked and focused on her again. "Were there any customers while I was out?"

Rosheen laughed, adding a new clue to the pile. "Of course not. There wasn't even any traffic." She held up the magazine. "At least I've caught up on all the gossip from 'Summer Bay' and 'Ramsay Street'. Where would I be without my daily dose of Australian soaps?"

Vera's bottom lip trembled slightly and Rosheen paused, her brow creasing. She liked him. Like, *really liked him.* Things were more dire than she'd realised.

"How about we close up this place and have a girls' night, just like old times," Rosheen said, setting the magazine down. "We can get some ice cream, chocolate, and crisps, then watch cheesy romantic comedies until we fall asleep. What do you say?"

Vera glanced around the shop. "I don't know..."

"*C'mon*. There's no one around. It's not like you're going to miss any customers if you close up a couple hours early."

Vera's expression crumpled. "Okay. Why not?"

Rosheen squealed and clapped her hands together. *Good girl*, she thought.

Grabbing a bright red plastic basket, she rounded the counter. "Let's shop! *My treat*."

---

Drew stood outside the pub, his hands shoved in the pockets of his jeans.

Vera hadn't been at dinner. He'd waited long after the other Exiles had disappeared for the night, hoping she was just late, but she never showed. Blue had to kick him out, cursing that he was a worse hoverer than Finn. Not liking the comparison, Drew had legged it.

The last shred of daylight glowed over the horizon —the muddy yellow faded into deep blue then melted into the black of the night sky.

He kept putting his foot into it with Vera. They seemed to be growing further apart, not closer, and he wasn't sure why, let alone how to stop it.

Across the highway, the lights were still on at Wally's garage. The roller doors were up and he could hear the old wolf tinkering inside.

He cast one last look at the darkened *Outpost* before crossing the road.

Wally was sitting at his battered workbench, a mess of machine parts set out before him. He was cleaning what looked like a piston with a grease-stained rag.

Drew didn't know much about cars or machinery, but it looked like a motorcycle engine. He'd seen *plenty* of those in his recent past.

"Hey," he said, stepping into the light.

Wally looked up from his work and beckoned the shifter into the garage. "G'day. You all right?"

He nodded. "What are you building?"

"I've had this old dirt bike sitting under a tarp in the corner for years," the mechanic replied. "Thought it was time to pull the old girl out and have a look. Got it from a bloke who used to dig near the Ridge."

"Lightning Ridge?" Drew asked. "What was he doing all the way out here?"

"Can't quite remember. Prospecting, probably. There's some tailing piles out east that still have some good pickings. We still get the occasional person who'll head out to fossick through the crap." The werewolf picked up another part and rubbed it with the same stained cloth. "You need to shift soon?"

"Yeah." Drew looked over his shoulder, but Solace felt quieter than usual. "I think I might go tonight."

"Good night for it." He looked up, his eyes flashing amber for a split-second before returning to normal. "Something eating at you, eh?"

"Ever since..." Drew sighed and lowered his gaze. "I haven't felt right."

"You're an alpha now, kid," Wally told him. "It's easy to forget, what with the Dust Dogs teleported who knows where. That turmoil you're feeling is your instincts looking for something to dominate."

"You think I'm trying to dominate Vera?" He snorted and crossed his arms over his chest. "I'd never do that to her."

Wally said nothing for a moment, continuing to tinker with the engine. "You know...wolves and dingoes aren't that different. We both have pack mentality, which makes going at it alone harder than it ought to be."

Drew shoved his hands into his pockets. "How do you handle it?"

"I focus on my human side and keep the wolf down until full moons." He set down the piston and turned on the stool. "I reckon it's a sight harder for you, being born to it. I wish I could offer more advice."

Drew thought about it for a moment, wondering if the old wolf was right. He could try to keep the dingo down until he had to shift. Blow off the pent-up alpha steam with one hell of a run, then he'd be good for a while. Keep things on the up and up with Vera.

"Maybe you're right," he murmured.

Wally glanced outside. "If you want to run tonight, you can leave your gear here. There's a lockbox out back."

"Yeah, I reckon I will." He turned towards the night.

"You're a good kid," Wally said behind him. "You're turning out all right."

Drew grunted. "If you say so."

---

Rosheen stood in Vera's underground kitchen and stared at the herbs hanging from the ceiling. It was like an upside-down forest...and the *smell*. Suddenly, an idea formed.

Wrinkling her nose, she unpacked the junk food from the calico shopping bags as Vera came into the room.

"You have so many herbs," Rosheen remarked. "I don't know half of them."

"That's because they're natives," the witch explained.

"Oh, that's right. Your *experiments*." She screwed up her nose again.

"Don't look at me like that. I remember you had a thing for herbs once."

"My favourite was always valerian," Rosheen stated. "You can mix it with so many things. St. John's wort, kava..."

Vera laughed. "Who were you trying to roofie?"

"You know I used to experiment with sleep paralysis," Rosheen reminded her as she opened the ice cream. "I was trying to pierce the veil by remaining alert between stages of consciousness."

"Did it ever work?"

She shrugged. "The jury's still out on that one."

"You never had *terminalia canescens* then," Vera said with a smirk, pointing to a bunch of dried leaves overhead. "When dried and steeped, it's more commonly known as jilungin dreaming tea."

Rosheen ran her fingers over the leaves. "*Ooh...* I'll have to try it before I leave."

Vera's expression faded. "Before you leave?"

"Of course! You didn't think I was going to stay here forever, did you?" She laughed as she opened a cupboard and found where Vera kept the bowls. "I love you, but that red dirt gets into *everything*." Glancing at the herbs, she waved a hand at the witch. "I'll fix the snacks. Do you want to get a movie started?"

"Sure." Vera disappeared and began rummaging in the next room.

Rosheen glanced over her shoulder to make sure she was out of view, then plucked some leaves from the dried *terminalia canescens* and grabbed the mortar and pestle.

"What do you want to watch?" Vera called from the living room as Rosheen ground up the leaves. "I've got *Dirty Dancing, Never Been Kissed, 10 Things I Hate About You...*"

"Dealer's choice," she replied, sprinkling the flakes over the ice cream. Waving her hand over the bowl, her magic fluttered over the crushed leaves and they dissolved.

Taking the bowls into the living room, Rosheen sat on the couch and handed the spiked one to Vera.

"Ice cream for dinner?" the witch asked, brandishing the TV remote.

"We're grown women," Rosheen replied haughtily. "We can eat whatever we want. *Go on*."

Vera laughed as she dug her spoon into the bowl. "Why the hell not? It's not like I'm trying to impress anyone anymore." The first mouthful went down without the witch suspecting a thing.

"Don't say that."

"It's true. He wasn't attracted to me for me," she muttered.

"Don't be so hard on yourself. You totally grew into your baby fat, Vera."

Her eyebrows shot up. "*Wow*."

"I didn't mean it like *that*."

"You were always prettier," Vera told her. "I may have been a Brinewold, but I was the poor little girl who lost her coven to the craglorn. You were always more beautiful, talented, and confident. No one even looked twice at me."

Rosheen stared at her, wondering if she was doing the right thing. As Vera ate another spoonful of ice cream, her eyes narrowed. It was too late for regrets now. She'd travelled to the arse end of the world for this and there was no way she was going back empty-handed.

"I didn't know you felt that way," Rosheen got out.

Vera sighed and swirled her spoon around in her ice cream. "I don't think you understand what it was like growing up in your shadow."

"I may have been prettier back then, but that was nothing compared to your magic...and that's *everything* to witches. I was always second to you." That's why it was so easy to write off Vera's disappearance as a victory. With her gone, Rosheen had ascended favourably in the eyes of the *Gealach Fola*. Suddenly, she meant something...until the time came for her to seek the Brinewold witch out.

Vera's head drooped and she blinked. "It's not a competition. It never should have been."

"Of course, it's a competition," Rosheen drawled. "Have you met my parents?"

"But you're not them." Vera set down the bowl and leaned back, her eyelids fluttering. "You don't have to subscribe, Rosh."

It was the first time Vera had used her childhood nickname and she almost faltered. *No*, she thought. *I came here for a reason.*

Vera slackened, her head falling to the side. Rosheen poked her arm, but the witch didn't stir. She was deep asleep and wouldn't wake until morning.

Smirking, Rosheen climbed off the couch and pulled on her boots. *Eyes on the prize.*

It was time to head out and see why this insignificant little town was so important to the last Brinewold witch.

Finn lingered in the darkness, holding a cloth-wrapped parcel against his chest.

It'd been a few days since he'd ventured towards Solace. After encountering that police officer at Blue's and spoke to Vera in the outback, he'd decided it was best for him to drown his sorrows in private for once.

Though, much to the camp's surprise, he'd cast aside his usual go-to—homemade *aru'de*, a rich fae wine—and picked up some tools and a block of wood instead.

He held the *lor'ashlar* close, hoping that if Vera ever found it hiding in the outback, she wouldn't be angry. It was a shrine sacred to his people and offering it to the memory of her coven was the only thing he could think of to mend what was broken.

*But why now?* He pondered the answer, not knowing why it took all these years to try to mend things with Vera. The only change he could think of was the arrival of one Eloise Hart. Something about the elemental and her powers had stirred his cold Unseelie heart. Either that or it was the increased vibrations from the seal.

Snorting, he looked down at Vera's ritual site. No matter the reason, he was here and he felt awful.

Like all things witch, fae funerals were deeply rooted in ritual. Bodies were cleansed by fire so they could return to the air. Then the ashes were buried at the base of a *lor'ashlar* in order to return them to the earth. Once the spirit was free of their mortal bodies, they would climb, gathering the wisdom of their life through the carvings on the *lor'ashlar* before they stepped through the veil into death itself.

Finn had none of those things to add to his shrine—he knew nothing of Vera's coven and the things they'd achieved—but he'd done his best.

He knelt at the site of Vera's ritual and set the shrine down, wiggling it into the rocky sand so it sat straight and true. Then, he pressed his hands against the earth on either side of the *lor'ashlar*.

"*Ashlar an lor, shride lei an val'ash,*" he murmured. *Honour the dead, for they give us life.*

It was a little insulting considering that magic-starved fae had literally sucked the life out of Vera's coven, but it was the prayer his people recited at funerals, and his people revered the dead. They were sacred.

From the ashes of death, new life was born. Nature was a never-ending cycle.

Finn stood, his head lowered, and listened to the stirring spirits. His heart leapt as he realised something lingered in the shadows behind him. His skin tingled and he spun on his heel.

He came face-to-face with an unknown woman. Blood-red magic bled from her and he felt his own stir in response.

Her hazel eyes flared in the moonlight as her lip curled. "*Fae.*"

"*Witch,*" he hissed, looking her over. She was pretty enough, but her unmasked hatred for him soured her otherwise flawless features.

"I didn't know this hellhole was harbouring fugitives," she drawled. "I'd ask if Vera knew, but something tells me she already did." The witch's gaze moved to the ritual site and came to rest on his *lor'ashlar.* "What are you doing here, fae?"

"I live here, so it's me who is asking you, witch. What are you looking for?"

The witch snorted. "What magic are you feeding off of to live so far from Ireland?"

Finn said nothing and stood his ground. If she wanted a fight, then a fight was what she was going to get.

He let his gaze rake over the witch, studying everything he could. It was clear this woman knew Vera, and if she was unaware of his presence, then what else hadn't the Exiles revealed?

*Nothing*, a small voice told him. *She knows nothing.*

She curled her hands into fists. "How many of you are there?"

"What happened between the witches and the fae has been over for a long time," he told her. "It has been put to rest."

"Put to rest?" the witch scoffed. "How many witches did you drain?"

"If you want revenge, I'm afraid you're too late," he drawled. "That ship sailed a long time ago."

She took a step towards him. "It's never too late for blood, *fae*."

Finn opened his arms and narrowed his eyes. "Then take your best shot. I won't stop you."

Hazel eyes stared at him, but she didn't call on her magic...not even a little.

"Be careful," the witch snapped. "Misfortune often befalls the unwary in the dark."

"Is that a threat?"

She smirked as she backed away. "Just a piece of friendly advice, *fae*."

*Friendly my arse*, he thought. *She's got an ill temper I don't like.* And that was saying something, considering his demeanour was as charming as a quagmire.

He lingered as the witch disappeared into the night, leaving him to ponder the brief, yet hostile encounter. The spirits were stirring, bristling at her passing just as much as he was.

What was she doing poking about out here? *She suspects...*

Finn looked towards the town, the glow of the artificial streetlights a murky blur in the night sky. Cops, unknown witches, and old wounds tearing open. Everything was happening all at once for a change.

Maybe it was time to go back to Solace and ruffle a few feathers after all.

## CHAPTER 14

Drew sniffed the air, his dingo senses taking over. Padding out from behind Wally's garage, he stalked through the shadows and headed north. When he was outside of the ring of artificial light surrounding Solace, he crossed the highway, bypassed the boab, and weaved into the scrub.

When he was a few metres into the wilderness, Drew caught a scent on the breeze. He stilled, his head turning towards the trail that ran behind the *Outpost* and into the outback.

It didn't take long for a solid humanoid shadow to appear. Luckily, it wasn't a spirit but it wasn't exactly anyone to be excited over, either.

Finn snorted as he looked down at the dingo. "Fancy seeing you here."

Drew said nothing, but it wasn't like he could make his thoughts known.

"Be careful," the fae told him. "There's a stray witch wandering around."

He tilted his head to the side.

"Don't look at me like that," Finn drawled. "I don't know who she is. We didn't exactly exchange phone numbers." He peered at the dingo. "Do you know her?"

Drew thumped his tail on the ground and nodded his head. *Rosheen. What was she doing out here? Did Vera know?*

"Well, well, well." Finn sighed and turned towards the darkness. "My duty is done. I'm going home."

Drew let him go, not wanting to spend any more time with the fae than he had to. They weren't exactly best mates, and neither of them were looking to warm up to the other any time soon. If anything, they were frenemies united by a single cause—the seal.

The shifter turned back to the trail, torn over his curiosity over Rosheen's wandering and his need to run to blow off steam. His spirit itched to feel the earth beneath his paws, to leap through the air, and to howl at the moon, but a growing uneasiness saw him turning towards the trail.

If Rosheen was prowling around in the dark, he ought to sniff her out and make sure she wasn't out to cause trouble. Her attitude stunk, and he still hadn't made up his mind if it was just a superiority complex that made her turn up her nose at everything or it was masking something more sinister.

He found her farther down the trail, lingering in a small clearing that was open to the starry sky.

Sticking to the shadows, he padded closer, lowering his head and focusing on the witch through the clumps of barbed spinifex and leafy shrubs.

As he closed the distance between them, his heart leapt as he realised where he was—Vera's ritual site. He'd heard her talk about it in passing, but hadn't seen it in person before. Now that he was here, his dingo eyes picked up on the traces of her magic—he knew it was her power because of the muted purple glow that clung to the rocks—and he knew it couldn't be anything else. Usually, Vera didn't practice complicated magic out in the open unless it was a special occasion. At least, she hadn't performed any spells that he knew about.

He lay flat on his belly under a scrappy shrub, watching Rosheen poke around the ritual site.

In the centre of the clearing was a little wooden carving that looked a lot like a totem pole with a little roof on top. What it was for, he didn't know, but he was beginning to suspect it was an offering left by Finn. There was no other reason he could think of for the fae to be out here, considering how lazy he was.

Drew watched as Rosheen walked around the clearing. She paused here and there, kneeling to touch the ground or run her fingers over a leaf. Her magic fluttered as if she was searching for something or trying to work out a puzzle.

Then she stood by the little totem pole and her aura began to glow. Drew's dingo eyes saw the subtle change—the air shimmering a deep crimson—and he lifted his head in alarm.

Sensing his movement, Rosheen froze. Her shoulders tensed, her gaze raking over the darkness.

Drew didn't dare move. He held his breath and waited to see what the witch would do next.

Rosheen dusted her palms on the length of her dress, then turned away from the clearing and walked into the scrub opposite to where he was concealed. He waited a moment, then slunk out of his hiding spot.

He crept around the clearing, sticking to the shadows cast by the moonlight, sniffing as he went. Catching her scent, he tracked the witch into the outback, careful to keep a safe distance.

The Milky Way gleamed above, the stars scattering across the sky like glittering crystal dust. The witch flittered through the trees just ahead, weaving around the scrappy trunks, forging a path to an unknown destination. Drew caught a glimpse of her before she disappeared, then another as she reappeared a few steps farther ahead.

His chase went on for a few more minutes until she slipped behind a small boab...and didn't reappear.

He padded up to the tree, sniffing the air as he went. Rosheen's scent had dissipated along with her tracks. Shoe prints led him to the base of the boab, then simply stopped as if she'd vanished into thin air.

*Damn it.* She'd given him the slip.

Did she know she was being followed? Drew didn't know enough about witches to be sure.

Lifting his head, he sniffed again, this time catching the stench of rotting flesh in the air. It was coming from the direction of Solace.

Drew's hackles raised, his senses warning him that a presence other than Rosheen lurked in the darkness.

He promptly forgot about the witch and made his way back towards the town, following the rancid scent. It didn't smell like any rot that he knew of, and his dingo nose was more than sensitive enough to tell the difference. Paired with his human mind, he was experienced enough to deduce if it was an animal, supernatural, or human...but the reek of this decay was new.

He reached the edges of Solace, circling around the ridge. As he approached the track that led down the rise towards the *Outpost*, he froze.

Shadows clawed through the trees, circling towards something that flashed white through the foliage.

*Eloise's van.*

One thought flashed through his mind as his predatory senses kicked in. *Kadaitcha.*

Then he felt her magic pulse.

Drew bounded forwards, letting out a piercing howl. The shapeshifting shadow spirits were closing in on the elemental, their inky bodies swirling as they swarmed the motorhome.

He sprinted through the underbrush and leapt, opening his jaws to snap at the closest shadow...and passed right through it.

Landing, he slid across the ground, his claws scratching the hard earth. He propped and turned, shaking his head as his entire body crackled with a weird static that popped and fizzed through his fur.

The door of the van crashed open and a panicked cry tore through the air.

*Eloise!*

---

Eloise stared up at the mountain, knowing she was asleep but unable to wake.

The peak was made up of black, volcanic rock, the boulders stacked up in a tall, haphazard pile. The pitch was darkened by the contrasting blue sky and the glow of the sun behind her, making the scene more ominous than it would've appeared at night.

*A daylight horror.*

She took a step towards the mountain, driven by some supernatural force beyond her knowing. Her limbs felt heavy, as if she were wading through thick mud, but the peak beckoned.

*Wake up.*

Eloise's eyes snapped open, her thoughts muddled.

She was back in her van, her memory foam mattress soft and familiar, but she frowned as her breath vaporised in the air. Sitting up, she shivered and rubbed her hands up and down her arms. It felt like she was in a refrigerator...but that wasn't right. It was almost summer in the outback. The nights were a little chilly, but not subzero.

Suddenly, she wished Kyne had stayed over. There'd been no dreams the nights he'd been with her, and certainly not any creepy temperature drops.

Her hackles began to rise as she leaned over and peeked out the curtain. That's when she saw shadows looming outside her van. Humanoid, inky blackness oozed out of the trees, their steps bringing them closer and closer to where she'd been sleeping just moments ago.

Eloise's body ignited with a wave of terror and her body began to shake. A dingo howled outside, the sound echoing across the outback. *Drew!*

Leaping out of bed, she forgot her fear and hauled the side door open, the metal whizzing on the runners. Cool air rushed into the van, making her skin prickle with goosebumps and her elemental senses spiked.

Human-shaped shadows swirled out of the trees and hurtled towards the motorhome. There were dozens of them, all driven into a sudden frenzy at the sight of her.

Eloise's eyes widened in shock as her brain caught up with her biological animal instincts. *Kadaitcha.*

When she was lost, she'd seen a single shadow spirit deep in the outback and that had been bad enough, but dozens? The world felt cold and dead, their presence leeching out all the baked warmth left behind by the blazing sun.

She only had a second to react as the kadaitcha raced towards her. Not understanding what she was doing, she forced her building elemental energy outward. The shadows recoiled as if they were hit by an invisible shockwave and scattered towards the trees, but the retreat didn't last long. They began to regroup and their featureless faces turned towards her once more.

There was an abrupt snapping and growling, then Drew leapt into the clearing, passing straight through one of the kadaitcha. He landed and shook his head as if the contact with the spirit had scrambled his brain.

"Drew!" Eloise cried as the kadaitcha began to swarm.

The dingo leapt towards her, standing by her side, and began to growl and snap.

How in the hell were they going to stop a wall of shapeshifting shades from devouring them? Eloise began to panic as she flattened her back against the side of the van.

*Think, Eloise,* she thought. *Think!*

Kadaitcha only came out at night. Night only ended with the rising of the sun. *That was it!*

Her gaze flickered down to the rear of the van, to where she'd stacked a pile of fallen branches.

Kyne had mentioned he liked to sit by a campfire

when he was out on his claim. The closest to nature he felt was when he had a fire and an unclouded view the stars, he'd told her. Elemental catnip. Since he was in Solace helping Drew build the dugout, she'd wanted to build him a fire so they could sit out by her van instead. Now her clumsy attempt at her first romantic gesture might just save her and Drew's lives.

"Drew," she murmured, "I've got an idea. I need a distraction."

The shifter didn't take his eyes off the kadaitcha as he stepped forwards. He began to bark, leaping towards the ring of shadows and snapping before leaping back. Then he did it again, forcing the sprits back.

Eloise dove for the pile at the back of the van, grabbing a branch. Hefting it aloft, she waved it at the kadaitcha and imagined the end bursting into flame, hoping her power would respond. It did, the spark lighting the dry and brittle wood in a smoky *whoosh*.

She swung the branch in a wide arc and the kadaitcha recoiled, scattering towards the shadows. Drew growled and snapped, chasing the malevolent spirits back towards the remote outback.

Eloise clamped down on her power, shutting out the elements as the branch continued to burn. Forced back and without anything to latch onto, the kadaitcha became confused and scattered into the wild. Drew ran after them, his dingo form darting through the scrub like a bolt of beige lightning.

Eloise brandished the branch for a long time, prowling the edges of the clearing in case they came back, but after a while it seemed they'd disappeared.

Heaving out a heavy breath, she set down the branch in the middle of the fire pit she'd started to build only hours before. Adding more wood into the ring of rocks, the fire began to grow, the light a welcome comfort after what she'd just witnessed...but she didn't begin to relax until Drew returned.

The dingo prowled out of the darkness and into the circle of firelight, his eyes reflecting silver and gold.

"Are they gone?" she asked. "I'm not sure how to tell. I haven't got to that part in the elemental textbook just yet."

The shifter nodded his head, then his body began to change.

Eloise hadn't seen Drew shift before, and she winced as his bones snapped. After a moment, she turned around, giving him privacy.

A moment later, his exhausted voice called out, "I'm done."

Eloise glanced over her shoulder and saw he was human again, but stark naked. Reaching into the van, she grabbed her dressing gown and handed it to him.

"Are you all right?" she asked. "That sounded painful."

"I'm the one who should be asking you," he replied, wrapping the grey fluffy robe around his naked body.

She made a face and sat on the step of her van. "Slightly terrified, but unharmed."

"They were..." He seemed to be looking for a confirmation.

"Kadaitcha," she murmured. "I saw one when I was lost." She shivered and Drew sat next to her. "Awful, cold, miserable *things*."

"Coen says they're shapeshifting spirits. Some people call them skinwalkers, but that word means different things in other cultures."

"Now it's just getting creepier," Eloise moaned. "Why were they so close to Solace?"

"And why were there so many?" Drew wondered. His brow creased, and he looked towards the darkness.

Eloise tugged on the sleeve of the dressing gown. "What is it?"

"I was going for a run," he told her, "but I ended up following Rosheen instead."

"Rosheen?"

"I saw her at Vera's ritual site," Drew told her. "Right after I saw Finn. If it wasn't for him, I would've thought she was a kadaitcha out to trick me."

Eloise's eyebrows rose. "You saw Finn?"

"The witches and the fae have bad blood."

"I know," the elemental replied.

"He warned me that she was lurking. I reckon they had a fight, or at least had words, so I found her and followed." He shrugged and looked sheepish. "I thought it was best to make sure she didn't disturb anything."

"Don't worry, I reckon you did the right thing." Her gaze went to the darkness, but the kadaitcha were long gone. "I have an uneasy feeling about her."

"You too? I thought it was just me."

Eloise felt a pang of relief tingle across her skin at his admission. He wasn't dazzled by her magically-charged beauty, which could mean anything, but she suspected his loyalty was firmly with Vera, no matter what. Maybe it was a shifter thing—unspoken pack rules or something.

"Rosheen arrived the day after her ritual," Drew added.

"Or did she?" Eloise murmured, hoping they were on the same wavelength.

The shifter looked up at her. "What are you saying?"

"It's all a little coincidental, isn't it? Vera cut her ritual short, the next day Rosheen arrives, then Vera's magic begins to go haywire. Plus, I found her lurking around the boab and she tried to get a vision from me... Think about it."

Drew wrung his hands, his expression troubled. "And everything that just happened... You think she used magic to attract the kadaitcha?"

"This felt like a distraction," Eloise replied. "A dangerous one."

"We've got no proof," he told her. "And I'm not about to put myself in the firing line again."

"What do you mean?"

"Rosheen said Vera's a powerful witch. So did Kyne. I don't fancy getting my head blown off my shoulders." Realising what he'd just said, the shifter winced.

Eloise's thoughts began to spiral. "Could that be it?"

"What?"

"*Power.*"

"I don't know..." Drew shook his head. "I don't like her much, but Rosheen was like a sister to Vera. Why would she want to hurt her?"

"This is the seal we're talking about. I don't know much about it, but it seems like all bets are off where its concerned, don't you think? That kind of power would tempt anyone who's not strong enough to resist."

"I don't know." Drew shrugged. "It all goes together a little too conveniently, but there are too many witnesses. Me, Finn, you. I didn't see her summon the kadaitcha, let alone do anything else."

"You're right." Her shoulders sagged. "Maybe I'm just overreacting. After everything that happened with the Dust Dogs... I guess maybe I'm just oversensitive."

"Maybe those spirits are just a side effect of the seal becoming more active?" Drew offered.

Eloise sighed. Maybe, but still seemed blatantly obvious to her. Rosheen was up to something. If that involved the seal, then they were in more trouble than the chaos brought by a swam of kadaitcha.

"I just don't want to go around accusing Rosheen without any proof," the shifter went on. "I care about Vera and I don't want to do anything to hurt her. She's been through enough...and maybe it's selfish, but I need her. She makes me want to grow the hell up, you know?"

She nodded. "I get it. I'm sure it was just a funky seal anomaly." Though as she said it, she knew she still wasn't convinced.

"Do you want me to go get Kyne?"

"No, no it's fine. They're gone now, and I don't want to worry him. I'll know if they come back."

"Do you want me to stay? I can shift and keep watch outside. I can see more when I'm a dingo."

Eloise smiled as she saw the shifter in a whole new light. "You're a good sort, you know that?"

He grimaced and scratched his head. "The jury's still out on that one."

"Oh, I don't know about that," she told him. "I'm pretty sure they've already ruled on it."

Drew grimaced, uncomfortable with her praise. "Go back in and get some sleep," he told her as he stood. "It's way too early and I still need to run, so I won't go far."

"Okay." She hopped back into the van. "And Drew?"

He turned, his face shadowed by the firelight. "Yeah?"

"Thank you. I don't know what I would've done without you tonight."

She thought she saw him blush, but she wasn't quite sure. "You're welcome."

Closing the door and locking it, Eloise hopped back into bed and closed her eyes. Sleep came eventually, and this time, it was dreamless.

The next morning, she woke to find her dressing gown outside, folded into a neat little square.

## CHAPTER 15

Kyne was worried about a lot of things lately.

He slapped another roll of white paint on the wall in front of him, sealing the chiseled rock inside Drew's dugout. Wherever the dingo shifter was, it wasn't here helping him.

He breathed deeply, his mask filtering the potent paint fumes. There was still so much to do in the interior, it wasn't funny. Plumbing, bathroom fixtures, kitchen, electrical...sealing the raw rock was the simple part.

"Kyne?" Eloise appeared as a silhouette at the end of the hall.

"In here," he called.

She ventured into the hall and looked at the dark dugout behind him. "You're painting all alone?"

"Yeah, I could do with a little help," he replied saltily. "Have you seen Drew?"

"Uh, there's a good reason he's not here yet," she told him. "There was an...*incident* last night."

Kyne dropped the paint roller back into the tray. "Incident? What incident?"

"Kadaitcha swarmed my van last night."

He froze. "Kadaitcha? In Solace?"

Eloise nodded and wiped the back of her hand across her brow. "It stinks in here, by the way."

Kyne took her arm and guided her down the hallway. "Let's go outside before the paint fumes get you." Once they were back in the sun, he pulled off his mask. "What happened?"

She told him the wild story about humanoid shadow spirits oozing out of the darkness like creatures straight out of a horror movie. Drew had been out running and had leapt to her rescue, helping her fight them off. Only fire and shutting off access to her power had finally driven them away.

"You didn't come and get me," he said.

"They were gone." She shrugged. "Besides, I didn't want to worry you." Eloise was too independent for her own good sometimes. He would've been there if he'd known she was in trouble.

"They were attracted to your elemental abilities," Kyne murmured. "But why were there so many?"

"That's what I want to know," Eloise said. "I know the seal seems to be more active than it used to be, but it seems a little coincidental."

He furrowed his brow. "What do you mean?"

"We're looking out for threats against the seal," she told him. "We're waiting for big mining to make a move on that iron ore, but what if we're looking in the wrong place? What if that threat is already here?"

"The seal could be its own worst enemy," Kyne mused. "Maybe we should ask Vera about it."

"I don't think that's a good idea right now."

"You think Vera's the threat?" he asked, raising his eyebrows. "No way. That's a hard no."

"No," Eloise said with an exasperated sigh. "*Rosheen.*"

Kyne scratched his head and looked down the hill towards the *Outpost*. If he was truthful about it, Vera hadn't seemed herself since the anniversary of her family's death. Rosheen could simply be a catalyst for something arcane they couldn't understand—the spark that ignited the fire, so to speak.

"Vera hasn't been herself ever since she arrived," Eloise went on. "Drew's worried, but he won't do anything because he doesn't want to rock the boat."

"No, before that," Kyne said, voicing his thoughts. "The anniversary of her coven's..." He coughed.

"Mourning is one thing, but things have only sped up since she came."

"Rosheen is abrasive at best, but a threat?"

"Drew said he saw her wandering around in the dark last night. Then the kadaitcha swarmed my van." Eloise raised her eyebrows. "Coincidence? Maybe, but with the seal at stake... I'm betting it's not."

This was getting messy. He needed to have a conversation with Hardy about it. If Eloise was right, then going to Vera would only alert Rosheen to their suspicions.

"I'm not sure this is a conclusion we need to jump to," he murmured. "If she is after the seal, then we need to be sure before we do anything."

Eloise scowled. "Isn't trying to kill me enough evidence?"

Kyne sighed and pulled her close. Holding her against his chest, his thoughts became even more troubled. Unless she'd actually seen Rosheen summon the kadaitcha, then they couldn't accuse her of it.

"I'm glad you're okay," he murmured, stroking a paint-flecked hand through her blonde locks. "I should've said that first."

"She's dazzled all of you with creepy sex magic, you know."

Kyne snorted. "Sex magic?"

"You don't notice it, but *I do*."

He drew back and ran his thumb down her cheek. "Eloise, I only want you."

"I know, but magic doesn't care."

Kyne sighed, not understanding where this was coming from. She really thought Rosheen was seducing all the men in town with magic. The witch was definitely beautiful, but he looked at her like he would a piece of art. Admire, but never touch. Could

Eloise be jealous? Their relationship was still new, but she didn't really seem the type.

"Promise me you won't go do something stupid," he said. "There's enough trouble brewing with the cops without a war with an unknown witch."

Eloise scowled, her brow creasing rather impressively between her eyes. "You can sleep at Hardy's tonight. I'm busy doing *intelligent* shit." She pushed him away and stalked across the clearing.

"What did I do?" Kyne threw his hand into the air as she stalked off. "Eloise!"

But she didn't turn around.

---

Hardy emerged into the morning sun and shielded his eyes. The sun hung low in the sky, the hour still too early for it to have climbed far.

He was thankful for the spell that kept him from burning into a crisp, because he would never be able to see how beautiful the outback was in the daytime with his vampire eyes. The night was just as stunning, but there was something about the bold, earthy tones of the red, blue, and grey hues that spoke to his heart, cold and dead as it was.

It'd been a long night underground, cut off from the stars, but at least things were returning to a semblance of normal in Solace.

Kyne was back and less salty about life. Wally was

working through the aftermath of his last transformation, making amends with Eloise and shoring up his mine after the Dust Dogs had dug into it. Blue was his usual no-fuss self. Drew was settling in just fine, despite his constant struggles with his dingo side. Eloise had brought a much-needed breath of fresh air, blowing into town in that motorhome of hers and obliterating all the cobwebs in her wake. Finn seemed to be doing what was right for the town for once in his life and keeping his distance while the police were sniffing around. Hardy *never* worried about Coen. The only hiccup was that Vera seemed to be slightly off-centre ever since Rosheen had appeared.

Every single one of the Exiles had a past—that's why they were called Exiles—so it stood to reason that Vera would be shaken up by the appearance of a witch from her old life. Rosheen was still here and nothing had blown up, so the going was currently good.

They all had problems, Vera was no exception, and Hardy had spent the previous night listening to Kyne's.

The elemental had slept on Hardy's couch, his excuse being that he didn't want to wear out his welcome with Eloise. He was working himself up into a sweat after asking her to move in with him—into a house he was going to build just for her.

It'd only been less than two months since Eloise had arrived in Solace, so it was a little too strong, but they were supernaturals. The normal 'rules' never seemed to apply when there was magic involved.

Hardy sighed. He had all the time in the world to worry about those kind of romantic relationship things, but lately, it seemed like even he had an expiration date. Old memories surfaced through the fog of time that was his past, and he shook his head.

Taking out his keys, he walked towards the rear of his shop. Cutting and polishing opal always seemed to calm his nerves...and soothe his throat.

He was so lost in his thoughts, that it was only by chance that he looked up and saw the strangest sight.

Vera was standing in the middle of the highway, not moving.

*What in the world?*

Hardy rounded the side of his shop and walked towards her. What was she doing?

"Vera?" he called, but she didn't respond. "*Vera?*"

He jogged out onto the road and stood in front of her, but she didn't notice him. She was facing north and staring into space, her eyes glassy. Hardy listened to her abnormally slow heartbeat and frowned.

He snapped his fingers in front of her face. "*Vera.*"

The witch started, her heart roaring into life. "Bloody hell. You scared me."

"What are you doing?"

"I don't..." She looked around, her confusion clear. "I don't know."

At first, Hardy thought she might've been under the influence of some kind of magical trance or amid a vision, but the longer he looked at her, the more worried he became. He'd never seen her stand in the middle of the highway before.

Checking his watch, he saw it was a quarter to nine. On the second Tuesday of the month, a road train ran through Solace at nine a.m. like clockwork. If he hadn't seen her, it would've been a close call.

"Are you all right?" Hardy reached out to lay a comforting hand on her arm, but the moment he touched her, he felt magic twist around him and grab hold. He recoiled as his skin sizzled and turned red. "Hell, Vera, that burns!"

The witch blinked and her magic subsided. "I'm sorry, I didn't realise..."

Hardy ran his hands over his bare arms as his lightly cooked flesh healed. "Don't forget there's only a spell between me and the sun."

"I..." she trailed off, her brow creasing, "I don't think I slept very well last night."

His brow furrowed as he looked her over. It didn't look like lack of sleep to him. Vera seemed confused and her grip on her magic was rather...*loose.*

"I'm sorry I was harsh with you yesterday," he told her. "I was just trying to get your spark back."

"It's fine," she told him. "I was angry and Clarke..." She sighed. "What a waste."

"That's his problem." He looked down the highway. "Let's get you off the road, hey? It's almost nine."

"Oh my God," she muttered. "Hardy, I don't know what I was doing. I don't remember walking out here."

"Well, first things first, let's get you off the road." Hardy wound his arm around Vera's waist and guided her towards the *Outpost*...and not a moment too soon.

They sat on the bench underneath the verandah as the sound of the approaching road train rumbled in the distance, coming closer and closer. Then it shimmered through the mirage as it reached the town limits. The huge black Mack truck was hauling three dusty silver trailers, and it barely slowed as it hurtled through Solace.

Hardy waited until it was in the distance before he spoke. "How long has this been going on?"

"This is the first time anything like this has ever happened," Vera replied, visibly rattled by the whole thing.

He didn't like the sound of that. Witches who lost control of their magic were trouble, and Vera was a rather powerful witch. If there was something going on, he had to address it. Not just because of the seal, but for her. She was family.

"What was the last thing you remember?"

She opened her mouth to reply, but hesitated. "I, uh..." She took a deep breath. "The whole morning is a bit of a blur."

"Last night, then?"

"Rosheen and I were sitting on the couch, eating ice cream and watching a movie."

"What movie?"

Vera tensed, her brow creasing in confusion as she tried to grasp onto her memories. "I don't feel so good."

Hardy wrapped his arm around her shoulders. "I'm taking you home."

"But I've got to open the shop…"

"Forget about opening today," he told her. "You're in no state to worry about business. What if Clarke comes back?"

At the mention of the sergeant's name, Vera scowled. "Fine."

Rosheen was clattering about in the kitchen when they ambled down the hall. Hearing them enter, she peeked her head out the door.

"What's going on here?" the witch asked, flashing an appreciative look at the vampire.

Hardy blinked as he swept the lime-green beaded curtain out of the way. "Vera's not feeling well. Her magic seems to be a little off today."

"Oh? Is it?" Rosheen abandoned whatever she was up to in the kitchen and came out to help Vera onto the couch.

"I'm not sick," Vera complained, waving them away. "I'm just tired."

"No one said you were sick," Hardy told her. "But you were standing in the middle of the highway."

"Oh dear," Rosheen murmured, waving her hands over the witch's head. "Your magic is a little wobbly, V."

Hardy scratched his head. "I'll say. She almost undid my daylight spell."

Rosheen raised her eyebrows. "Maybe we had a little too much ice cream last night after all."

Vera pinched the bridge of her nose. "Stop speaking so loud. I've got a headache."

Hardy raised his eyebrows, his worry deepening. Glancing at Rosheen, he nodded towards the door. "A word?"

Vera didn't seem to hear him, so he ventured outside with Rosheen.

"In all the years I've known Vera, I've never seen her sick," he said as they stood in a block of shade cast by the *Outpost*. "Not even a hint of a cold."

"That's witches for you," Rosheen said. "Biological illnesses are rare, though we're not immune."

"Sure, but this seems magical."

"Oh, no doubt."

Hardy thought about the seal and wondered if Vera had a magical illness connected to it. He was well-aware that nothing seemed off limits where it was concerned, but he couldn't tell Rosheen that. Vera seemed to trust the witch, but not enough to vouch for her with the Exiles yet.

"Do you know what's causing it?" he asked instead.

Rosheen glanced towards the outback, her gaze following the trail. "Has she done any magic lately? Any rituals?"

"It was the anniversary of her family's death," he replied, knowing she already knew all the details. "I know she goes into the outback to honour their memory. I assume it involves magic."

"Hmm..." Rosheen's expression was thoughtful for a moment before she turned back to him. "Her father was a Nightshade. They were one of the five great covens. He was a good man, but the coven itself was known for their predilection for dark magic. They don't exactly follow the rules, if you know what I mean."

"Do you think Vera has a susceptibility to it?" Hardy asked. "Could that be what's causing her to... zone out?"

"It's possible." Her brow furrowed. "I've sensed something strange in the air ever since I arrived. There wouldn't be spirits lingering around here, would there?"

"What kind of spirits?" Hardy asked, hedging around the question. Their conversation was straying too close to the seal for his liking.

"Any kind, I suppose."

Hardy didn't see the harm in telling Rosheen about the kadaitcha and the other spirits—otherwise known as the Min Min—that lingered in the outback. They certainly weren't linked to the seal—they'd be here no matter what.

"There are some that appear in the outback," the vampire told her. "There's been sightings over the years, but they don't come near the town. Mysterious lights and other shadows."

"It's no wonder," the witch said with a snort. "They all probably died of boredom."

Hardy raised his eyebrows. For a moment there, the witch almost seemed *nice*. "Well, people do go to extremes for power and wealth."

Rosheen narrowed her eyes as if he'd pinched a nerve. "Well, there is a possibility that all of that energy has stirred something in Vera. Especially since she was out wandering in the dark doing rituals and whatnot. I can do a cleansing with her. That should help set her magic right."

Hardy glanced back towards Vera's dugout. "Should we be worried?"

"Not at all. Consider it witchy maintenance." Rosheen clicked her fingers. "Like an oil change."

He held onto a sigh and shrugged. "I'll come back later and check on her." He pointed towards his shop. "I'll be in the workshop all day. Let me know if anything changes."

Rosheen smiled, the air glittering around her. *Gosh, she was pretty.* "Of course. I'll take good care of her, I promise."

Hardy stared after her as she went back inside and only turned when the door had long closed. He walked across the side road in a daze, his boots shuffling across the asphalt.

Sensing someone approach, he turned to find Drew following the shade of the gum trees behind the workshop, the shifter's footsteps as light as a dingo's.

"Hey," the vampire said, his mind clearing. Maybe it wasn't the best idea to tell him that Vera wasn't feeling well. He'd be over there in a flash, and he got the feeling Drew wasn't a fan of Rosheen. Mix his alpha status into the pot, and there'd be trouble. "Kyne's already gone up the dugout. Said something about painting."

"I actually wanted to see you."

Hardy stilled, his keys hanging from his fingers. "What now?"

Drew's gaze shifted to the *Outpost*. "I think we may have a problem."

## CHAPTER 16

Eloise strode away from Kyne, her anger reaching boiling point.

Her boots stomped on the packed earth, sending out short bursts of elemental energy into the rock below. He was right when he said he should've led with asking if she was okay. Was he her boyfriend or not?

Those kadaitcha were scary as hell. Seeing a dozen shadow people swarm out of the darkness was something out of a horror movie. A solo woman sleeping in a van in the middle of woop woop had more than enough to deal with without all that.

As she approached the highway, she spied Drew and Hardy lingering in the shade behind the opal shop. Hoping they were discussing last night's tussle with the kadaitcha, Eloise turned up the path behind the *Outpost* and approached the boab on the north side of town.

If anyone could help her make sense of what had happened, it was Coen.

No matter how many times she saw it, the boab was always an impressive sight. The bottle-shaped tree was the largest of its kind she'd ever laid eyes on. Not only did it hold magic of its own, but it concealed the entrance to the tunnel that led to the seal itself.

Eloise took the eagle feather from her shirt pocket and twirled it around in her fingers. The brown and white plume was fraying a little, and she wondered if its magic was fading as well.

Eloise looked around, her gaze raking over the green scrub, the ochre dirt, and the lonely highway. Nothing stirred and her elemental energy didn't sense any unwanted eyes, so she clutched the feather and called, "Coen?" She listened a moment but there was only silence. "Coen, are you there?"

"Hello."

Eloise turned to see Coen peeking around the trunk of the boab, his curled hair falling into his eyes. He really was childlike sometimes, his cheeky grin warming her heart and making her smile.

"Hey." She looked around, but the kangaroo he usually travelled with was absent. "Where's *Marlu*?"

"*Marlu* rests with her joey," he replied, rubbing his stomach.

Eloise's heart warmed. "*Aww*, she has a joey?"

His grin widened. "A boy who sits safe and warm in her pouch." He sat on an exposed root and patted the space beside him. "Sit. The boab will comfort your unsteady heart."

Her smile faded. "You can tell?"

Coen grinned and patted the root again. "You summoned me."

Eloise sat, letting out a heavy breath. "There's a new witch here. A friend from Vera's past."

Coen blinked as he studied her. "But not *your* friend?"

Eloise shook her head. "Nope," she popped the 'p' and narrowed her eyes. "I have...*misgivings.*"

Coen tilted his head, his eyes sparkling. "You want to ask about the witch?"

"No, not exactly... Kadaitcha attacked me last night. Drew was out running and he helped drive them off, but it was a close call."

"Kadaitcha in Solace," Coen mused, looking troubled. "Very close, but Drew has spirit eyes. He will see if they return."

Eloise frowned. "Spirit eyes?"

"His dingo eyes can see many things if he opens them wide enough."

"Like kadaitcha?"

Coen swept his arm across the sky. "Many things."

"Fair enough," she murmured. "What are kadaitcha? They must want something?"

"Kadaitcha are malignant spirits," he explained. "Kadaitcha is a word found in many mob's language. It is also a name used for a mission of vengeance by the living. *Punishment*."

She shivered. "Punishment?"

Coen nodded. "Only a person with vengeance in their heart can summon them...or choose to become one. This land is old, many die here when the white fellas came."

Eloise's skin prickled. It was a truly awful time in Australia's early history, one she wished had never happened. *If only...*

"You see the path," Coen added. "Your magic opens your eyes."

"Someone with one hell of an axe to grind," she stated, forcing herself to think about the kadaitcha again. "There had to have been at least a dozen of them. Why would they come after me?"

"You walkabout close to the Dreaming," he told her.

"Of course." Andante had warned her that spirits were attracted to her because of her affinity with the fifth element—ether, or *spirit*. Where was Andante now? Likely still living in her cave, hidden away in a pocket of space and time, oblivious. "Do you think someone summoned them last night?"

Drew had seen Rosheen wandering around in the dark right before the shadows had swarmed her van. That was too much of a coincidence... But if Rosheen was responsible, what axe did she have to grind with Vera that Solace was being dragged into it? Did the witch know about the seal and was making a sly play for it? It didn't matter if she found it, Kyne was the only one who knew where the key was hidden. *Unless...*

Her creepy sex magic!

"I can't know that," Coen replied. "I didn't see that in the Dreaming."

Eloise straightened up. "But you saw something?"

The Indigenous man nodded. "I saw the emu set in the sky. It was being chased below the horizon by the lawman."

*Sergeant Clarke.* With all the fuss kicked up with Rosheen and the kadaitcha, she'd almost forgotten about the cops and their Dust Dog investigation.

Eloise sighed. "Are you saying...?"

"The policeman who came to Solace still has questions. He is still close."

That didn't sound good at all. After his attempts to trick information out of Vera by catching her heart, Eloise had hoped he would've got the message. They weren't talking about Craig Roth and the Dust Dogs—they couldn't without revealing the supernatural truth about Solace *and* Drew's involvement. Besides, that wasn't the only thing she worried about—Rosheen was a loose cannon.

This was getting messy, but messy was the order of the day in Solace.

"Do you know anything about Rosheen?" she asked. "Can you see that kind of thing?"

Coen shrugged. "Sometimes."

"I can tell you something," a voice said behind them.

Eloise let out a squeak of surprise as she turned to see Finn slink out from behind the cover of the scrub.

"Ah, there you are," Coen said, grinning up at the fae. "You're slow like a wombat."

Finn snorted and knelt in front of them. "I choose to take that as a compliment. Wombats *are* fat and slow, but they're also cute as a button."

Eloise raised her eyebrows, disturbed that Finn had uttered the words 'cute as a button'.

"I saw a witch last night," he went on. "One of Vera's friends, I'm guessing. She was *lurking*."

"*Rosheen*," Eloise muttered. "What was she doing?"

The fae grinned. "I like that you went straight for the witch's jugular and sidestepped mine. I knew you were special, desert pea."

"He was leaving an offering to Vera's coven," Coen declared.

Finn squirmed, shooting a glare at him. "Did you have to say it so loud?"

"Yes."

Eloise sighed. At least the fae was trying to make amends for his people's past. "What happened with Rosheen?"

Finn snorted. "What kind of name is Rosheen anyway?"

"An Irish one." She waved her hand at him to stop him from stalling. "*C'mon*."

"She wasn't pleased to see me," the fae replied. "Our people have animosity, as you know. That new witch didn't know I was here, and it was a rude shock to the both of us. It could have easily ended up in a fight to the death."

"What did she say?"

"I believe she said, 'misfortune often befalls the unwary in the dark', or something equally ominous."

Coen was listening to their back and forth with interest, his chocolate-coloured eyes sparkling with a light that seemed to echo the stars.

"Well, I don't know about you guys," Eloise said, "but that's all the evidence I need."

"Evidence of what?" Finn asked. "That witches are meddling busybodies who love slam poetry?"

"*No.* A swarm of kadaitcha attacked me last night."

"Well, well, well..." the fae drawled. "I rest my case." He looked up at Coen. "What say you, walkabout man?"

Coen shrugged. "I didn't see."

Finn rolled his eyes. "The only time he has nothing to say is the one time we want his input."

"Hang on," Eloise said. "That's your opinion, but I listen to *everything* Coen has to say."

"You should watch where you step," the Indigenous man told the fae. "The water in the billabong rises."

Finn stood and shook out his dreadlocks. "And that's my signal to leave."

"Wait," Eloise said. "Keep an eye out for Rosheen. I

think she's up to something. I've got a dreadful feeling that the kadaitcha swarming my van wasn't an accident. Kyne, Hardy, Wally, and Blue...they all seem to be dazzled by her, too."

Finn narrowed his eyes. "I won't come back to Solace while the cops are still lingering. I've done enough damage apparently, and if that witch sees me again, I'm charcoal. I'm sorry, desert pea, but this is one fight I *don't* want to make worse." He spread his arms wide. "It's a Christmas miracle!"

Eloise and Coen sat together in companionable silence as Finn walked away into the scrub.

"I'm sure he doesn't mean to be awful like that," Eloise said after a moment, attempting to apologise on Finn's behalf. "He's a long way from home."

Coen laughed as if he knew an amusing truth but said nothing.

"I'm worried about Rosheen's intentions," she went on. "The kadaitcha *may* be a side effect of the seal becoming more active, but I don't think we should take any chances. Are you able to keep an eye on the spirits?"

"I will watch, but I don't always see," he replied. "The Dreaming is always moving—up and down, side to side. Backwards and forwards. The river ebbs and flows. Never sits still."

Eloise rubbed her eyes, remembering the dreams that had brought her to Solace. They were still playing out, but now that most of them had come true, they were beginning to change, though the mountain still loomed.

"Coen... I..." She frowned, not knowing how to broach the subject of the mountain.

"Yes?"

"I have this dream. It's..." Her brow furrow deepened into a chasm. "There's a mountain made of black volcanic boulders."

"What does it do?"

"Nothing... It *looms*, I suppose."

Coen turned thoughtful, his eyes dreamy. "A looming black mountain."

"You helped me when I was lost. You seemed to know... Maybe there's something you've seen in the Dreaming? Something to explain it?"

"I haven't seen a mountain," he replied, his expression clearing. "Maybe the Dreaming hides it from me, or it's something I don't need to know."

"Yet..." she said, hoping that was the truth of it.

"Yes," Coen said with a smile. "Maybe not just yet."

Eloise mulled over all the troubling revelations, but it only made her stomach churn. If there was a solution, she wasn't sure what it was, let alone the correct path to take. Rosheen, the kadaitcha, Sergeant Clarke... Maybe all she could do was watch and wait.

At least Drew seemed immune to whatever illusion Rosheen was casting on all the men in town, but he'd also said they didn't have any evidence. A thinly veiled threat aimed at Finn wasn't enough to incriminate her, either.

Coen watched her with a troubled expression, and it only made her want to throw up.

"I will watch the currents and read the stars," he assured her. "You have my promise, Eloise Hart. The emu has come down to rest by the billabong, and so we will see."

Eloise sighed and offered him a thankful smile. "It seems I have work to do," she murmured, thinking about her forgotten mural project. The water tank would have to wait. "I better make a to-do list."

Coen chuckled and leapt to his feet. "I will come if I see a message."

"Okay." She stood and straightened her hat. "You better get back to *Marlu* and her joey. Thank you for coming." Eloise turned, but Coen had already disappeared.

Shaking her head, she made her way back down the trail towards Hardy's opal shop.

***

Vera Walsh was searching. Ever since her parents died and her coven had gone down with them, she'd been cast out into the heaving water, struggling to keep afloat.

And somehow, she'd ended up with the *Gealach Fola*—otherwise known as the Blood Moon witches.

They only wanted her because she was the last living member of the Brinewold coven...and the last link to Nightshade magic. A two-in-one deal that could not be beat.

Her thoughts drifted as she drove along the straight stretch of highway, hurtling farther and farther towards the red heart of the Australian Outback. What had drawn her here was a mystery, but she thought it was the last place the Irish Witches would think to look. She would never belong to another coven again, not even the *Gealach Fola*.

People sucked, but witches sucked even harder. It was always about magic and power. The prestige of the last Brinewold-Nightshade was the only reason they'd taken her in. Too bad it'd taken so long for her to realise that having magic wasn't as magical as picture books made it out to be.

In the distance, a large green road sign came into view. It grew larger, the white writing sharpening. At the top it read, 'Solace - 5kms', then 'Lightning Ridge - 224kms'.

It was an omen. Solace was exactly what she was looking for—the sentiment, not the town.

As she drove the five kilometres into Solace, she scowled. Was this it? Four buildings, a rusted windmill, a bloated boab tree, and nothing but ochre dust and washed-out green shrubs as far as the eye could see?

Still, something made her pull over in front of the general store.

Vera began to climb out of the car, but hesitated. She hung halfway out of the door, one foot still firmly planted inside in case she needed to make a quick getaway.

The front of the building was a patched together mess of faded signage and hasty repairs. It looked more like an abandoned shed than a general store. Definitely a man's world, this *Solace*.

Deciding nothing was going to jump out and grab her, she set both feet on the ground and hopped up onto the old wooden verandah that ran the length of the front façade.

As she was about to try the door, she saw a scrap of white paper was taped on the inside of the glass. A message was scratched out on it in black Texta. Whoever had written it had terrible handwriting, but she got the gist of it. 'If unattended, please call Wally', followed by a mobile phone number.

Vera took her battered prepaid phone from her pocket and scowled. There was no signal, just 'SOS Only'.

Sighing, she turned and looked up and down the lonely highway. For a long moment, she imagined she was the only human being left on the planet. Nothing stirred, not even the wind.

Spotting two petrol bowers at the garage across the road, she locked the car and made a move towards the open roller doors. Maybe there was someone there who could help her.

But the moment she stepped on the white line in the centre of the asphalt, she felt magic stir deep in the earth beneath her.

"Hey, Vera."

She blinked, turning to see Hardy step up onto the verandah beside her. The memory faded, her consciousness returning to the present.

"I wanted to see how you were doing," the vampire went on. "I didn't have time to see you last night."

Vera sighed. "Rosheen turned you away, didn't she?"

"Something like that."

She looked back at the highway, staring at the spot she'd been standing the first time she'd felt the seal. Strangely, it was the same place Hardy had found her the day before. It was obvious she was gong trough something, but what?

"I feel...nostalgic," she told the vampire. "The headaches are gone and my magic seems okay, but my thoughts..."

"I know all about nostalgia," Hardy said. "I have a lot of memories to sift through. Some I'd rather not, too."

"*Hmm.*"

"Will you be all right?"

"I will be. Rosheen's cleansing helped set my magic right. You don't have to worry about the..." She nodded towards the road. "I just need some time to reflect on my past. I'm not sure what I want to do."

Hardy took a step closer. "What do you mean?"

"I may not be magically linked to the Irish covens, but..." She sighed. "I don't know. Do I have a responsibility to them? Maybe. Do I need to go back and make things right with the *Gealach Fola*? Maybe. I did run out on them without a word."

Hardy stared at her, unblinking. He'd become a vampiric statue, his undead status turning him to stone. "You're thinking about leaving?"

"No." She shook her head. "I'm..." she trailed off, her heart heavy. Was she? It was clear she was at a crossroads.

*You know you want to*, a voice echoed in the back of her mind. *You could be great. You could be matriarch of the new world.*

"Vera, if you ever need to talk..."

"I know," she replied. "I know."

Hardy straightened up. "I've gotta go to the workshop. You going to be okay?"

"Yeah, Drew's helping out today. He's inside opening up."

He snorted. "*Look out.*"

"It's all right. We've reached an understanding."

"You sure about that?"

Vera managed a smile and waved the vampire away. "Enough. Off with you."

No sooner than the vampire was gone, that she heard an engine as a road train approached from the south. Vera lingered, not wanting to go inside and deal with Drew's questions just yet. A moment of blessed peace was the order of the morning.

But instead of a truck, it was a convoy of another kind. A convoy that raised her stress levels for another reason entirely.

A line of bright, shiny police vehicles filed along the highway, the sun glinting off metal as they passed. Two 4WDs, a divi van, and a black transit all headed north.

*Still after Roth.*

And bringing up the rear, like a cringeworthy punchline, was a familiar 4WD...that pulled off the highway and parked in front of her. Sergeant Clarke sat behind the wheel and took off his aviator sunglasses as he killed the engine.

Vera didn't move, but her scowl deepened as he got out and approached her. At least he had the good grace to look sheepish about it.

Clarke took off his hat and lifted one booted foot up onto the verandah.

"What can I do for you, sergeant?" she asked coolly, crossing her arms over her chest. "I have nothing to say to you, you know."

Clarke grimaced. "We're searching the Dust Dogs squat," he explained. "Forensics, sniffer dogs, the whole deal."

Her scowl softened slightly. "Sniffer dogs?"

Clarke nodded. "They've been used for drugs in the past, and if there's foul play...." He shrugged. "Anyway,

I don't want to worry you with all of that. I just wanted to stop by and apologise for the other day. I shouldn't have used our date to get information out of you. I'm sorry."

*He's sorry*, the voice chortled. *He's sorry!*

Vera pursed her lips. "It was a rotten thing to do."

He wrung the edge of his hat, his brow furrowing. "Yeah, not one of my finer moments."

Vera balled her hands into tight fists as her magic tingled down her fingers. What she wouldn't do to zap his arse right about now.

*Do it.*

Clarke looked towards the road, unable to meet her gaze. "Look, Vera, I'm sorry about how it went down. I never meant... I'd like to try again, if you're up for it."

She lifted her fist, her lip curling. It would be so easy to—

The door opened behind her, the bell ringing furiously.

"What are you doing here?" Drew bellowed. "Haven't you done enough damage?"

Vera closed her eyes and said a prayer. *Here we go...*

## CHAPTER 17

Drew shoved the tray of money into the till and slammed it closed. The whole bench shuddered and his alpha anxiety rose as he caught sight of Hardy talking to Vera outside.

They were standing on the veranda of the *Outpost*, having what looked like a deep and meaningful conversation.

Drew had only spoken with her once like that—namely, a couple of weeks ago when he'd been all busted up after fighting Roth and the Dust Dogs. Once things had calmed down, it was right back to the status quo—constantly butting heads. Didn't help that he was an alpha without a pack.

Scowling, he thought over the conversation he'd had with Hardy yesterday afternoon about Eloise and the kadaitcha. If the vampire cared that their latest arrival had almost been swallowed whole by a swarm of shadow people, he didn't show it. He was dismissive about Rosheen, too. Maybe Eloise was right about her trying to use magic to trap all the men in Solace. If that was true, then why wasn't he under her spell?

His spirits lifted when he saw Hardy was gone, but when the police 4WD pulled up out front, any spirit he had was dashed. Sergeant Clarke had made his inevitable return.

Drew scowled as he watched him talk with Vera.

The guy wasn't genuine. He didn't care about her. At least Clarke had the decency to look like he was packing it.

Then he saw Vera lift her fist, her hand crackling with purple magic, and his scowl disappeared. *She was going to zap the bugger!*

Drew leapt over the counter and pushed the door open with a violent jab. "What are you doing here? Haven't you done enough damage?"

As Clarke turned, Vera lowered her fist.

"Drew," the cop began, but Drew wasn't in the mood for this bloke's excuses.

"You've got some balls showing up here after what you did to her," he snarled, his alpha showing. "Breaking her heart for *information*. We already told you everything. Rack off already."

Clarke straightened up to his full height, but was still an entire head shorter than Drew, who was up on the verandah. "I think I better leave."

"No shit, Sherlock," Drew drawled.

The sergeant glanced at Vera, who'd become silent.

"Think about what I said... If you change your mind, you know where to find me."

The shifter narrowed his eyes. "Yeah, sifting through a pile of steaming dingo shit."

"*Drew*," Vera muttered.

"It's fine," Clarke said, backing away. "I've got to go assist with the search anyway."

"Yeah, you better." Drew scowled at the sergeant as he got into the 4WD, reversed, and took off up the highway.

"Search? What search?" he asked.

"They're shaking down the Dust Dogs camp," Vera said.

"*Whatever*." Hardy had wiped the place of evidence, so the cops were the least of their problems. But moment the 4WD was out of view, Drew turned to the witch, his anger palpable.

"What do you think you're doing?" he raged. "You almost outed yourself to a stinking pig!"

"Like your behaviour was any better," she snapped.

He shook his head. "What's going on with you, Vera? Ever since Rosheen showed up, it's like you're a different person."

"This has nothing to do with Rosheen!"

"She's a bad influence on you!"

She sighed and dragged Drew into the *Outpost*. Making sure the shop was empty, she said, "True, she's a little arrogant and not made for the outback, but she's—"

"You've only got sicker the longer she's been here," he interrupted. *She was making excuses for her!*

"Excuse me?" Vera put her hands on her hips and glared with the force of a million nuclear bombs. "I'm not sick. Why would you think that?"

"It doesn't matter why, only that you are. And I'm not the only one!"

"Yeah, then who else?"

"A swarm of kadaitcha attacked Eloise the other night right after I saw Rosheen lurking in the dark. She says Rosheen is using magic on all the men in town."

Vera listened in open-mouthed shock. "Magic? Kadaitcha?"

"Yeah, *kadaitcha*," Drew exclaimed. "If I wasn't there to help her, who knows what would've happened!"

"Why didn't anyone tell me?"

"Because you've been brainwashed by Rosheen!"

"Rosheen and I have history, but brainwashing? She's been helping me!"

Drew jabbed a finger towards the verandah. "Did that look like it worked? You were about to smack that cop down with your magic! A *cop*, Vera. A bloody cop who could out us all!"

"I wasn't going to do anything!" she cried.

"Rosheen needs to go before things get worse. If you can't see that, then I'll see it for you."

"Careful, Drew, your alpha is showing," she drawled.

Fighting with Vera was the exact thing he was trying to avoid when he told Eloise he didn't want to go around accusing Rosheen without evidence, but it was far too late for that. Seeing Vera raise her magic to attack Clarke was the straw that broke the camel's back. Eloise had already done so much for him and for Solace, but it was clear she was still out there fighting the good fight while the rest of them were easy pickings.

He lowered his voice. "Rosheen is the problem, Vera."

"She's the last link I have to my family, I—"

Drew scoffed, "Yeah, some family."

"You don't know what you're talking about," she hissed. "You have no idea what it was like for me when my family died."

"The Dust Dogs murdered my entire pack, remember?" Drew snorted. "Kick me in the guts, why don't you?"

Vera's cheeks reddened. "Drew, I—"

He didn't want to hear her apologies. "Rosheen's after something, and if it's not the seal, then it will be soon."

"No." Vera shook her head. "No, I don't believe it."

"If she tries to hurt you or anyone else in Solace again, I will kill her." He breathed deeply, his dingo rising. "And that's not a threat, Vera... *It's a promise.*"

"Stay out of it," Vera warned. "This is witch business."

"You're my pack," he said. "You told me so yourself."

"But you're not our alpha, Drew. There's a difference."

"Someone has to fight for you." He lowered his gaze to her lips, wondering if that's what his feelings were about.

"Get away from me," Vera hissed. "Get a clue, Drew. I don't need your help or your stinking dingo dominance." She spun on her heel and stalked out of the *Outpost*, shoving the door open so hard she almost broke it off the hinges.

Drew didn't stop her. He knew better than to confront an angry witch, lest he get his arse beat.

Eloise was right about Rosheen. He saw it plain as day. If Vera saw what was happening, she didn't want to acknowledge it, but she probably didn't know. He'd bet a million bucks that the witch's 'cleansing' was nothing more than a ruse to make Vera sick.

But what could he do about it? He knew nothing about magic. Hardy was no help, and Kyne was probably under the same spell along with Wally and Blue.

Eloise might help, but she was as new to her magic as he was to Solace. Besides, after the other night with the kadaitcha, he didn't want to put her in any more danger.

And he could forget about Finn and the fae—they wouldn't help a witch, not even Vera.

He was truly on his own.

———

Sergeant Andrew Clarke leaned against the bonnet of his police issue 4WD and watched the commotion unfold in front of him.

A pair of constables—a man and a woman—were carrying out a bag full of unregistered shotguns and rifles, but it wasn't the only thing they'd found and far from the last.

The Dust Dogs' squat was a mash up of old corrugated iron buildings, lean-tos, rusted-out machinery parts, and fire pits. They'd been living here for quite some time but had left everything behind. Tools still filled the garage, clothes were in drawers, beer was in the fridges, and other valuables were left lying around.

"Clarke," a man called as he walked over.

Clarke leaned against his 4WD and crossed his arms over his chest as Detective Landry came to stand with him. The guy was five years his senior and an exemplary cop, but his approach was 'bull in a china shop'—a tactic that was more suited for the city.

"I don't get it," Landry said, pushing his sunglasses up. "They just left all their shit here. Wallace just found five kilos of ice in the caravan at the back. What bikie gang ups and leaves hundreds of thousands of dollars' worth of drugs?"

"Stuffed if I know," Clarke replied. "Bigger and better things?"

"Bigger things? Not likely. It stinks of foul play."

"Last I heard, there were at least twenty guys living out here. If it were a mass murder, there'd be evidence. Signs of a struggle. Blood. The dogs have found nothing."

Landry snorted. "Stranger things have happened in the outback. How's recon going in that town?"

Clarke raised his eyebrows. "Solace?"

From the moment he'd got out of the car, Clarke knew it differed from any other small outback town he'd visited. There was something in the air that smelled slightly off. Not in a bad way, just a curious feeling that had his hackles tingling.

There were eccentrics, then there was the population of Solace. The publican was normal enough, but the dreadlocked guy was next-level strange. He was more suited to live in a share house in the artsy Sydney suburb of Newtown than the outback—and he damn well had the attitude for it.

The young woman, Eloise Hart, seemed out of place amongst it all, but she seemed like one of those 'van lifers' who were popular on social media these days. It wouldn't surprise him if she had a following somewhere she was 'influencing'.

The old mechanic reminded Clarke of the rough as guts men in the Ridge, and the miner Kyne much the same, but it only got stranger from there. The opal buyer gave him the creeps. He'd appeared out of thin air, moved silently, and stared unblinkingly as they'd spoken...kind of like a predator locked onto its prey. A hawk circling a rat.

Drew was aggressive, foul, and quick-tempered. His attitude was a cause for concern, especially where Vera was concerned. He was an alpha male of the worst kind. A dog without a pack.

And Vera... *Vera Walsh*. His brow creased at the thought of her. He'd blown his shot big time, but his experience was telling him there was something she was holding back, something big.

That window was fixed in the space of a day...and it wasn't a small one, either. Solace was remote and glass like that was a special-order kind of thing. This morning, he was sure he'd seen—

*No way, purple electricity? C'mon, Clarke, you're cracking up, mate.*

It was obvious Solace and the people who lived there held secrets, but if it was linked to what'd happened here, there was no evidence. At least not any he'd found.

"Andy?" Landry prodded.

He sighed and shook his head, deciding to keep it to himself for now. At least until he could make sense of it all. "They're a unique lot, but that's part and parcel out this way. They were forthcoming enough and drew a hard line where Roth and his gang are concerned, but I haven't been winning myself any points."

"You push 'em too hard? Step where you weren't wanted?"

"Ah…" Clarke sighed, knowing he was going to cop a ribbing when he got back to the station in the Ridge. "The woman who owns the general store—"

"I knew it," Landry said with a grin. "You got yourself entangled with a bird. Rookie mistake, mate."

"Yeah, well, I didn't handle it so good. She caught on that I was fishing for information."

"Of course, you were. You turn up in uniform… what do they expect?"

"I took her on a date."

Landry snorted and began to laugh. "Oh, *mate*." He clapped Clarke on the shoulder. "There's a doghouse over there with your name on it." He pointed to a rusted cage in the middle of the camp. "Business and pleasure don't mix, especially in our line of work."

"Rack off, Landry. Forensics pull up anything useful yet?"

"Not a drop of blood, sweat, or shit," the detective told him. "Plenty of other illegal crap to charge 'em with, but their disappearance?" He blew a raspberry. "The dogs have had a field day, but all they sniffed out was drugs."

"Five kilos of ice isn't a bad haul," Clarke said. "At least that won't be getting out." Drugs and alcohol abuse were devastating to outback communities, so in his eyes, it was a win. A small one, but a win, nonetheless.

"I have a feeling this is going to end up a cold case," Landry said. "I like my cases hot and closed." He clapped his hands together.

"Not much we can do about that. Have you contacted the station owner yet?"

"Yeah, they had no idea there were squatters, but this far out, how would they?"

Walawala Station was over 150,000 hectares of sheep and cattle grazing land that straddled the New South Wales and Queensland borders. The dingo-proof fence cut through a swathe of it, so a vast amount of the station was unoccupied by livestock.

"Due diligence. I'd be checking with their employees. Someone has to have been getting a kickback." Clarke pushed off the side of the 4WD and walked towards the constables. "Get back to work, hey? You might sniff out a lead yet."

Surveying the assembled weapons lined up in the ute's tray, he asked, "What have you got?"

"Two handguns, three rifles, four snub-nosed shotguns," the male constable told him.

"Unregistered?"

"Yep," the woman replied.

"Patterson's bringing out some machetes and a box of hunting knives," the man added.

Clarke looked around the camp and grimaced. His confusion was only deepening the more they combed through the property. There was a treasure trove of convictable evidence just laying about, but no clues as to why Craig Roth and the Dust Dogs had up and left.

"Any theories?" he asked the constables.

"None that make any sense," the woman replied.

"Could be alien abduction... if you believe in that sort of thing," the male constable said with a snort. "But try to prove that in a court."

"Supernatural..." Clarke murmured, his thoughts turning to Vera. "Bloody feels like it."

# CHAPTER 18

Rosheen ran her fingers over Vera's altar and smirked.

It sat in the second bedroom of the witch's underground hovel and took up all the available space. Shelves lined the far wall, all covered in various bits of crystal, dried herbs, flowers, eucalyptus leaves, rocks, and sticks. Below was a mishmash of crates and boxes draped with purple and blue material. Candles, crystals, and incense had been arranged in a specific pattern, and in the centre was a large silver bowl. A mirror with a gold gilded frame leaned against the wall, reflecting the sun and moon tapestry hanging opposite.

Rosheen looked down at the worn Turkish rug and the padded pillows on the floor and curled her nose. Vera's altar reminded her of a hippie commune and not at all fitting for Irish witch royalty.

Changing the orientation of the crystals on the

altar, she felt the energy shift, but it wasn't enough. When she'd decided to find Vera, she knew she'd be in this for the long haul but had no idea it would be spent in the middle of nowhere.

Red dust got into everything—it stained her clothes, turning her favourite cream linen dress a putrid shade of rusty brown—and the *flies*. There were thousands of the disgusting insects. If it wasn't for her magic, she would've eaten half of them...that's if they didn't crawl up her nose. *Ugh.*

And the *heat*. It was blistering, sweaty, and unbearable. Solace was an awful place. It stunk like something had crawled into the sun and died.

This was taking too damn long.

Vera had to cross over before Rosheen could convince her to leave Solace. How aware the witch was of her Nightshade legacy's attempt to take over wasn't clear, but her subconscious was fighting back, and it was becoming an issue.

If Rosheen had the full strength of the Ascendants behind her, then the deed would've already been done, but she was on this mission solo. She could do it, but it was going to take more time than she'd originally planned. The Exiles were a rather frustrating complication.

The human was easy...he was too old and slow to pose any real threat. The werewolf was only powerful when the moon was full, otherwise he was all bark and no bite. Her magic worked seamlessly on their perception.

The elemental Kyne was a little more complicated. His love for Eloise had needed some brute force to break through, but dazzling the vampire Hardy was easy as pie.

Drew on the other hand... He was impossible. No matter how hard she tried, his head was too thick to crack—whether it was stupidity or his shifter magic, she wasn't sure—and Eloise's affinity for spirit magic had made her sharp as a tack. Not even an army of shadow spirits could get rid of those two.

Then there was the fae. The *monstrosity*. He didn't belong in this world. They should never have come here.

The aura she'd felt around the boab had to lead to a place of power, otherwise the fae wouldn't be here. He couldn't survive so far away from the portals without access to magic—and he certainly wasn't feeding off Vera.

There was no other explanation. The boab tree was hiding some kind of magical artefact, which meant she was about to get a two-for-one.

Rosheen stared at her reflection in the mirror and raised her hand. The candles ignited, spreading a warm glow over the altar. Beautiful, powerful, cunning. She was a true witch of the *Gealach Fola*. The blood moon would rise over this awful hole and all would be revealed.

The time for reckoning was approaching and if she didn't return soon... She turned another crystal, her smile spreading. It was past time to give Vera a little shove.

"Come, sister," Rosheen said, calling on her magic, "it's time to come home."

Her smile widened as the candles flared, the long, thin flames reaching towards the ceiling.

She never was patient.

***

Vera stormed out of the *Outpost*, her anger reaching boiling point. Her magic crackled and she shook out her hands as purple sparks raced across her skin.

She'd argued with Drew so many times, it was becoming a bad habit, but this time... Accusing Rosheen of summoning those kadaitcha? She had the power, but she wouldn't do that. She *wouldn't*.

She looked across the road at Hardy's shop. The wind picked up, blowing hot air around her is swirling gusts that buffeted her hair. Pulling a curled strand away from her face, her expression fell.

Hardy had been a little vague lately, and Kyne and the others had been rather lax in their duties around the seal. They were complacent when they should've been alert, but it could be because she'd vouched for Rosheen...but the *Gealach Fola* were known of their illusion magic. The power drawn from the blood moon cast all in deathly shadow.

Vera had vouched for her. She swallowed hard as her temples throbbed with the onset of another headache.

*No shadow is more deadly than the Nightshade*, the voice whispered, the sound so faint, Vera wondered if it was just a trick of the wind.

Something wasn't right.

Vera walked around the back of the *Outpost* and opened the door to her apartment.

She froze as she looked down the stairs into the maw of a rose-coloured shadow, the scent of Rosheen's magic tainting her home in a wash of coppery blood. Whatever was about to happen wasn't going to end well.

Vera glanced over her shoulder, wondering if she should warn the Exiles, but in her heart, she knew they wouldn't be able to help her, not with this. This was witch business.

Taking a deep breath, she stepped into the haze, her movements sluggish in the thick air.

She found Rosheen kneeling before her altar in the spare bedroom. The candles were lit, the long, thready flames almost reaching the stone roof above, and most of the crystals were realigned, their energy skewed towards something dark and bordering on dangerous.

"Rosheen."

"There you are," she murmured. She rose, the energy pulling at the shadows cast by the candlelight.

"What are you doing?" Vera asked. "Have you been messing with my altar?"

"Only a little." Rosheen smirked, her eyes darkening.

Vera swallowed hard, her magic warning her that danger was close. Was Drew right? Rosheen was her sister. Her *sister*.

"I think it's time you tell me what you're really doing here, Rosh," she murmured.

"Took you long enough," the witch drawled, flicking her hair over her shoulder. She looked bored, but Vera knew better than to underestimate the *Gealach Fola*. "You were always a pushover, Vera."

She narrowed her eyes and stepped into the room. "It's been a long time. I'm not the same witch I was when I left Ireland."

"No, you're even more pathetic." Rosheen looked her over with open dislike, her lip curling savagely. "You don't even see it."

"See what?"

"You hear them, don't you?"

"Who?"

"The Nightshade ancestors...they speak to you." As Vera shook her head, Rosheen snorted. "Don't deny it. I've seen it written all over your face. They spoke to you even before I arrived."

She was right. Vera had triggered something

during her remembrance ritual in the outback. Ever since, she'd had headaches, memory loss, and her magic had been on the fritz. Now she was wondering how much of it was because of Rosheen's exploitation.

"What are you doing here?" Vera asked. "And drop the lies. I won't tolerate it."

"Well, as long as we're being frank with one another, maybe it's time you tell *me* the truth."

"What truth?" There was plenty Vera had lied about, and she could justify it as much as she wanted, but she'd deliberately kept things from Rosheen. The seal, being the current number one on the list. With how the witch was behaving right now, Vera was glad she'd kept that tidbit to herself.

"Why you left, of course. All I ever did was love you like a sister."

"I told you—"

"You told me what you thought I wanted to hear," Rosheen snarled. "*Whatever*. It won't matter, not after today."

Vera hesitated, her magic flaring in warning. "What do you mean?"

"The old ways are dead and gone," Rosheen said. "The Brinewolds are gone, save for you. I can count the remaining Crescents on one hand, the Nightshades had their magic stripped, and the other covens are shadows of their former glory. They have no power, not anymore. They only live to grovel like animals at the feet of the fae queen and her blasphemous court.

The Ascendants will rise and lead the witches of Ireland into the new world."

"Ascendants?" Vera asked. She'd heard that name before, and it struck nothing but dread into her heart. "Rosheen, *no*... You joined a cult?"

"The old ways almost led us to extinction. The fae—"

"Now I see," Vera interrupted. "This is about power and revenge. War with the fae, but not before a civil war between our own kind." They'd been looking for her for a very specific reason—her Nightshade blood was prone to dark magic. Paired with the Brinewold, Vera could summon the power they needed to take their plans to the next step, but they had nothing without her. "The Ascendants fight in the shadows like cowards for all the wrong reasons. They're terrorists! I'll have no part of it!"

Rosheen swirled her arms in the air and her magic rushed forwards. It collided with Vera and she flew back, the force of the blow pushing the air from her lungs. She hit the bedroom wall, her head cracking against the stone, and she gasped for air.

"What are you doing?" Vera rasped. She went to lift her hand to retaliate, but her heart twisted with dread as she realised she was stuck, pinned against the wall.

Now Vera realised why Rosheen had realigned the crystals. It was a trap.

"Like I said," Rosheen drawled, "you were always a pushover."

Shadows peeled away from the wall and crawled towards Vera. They curled up her legs and around her arms, slithering like cold snakes, forcing her back against the rock. Vera thrashed, but she was stuck like a fly in a web—and struggling only made it worse.

Rosheen stood before her, her expression menacing in the candlelight.

"No!" The shadows clawed at Vera's mind, tearing at her magic. "Rosheen, don't! You're better than this. You're—"

"You'll see," the witch snarled, lifting her hand into the air. "This is right. This is *just*...and you will help me." She closed her fingers into a tight fist, her magic closing around Vera. "We'll start with the magical artefact you're hiding in this putrid cesspool of a town."

"Rosheen, *no*. You don't—" Vera choked, her eyes widening as the shadows swarmed inside her mind, calling forth the Nightshade.

She had to stop her from finding the seal! Her power was dangerous enough in the wrong hands, but if the Ascendants opened up that rock and let out whatever was locked away down there, they were all doomed.

"Stop fighting, Vera," Rosheen said. "It's inevitable. I saw to that."

"You've—"

"Been poisoning you with your own herbs?" Her grin twisted. "Yes, yes I have."

*Oh, Drew, I'm sorry*, Vera thought. *You were right and now—*

"You'll never win," she rasped. "The Exiles—"

"Were easier to crack than an egg," Rosheen interrupted. "It's already over for them, but it's only just beginning for you and me. Come forth, sister. It's time to claim what is ours."

Blood magic swirled, digging into Vera's mind like red-hot barbs. She thought she screamed, but her mouth opened silently, then...

Vera blinked. A deadly calmness soothed her heart as the world took on a steely grey hue.

"Now I see," the voice said through her. "And now I speak."

Rosheen smirked, her smile signalling her work was done. "Now, dear sister...tell me *everything*."

## CHAPTER 19

Finn looked up at the Milky Way, watching a satellite float serenely across the sky.

The stars appeared much the same as they did on Earth, though without the artificial machines rotating the planet.

The fae world was a parallel universe, one that had evolved differently—though what event had occurred to separate the two was a mystery not made for mortal beings. There was magic here, but it was rare and bizarre. His homeland was seeped in it. The air felt soupy with the promise of magic and it filled his lungs every time he'd breathed in.

At least that's how he remembered it. A thousand years was a long time to be away.

He lounged in the curve of a fallen gumtree, the twisted wood propping up his back. Feeling the slither of scales underneath his shirt, he lifted his collar so the death adder could work its way out into the air. The snake draped itself around his neck, its tongue flicking as it scented the air.

Finn's magical talent was best spent beast-charming. Sometimes he preferred the company of animals, despite his ability to force his friendship on them. People were hard work. No matter how wonderful things like love and friendship could be, in the end, they lied, cheated, hurt, and destroyed. Staying away from Solace and the world at large was a simple act of cutting out the middleman.

Though he was softening towards the Exiles after the arrival of a certain desert pea—Eloise Hart and her oblivious superpowers. She'd sent those mangey Dust Dogs across the void with a flick of her wrists. Maybe she could do the same with that witch Rosheen.

Finn snorted and wondered how much longer he'd have to keep away from Solace. He was missing his favourite dish. Blue had a rather tasty knack for cooking deep fried potato.

Sensing someone was lurking in the dark, he turned, doing a double take when he saw Vera standing in the moonlight a few paces away.

They looked at one another for a long moment, but she was silent and unmoving.

"Vera?" He stood and took a step towards her. "What are you doing out here? Aren't you supposed to be babysitting that witch?"

She didn't reply. Instead, she raised her hand and clenched her fist. The moment her fingers came together, the snake jerked, its neck snapping. It slithered off Finn's shoulders and tumbled to the ground, dead.

He stared in shock at the corpse of the adder, his chest heaving. *"What did you do that for?"*

"It's past time we settled our differences," she said, her voice sounding strange and vacant. "Don't you think?"

He swallowed. The air tasted foul, like rust and sickly-sweet rot. Darkness, that's what it was. Deadly nightshade. Her magic was tainted, and he was her first target. Honestly, he wasn't in the least bit surprised.

"You really think you can go up against an Unseelie and win?" he asked. "I will fight if I have to. You know what we're up against."

"Oh, I know." Vera's lips thinned. "But you're forgetting one thing, Finn..."

"Yeah, and what's that?"

"I'm with the Nightshade now." She raised her arms and a wild wind rose, whirling around him. The threads were entwined with purple sparks, Vera's magic twisting in the tornado that drew ever closer, suffocating him.

Every breath drew dust and magic into Finn's lungs, choking and numbing his limbs. He stumbled and gasped for air, his knees crumpling beneath him. Before he understood what was happening, he was lying flat on his back.

He stared up at the sky, unable to move. Except his eyes, which he darted around wildly, trying to see what was going on.

"Vera?" His tongue felt thick and he slurred his words. "*Addrei. Addrei, ak'ande lir...*"

"Quiet," a voice hissed. "Enough with that foul language."

A shadow fell over his prone body and an ugly face blotted out the stars. Rosheen smirked down at him, her lips curving upwards.

"Oh, it's *you*," Finn rasped. "Colour me *not* surprised."

His gaze moved to Vera, who stood behind the auburn-haired witch, her eyes black and emotionless as she stared down at him.

"What has she done to you?" he choked out.

Vera said nothing, she simply continued to stare. Rosheen had done something to her, that he was sure of.

Finn knew they had their differences, but Vera would never do anything to harm him or the other fae. She'd never use her magic like this. *Ever.* In all the years he'd known her, Vera Walsh had shied away from using her magic, only doing the smallest of spells and saving the good stuff for her yearly ritual.

"Where are the other fae?" Rosheen demanded.

His heart clenched. "I don't know what you're talking about."

"Don't play games with me," the witch snarled, tightening her magic around his throat.

Finn gasped, his neck elongating as if held by invisible hands. "My stellar personality is incompatible with other people," he rasped. "I can't handle not being the centre of attention. Other fae would ruin my ability to shine."

"You can drop the act," she told him. "Unluckily for you, Vera told me everything."

"You corrupted her," he fired back. "It's plain as day."

"I only brought forth what was already there. Vera was already corrupted, *fae*. Her legacy is darkness, just as yours is parasitic. You drain the magic from our world and our people. You don't belong here and if you can't go back, then there's only one thing you're good for."

Her magic pulsed again, but this time, Finn felt his power fade and he let out a moan of agony. She was channeling his magic, drawing it from him and into her.

"Now you know how it feels to have your magic stripped away," Rosheen snarled. "How it felt when the craglorn sucked the magic out of Vera's coven. And when the last drop leaves your body, you will know what it feels like to die a *true death*."

"You'll never find them without me," Finn snarled. "I made sure of it." He felt the drain on his magic stop.

"A fae's magic isn't bound to their life. If you weren't so blinded by your racism, you'd know that, witch."

"He's right," Vera said, her voice chillingly vague. "When a fae casts a spell, it's forever."

"And when a witch casts, their spells are bound to their life," Finn drawled. "Guess what I'm going to do once I'm free?"

Rosheen tightened her grip on her magic and he felt his flesh warp.

"We can use him," Vera said. "We'll need as much magic as we can gather for the next stage."

Rosheen stood, her eyes narrowing. "What do you suggest, sister?"

Finn gasped as his body drew on the power of the seal, renewing his magic.

Vera smiled, though her eyes remained dark. She didn't need to say it. They all knew.

He'd just become a glorified battery.

---

Vera knelt in front of her altar, staring at her reflection in the mirror. Candles burned on either side of the antique, the glass surface marred with black splotches where moisture had gotten into the backing.

Her eyes glowed with a new understanding, the spirit within her channelling more power than she'd ever felt before. She knew she made her own choices, but the Nightshade guided her hand. It whispered to her when she called, it told her what to do.

It was more than magic. Her father had warned her long ago not to trust it, but he was dead and gone.

"There you are," Rosheen said as she stepped into the room. "We've got some unfinished business, sister."

Vera curled her lip. She should feel grateful her sister had called forth her legacy, but the witch was just as arrogantly annoying as she'd been when they were teenagers. Only one of them had grown up, and it wasn't Rosheen.

"If we want the seal, then all we have to do is grab Kyne," Vera said as she rose. "He's the one who hid the key and the only one who can retrieve it."

"I know you're itching to use your magic, but we have to plan this carefully," Rosheen said. "The last thing we need is the entire town going up against us. The best laid plans are the ones done in secret...and by the time we're ready, they won't see what's coming."

Vera sighed and flexed her fingers. She could feel her Nightshade legacy building inside of her, and with the addition of Finn as a conduit to the seal, it felt as if she could take on the entire world. Screw the Ascendants and screw the *Gealach Fola*.

"Act natural," Rosheen told her, smoothing her hands through Vera's curls. "We don't want those pesky Exiles working out that something's up with their favourite neighbourhood witch."

"It doesn't matter," Vera said. "Thanks to Finn, they won't be able to stop us."

"It's not about power," the witch explained. "We still have the police to contend with. We can't launch a hostile takeover while a whole forensics unit is digging through dingo droppings twenty minutes north." She sighed and rolled her eyes. "I hate to say it, but we're on the same page where those shifters are concerned. The enemy of our enemy is *not* our friend."

"Don't worry about Sergeant Clarke," Vera said with a smirk. "I've got him wrapped around my little finger."

"Well, we do have to worry about Eloise and Drew. My magic didn't work on him, and I'm not into women. The rest of them were so easy, it was like dangling forbidden fruit in front of a group of horny teenage boys."

Vera snorted, not wanting to know about Rosheen's sexual conquests—the list was likely long and dirty. "Eloise Hart is a wallflower of the worst kind," she said, instead. "She doesn't know how to relate to people, let alone have a romantic relationship. The moment Kyne looked at you, her insecurities took over. One little push in the right direction and she won't be a problem."

Rosheen's eyes shone. "Well, well, well... I know what I'll be doing today." She smoothed her hands over her dress and licked her lips. "A two-for-one deal."

"Leave Drew to me." She looked towards the front

door. "I'll open the *Outpost* as normal and he'll come running to apologise for yesterday. When he does, I'll take care of him."

"And what about that other man? The one with the kangaroo as a pet?"

"Coen?" Vera raised her eyebrows. "He only comes when he wants something. By the time he realises what we're up to, it'll be too late. I wouldn't worry about him. Coen is a dreamer."

"You know them best, sister." She fluffed up her hair and trussed up her boobs. "Now, how do I look? Kyne is smoking hot, and I want to please him just as much as I want him to please me."

Vera snorted. "You were always prettier than me."

"Aw, thanks." Rosheen grinned, the veiled insult going straight over her head. "Today is going to be a great day. I can feel it."

Vera lifted her hands and straightened her rings, her gaze tracing the sharp black tattooed lines across her fingers. Talismans, focal points, runes, and sigils, all designed to help her bind her power. Fat lot of good they did.

"We'll have everything we need by tonight," she murmured as her magic simmered. "And no one will be able to stop us." Stepping around Rosheen, Vera walked towards the door. "Good luck, sister. I'll meet you at the seal at sunset."

Vera unlocked the door of the *Outpost*, wondering what had ever crossed her mind when she'd decided sinking her life savings into a hole like this was a good idea. There was nothing and no one around to make Solace interesting. The seal was a means to an end. Who cared what lay underneath it?

She turned on the lights and curled her nose as she looked over the aisles of junk. Picking up a Cherry Ripe chocolate bar from the rack beside the till, she tore it open and bit off the end.

Vera knew it was important to maintain her façade, but it was infuriating. There was all this magic running through her veins, and she couldn't use any of it. Not yet.

The door opened behind her, the bell ringing annoyingly.

"Vera?"

She paused. She'd been expecting Drew to come running, but it was Sergeant Clarke who'd returned first.

Vera turned, chewing on the mouthful of chocolate. Not who she was expecting, but maybe it was an omen—the universe's way of granting her a chance for revenge.

He glanced at the Cherry Ripe in her hand. "Breakfast?"

She shrugged. "I needed a pick-me-up."

"Listen, Vera—"

"How did your snooping go?" She tilted her head to the side. "Find any dirt on the Dogs?"

"Uh..." Clarke scratched his head. "The investigation is ongoing."

Looking him over, Vera couldn't underestimate his value. If he knew something, there was only one way of getting it out of him. She tossed the last of the Cherry Ripe into the bin and reached out.

Clarke's brow furrowed in confusion as her hand closed around his wrist, but she didn't care. The vision slammed into her, bright and clear, fuelled by the magic channeling from the seal.

It was worse than she'd expected. Clarke was no longer interested in the Dust Dogs, but in Solace. In *her*.

He'd been snooping, and not just a little bit. He'd done a full background check, which included pulling old newspaper clippings about the mass murder of her coven.

*Solace wasn't what it seemed. There was eccentric, then there was Solace. Drew was suspicious. Hardy was old-fashioned. The mechanic was cagey. The miner was hiding something, and it wasn't black opal.*

Vera let Clarke go and curled her lip. Rosheen was right about the police and their snooping. They were a problem, but luckily for her, Sergeant Clarke had genuine romantic feelings she could exploit for a little added fun. Served him right, after all.

"Vera?"

"I know the thoughts running through your head," she told him, her voice bland. "Could they be real? That's what you're wondering, *Andy*. When you looked up the news reports, it only led to more outrageous speculation. Were they devil worshippers? Witches? Was it a magic spell that turned them into withered corpses? What kind of murderer had the power to suck the life out of a dozen people in the span of five minutes? It had to be supernatural, right? No one could mummify that many people on their own, and in broad daylight no less."

Clarke blinked in surprise. "Vera, I don't—"

"Oh please, you're a cop, Andy. You're supposed to be smart." She leaned closer. "*Figure it out.*"

He sucked in a sharp breath. "You're... You're a witch."

Her lips curved into a sly grin. "There you go. Wasn't so hard, was it?"

"I-I don't understand."

"They never do," she said through an exasperated sigh.

His brow creased. "Vera, what happened to you?"

"You were right about us, Sergeant Clarke," she told him. "The Dust Dogs didn't just ride off into the sunset. Eloise Hart made them disappear with her elemental magic, but not before Dingo Drew shot Roth in the head with a shotgun." She clapped her hands together, making Clarke jump in surprise. "There wasn't much left after he was done with him, but the guy deserved it. Craig Roth was a blight. *A disease.* He got what he deserved."

"Why are you telling me this?"

Vera reached towards him, her smile widening. "The truth will set you free, Sergeant Clarke...or in this case, make you disappear."

A violent gust of air whooshed around them and in a blink of an eye, they stood in murky, underground darkness. The only light came from the cracks in the metal sheeting that covered the top of the shaft, and the air was cool and dry—a steady twenty-four degrees Celsius.

Clarke looked around, unmasked panic in his eyes. "Where are we?"

"In an *abandoned* mine outside of Solace," Vera replied, air quoting the word 'abandoned'. "Charming, isn't it?" She wrinkled her nose. "Smells a little like wet dog, though."

He backed against the wall, his eyes darting this way and that. "Wet dog?"

"Careful," she told him. "There's a full moon coming up and Wally O'Brien is a werewolf."

"He's a *what?*"

"It's important to remember that werewolves are carnivores...and they don't discriminate."

Clarke lunged forwards, finally understanding the danger he was in. Unfortunately, he slammed into an invisible wall. He blinked in surprise, and then tried again.

Vera laughed, enjoying his wide-eyed confusion. "Try all you like, but you'll never get out...and no one will hear you scream."

"Why are you doing this?" he demanded.

"Because I can," she said simply, the Nightshade guiding her hand. "You're stuck here until dinnertime, sergeant. *Bon appétit.*"

Then she disappeared in search of her next target.

## CHAPTER 20

Kyne knocked on the door of Eloise's motorhome, trying to think of the perfect thing to say to her. It wasn't like he'd spent the last two days mulling over it, but women were never his strong point. Give him a slab of rock and he could sing it to sleep. People, on the other hand, were unpredictable.

He needed to stop psyching himself out. This was Eloise. A couple of weeks with her had shown him what a happily ever after looked like for an elemental outcast. Talking to her was supposed to be the easiest thing in the world, right?

"Eloise?" he called. "Are you there?"

A rustling sound came from inside, footsteps, then the side door whizzed open.

Eloise stood inside, her eyes sleepy and blonde hair messed-up. She was wearing her unicorn pyjamas—the ones she only wore when he wasn't around.

"*Kyne*, it's ten to six," she complained, smoothing

her palms self-consciously over her purple unicorn-covered T-shirt. "What kind of time do you call this?"

He offered her a sheepish smile. "Grovelling time?"

"Took you long enough," she muttered, her shoulders sinking.

"I thought I'd give you some distance," he said. "You were angry, and I was clueless… Didn't seem like a good mix."

She looked him over, then she twirled her finger in the air. "Turn around, I'm going to get dressed."

"Are you sure?"

Her eyebrows rose. "Don't push your luck."

Grimacing, he turned to face the bush while Eloise changed out of her pyjamas.

"I'm sorry I was dismissive," he said, angling his head to the side so his voice wasn't muffled. "I've had time to think and I should've been more concerned about the kadaitcha."

"*You think?*"

"I know, I know," he went on. "I'm glad Drew was there to help you."

A cabinet door slammed from inside the van. "And the other thing?"

"I, uh…"

"*Kyne.*"

He turned to see her stick her head out of the door, the force of her scowl burning right through him. In place of the purple unicorns, she was wearing a pair of tight leggings, a long singlet, and a red-checkered shirt.

"You need to think logically, with your *head*...not with Little Kyne," she went on.

Kyne glanced down and recoiled as he felt her palm slap him on the ear. "Ow!"

"*Pig*."

"*Fine*, I have doubts," he declared, throwing his hands into the air. "Rosheen is an outsider, but we'd already set other things in motion. Clarke came because of our fight with the Dust Dogs, and Vera's been unsettled since the anniversary of her family's death. Rosheen appearing has just added a little more fuel to a fire that'd already been burning long before she got here."

"A little?" Eloise scoffed.

Kyne shrugged, still not seeing what the big deal was. It wasn't like Rosheen knew about the seal—what would she need it for anyway? "If you and Drew are so concerned about it, then we'll have a town meeting."

Eloise paused for a moment, thinking over his proposal, then nodded. "Finally, some sanity. You want some tea?" She began fussing in the kitchen cabinet and took out a blue collapsible kettle—the little twelve volt kind that ran off the batteries in her van.

"Yeah, uh..." Kyne trailed off, his gaze moving to the gumtrees. Suddenly, the outback didn't feel so lonely. "Actually, how about we head down to Blue's for breakfast?"

Eloise put the kettle down. "Will he be up at this hour?"

"Sure, I'll give him a ring to let him know we're coming." He looked towards the trees again. Something was lurking, but he didn't want to spook Eloise, especially not after her ordeal with the kadaitcha. "I've got to sort some stuff out up at Drew's dugout, so I'll meet you there?"

Her eyes narrowed. "What kind of stuff?"

"The kind of sticky stuff that needs all day to set," he lied. "Oh, can you get the others to meet us? I'll text Hardy, but can you ask Drew and Wally?"

"What about Vera?"

Kyne hesitated for a moment. If Eloise was right about Rosheen, then alerting Vera would tip the witch off. "We rarely see Vera this side of nine a.m. I reckon we don't mess with a witch's body clock unless we want to get zapped."

"Right..." Eloise shook her head, and he gathered she was on a similar wavelength.

"I won't be long." He tipped his hat and took the trail towards the ridge.

As he walked up the rise, the sensation he'd felt back at the van only rose. He crossed the road and approached Drew's dugout, listening.

The yard out the front was a mess—planks of wood were stacked to one side, sawdust had gathered underneath their makeshift workbench, and a pile of rubbish had been stacked to one side, ready to be burned. Drew was nowhere in sight, but he wouldn't be here this early.

Kyne stood in the clearing and waited. His elemental powers stirred, calling the breeze and the sounds it carried towards him.

Footsteps crunching on rock approached, and he turned as Rosheen stepped through the break in the trees.

"You're out early," he said.

"I like to see the sun rise," she told him. "They're so pretty out here. The colours are richer than in Ireland."

"I thought you found Solace boring." He twitched, an annoying itch tingling the base of his skull.

"Let's be real, there isn't much to pass the time, not like the city."

Kyne shrugged. He was already forgetting what Eloise had told him about Rosheen. Why she didn't like the witch was beyond him. Maybe she was jealous.

"What do people do in the city anyway?" he asked. "Can't see the fascination."

"There's plenty... Maybe we can go to Sydney together."

"I can't see the attraction for an earth elemental. The place is all concrete and asphalt. I'd rather dig opal."

Rosheen's eyes lit up. "An elemental who mines opal? *Fascinating*. Women love pretty rocks."

Kyne shook his head. There was an annoying buzz in his ears he couldn't seem to shake. He'd given Eloise an opal. He blinked, remembering he was supposed to meet her at Blue's for breakfast.

The buzzing seemed to fade, and he looked up at Rosheen.

"Is there something I can help you with?" he asked.

She raked her gaze over him, her smile widening. "Oh, I'm sure there are plenty of things you could *help* me with."

Kyne blinked again, his concentration slipping. She *did* look pretty in that dress...

"C'mon," she purred, undoing the top button. "Come a little closer."

He took a step, closing the gap.

Rosheen knocked his hat off his head and it fell to the ground with a dull thud. He went to pick it up, but she grasped his face and went to kiss him.

Kyne tore out of her grasp. "Bloody hell," he cursed. "Rosheen, I'm with Eloise."

"So?" She pouted and went to place her palms on his chest, but he grabbed her wrists and pulled her away.

"So, I don't cheat."

"An elemental with no control over her powers, who erases memories and alters emotions... I bet she hasn't put out yet."

His scowl deepened. "What the f—"

"Men have needs, Kyne," Rosheen purred. "And I'm more than happy to help you satisfy them."

"*Everyone* has needs, and mine are satisfied plenty," he drawled. "You need to back off, Rosheen. I won't ask again."

She rolled her eyes, her expression turning sour. "I'm getting tired of you people. Do I have to use brute force on everyone around here?"

Kyne jerked back as he saw blood-red magic coil in her hands, but before he could make a move, a kangaroo burst out of the tree line and leapt between them.

Rosheen lost her grip on her magic and let out a cry as she stumbled backwards.

"*Ha!*" Coen shouted, jumping out of the scrub and waving his arms at the witch like he was trying to herd a wild buffalo. "*Ha!*"

If he wasn't in such dire straits, Kyne would've laughed at the absurdness of the entire situation, but he was too stunned to move.

Rosheen, on the other hand, wasn't so shocked. She took one look at Coen waving his arms in the air, turned towards the outback, and didn't just run, she *sprinted*. She darted between clumps of spinifex and ducked under low-hanging branches, taking a straight line into the sunburnt country.

Whatever she saw to make her turn tail so fast, Kyne had no idea. But right now, it didn't seem to matter. He blinked, breaking free of his stupor, and went to pursue her, but Coen grabbed his arm.

"Stop," the Indigenous man said with a shake of his head. "Not safe."

Kyne let out a groan and fisted his hands into his hair. "Eloise was right. How was I so blind?"

"Magic," Coen stated. "She tricked you."

"Can you see it? Is it still around me?"

"Yes." The Indigenous man nodded. "It already fades. *Marlu* stopped her before she could make more."

Kyne snorted and ran his hand over his face. Damn that witch. Odds were, Rosheen already knew about the seal. Why else would she try to seduce him? He was the one who knew where the key was and if she knew that, then Vera... *Shit*. It was a good thing the Exiles were gathering at Blue's right now.

Kyne sighed and turned back to Coen. "How did you know I was here?"

"Eloise asked me to watch," he said with a grin. "She worries about Rosheen. Finn, too."

"Finn's got his fingers in this? That explains a lot," Kyne said, glancing towards the scrub where Rosheen had fled.

"I understand now," Coen went on. "The emu rests at the billabong...but watches at the same time."

"Fair enough." Kyne blinked and retrieved his hat. "I reckon you need to keep an eye on the seal for now. I've got a bad feeling something's wrong with Vera. I've got to go talk to the other Exiles...unless you want to come with me?"

Coen shook his head. "No. I want to watch. The Dreaming ebbs, warns."

He didn't like the sound of that. "Let me, Eloise, or Drew know if you need help. Until we can make sure

Rosheen's magic isn't influencing the others, we can't take any chances."

Coen nodded and looked to the kangaroo. "See, *Marlu*? I told you."

Kyne frowned, but he was long past trying to decipher Coen's ramblings. He looked towards Solace, his thoughts already trying to formulate a plan. "I'll see you later, then?"

When he got no reply, he looked back, but Coen and the kangaroo had vanished into thin air.

---

Coen lingered in the abandoned mine underneath Solace, humming softly to himself as he lounged on a rock in the far corner—the farthest point away from the anomalous bluestone rock.

The cave that held the seal carried its own strange light, casting the otherwise dark space in a warm glow. Coen didn't like to spend much time down here, being so far away from the sky and the *marlu*.

He felt the roots of the great boab tree coil through the earth, reaching towards the strange rock that held the sleeping power at bay. What it was, Coen didn't know. It was beyond anything he understood, and he knew a lot of things. The stars and the spaces between told him stories as the Dreaming carried him to and fro, but none knew of the mystery under the bluestone.

Andante knew things, but she was lost in her own

time—a traveller between worlds. She would rather stay in her cave and be forgotten while Coen preferred to travel as far as he could.

He looked up as he heard someone approach, the sound of footsteps carrying a warning. He raised his head as the figure appeared.

Vera.

Coen felt the shadow inside her—all purple and swirling—and he squinted to sharpen his sight. It was magic, but it *lived*. Witches were strange creatures to him, but this was stranger still.

She stood before the seal, standing as still as a statue as she stared at it. The shadow pulsed, its magic twisting tighter and tighter. It controlled her, Coen realised. It was Vera...but it wasn't.

He waited to see what she would do, wondering why the shadow had led her here. The seal's true purpose was out of reach without the key to unlock it.

After a long moment of staring, Vera bent over and reached out her hand. Shadow and water didn't mix.

"You shouldn't touch it," Coen said, startling the witch.

Vera spun and laid a hand over her heart. "Coen," she said. "I didn't see you there."

She wouldn't, but that didn't matter. He promised Eloise and Kyne he'd watch the seal, but he'd expected Rosheen...but maybe he was already looking at her.

"What are you doing?" he asked, standing.

"I, uh..." Her eyes narrowed. She was trying to think of a good reason, but Coen knew she had none.

"This place isn't for you," he told her. "The shadow won't mix."

She tilted her head to the side. "Shadow?"

"You know what I talk about. Your false mob has cursed you."

Her expression twisted. "False mob?"

"This place isn't for you," Coen told her.

"And who died and made you lord and protector of it?"

"Spirit is sacred." He angered, and it was an unpleasant feeling. Coen was never angry.

"Oh, who cares," Vera drawled. "Everyone wants power, Coen. Even you." She called on her magic, filling the cave with overwhelming purple shadow.

It rushed towards Coen, but he was ready—he'd already seen the spirit rise within her before she'd raised her hands.

He leapt onto the currents of the Dreaming and soared through the spaces between the stars, then landed behind her. With a great cry, he landed a blow on the back of her head, striking the shadow where it held her the tightest.

Vera gasped, then fell to the cave floor like water.

Coen knelt and pressed his palm against her forehead. The shadow was silent.

"You're wrong," he murmured. "Power isn't peace."

*If not power, then what do you want?* the shadow asked.

Coen didn't reply. Scooping Vera into his arms, he lifted her up and into the Dreaming, travelling the currents to the surface.

## CHAPTER 21

Eloise's anxiety spiked as she pushed open the door to Blue's pub.

Her confidence was growing since she'd arrived in Solace, but the current turn of events wasn't helping much.

Wally and Drew were sitting at the bar, and beyond, she could hear Blue fussing in the kitchen. The shifter was scowling, making it clear they'd been arguing.

"Eloise," Wally said as she let the door swing closed behind her. "You're out and about early."

Her lips thinned and she shook her head. *Dammit Kyne.* "He didn't call you, did he?"

"Who?" Blue asked, sticking his head through the open kitchen door.

"Kyne."

"Was he supposed to?" the publican asked. "Ah, never mind. I'll fire up the cooker."

Drew turned around on his stool, his forehead creasing. "Everything okay?"

Eloise sighed. "Kyne agreed to a town meeting, but now I'm beginning to worry he was accosted along the way."

"A town meeting, eh?" Wally said, scratching his head. "Whatever for?"

"You're seriously out of the loop, old dog," Drew told him. "Or seduced up to your eyeballs with Rosheen's witchy juju. I've been trying to tell you all morning that Vera's sick and Rosheen—"

"You're jumping to conclusions," Wally snapped. "That sweet witch wouldn't harm a fly."

"You're whacked, old dog," the shifter retorted. "High on blood moon pheromones. No wonder she got you so easy."

The mechanic's face reddened. "You should show more respect for your elders, you flaming galah!"

"Stop it!" Eloise exclaimed. "Fighting won't solve anything, not while there's magic involved. We can discuss this together. Anyone got Hardy's number?"

"I've got it," Drew said, leaping off his stool. "About time we sorted this mess out." He fired a foul look at Wally as he picked up the receiver from the landline phone on the wall.

Eloise sat at the closest table as the shifter went behind the bar and called the vampire.

"Has anyone seen Finn?" Blue asked. "It's been few

days since he's been in for his usual bowl of chips. It ain't like him."

"I saw him like the day before yesterday," Eloise replied. "He's keeping a low profile while Rosheen is hanging around." Good thing, too.

"Hardy's on his way," Drew said, sitting back down. "Should I go check on Kyne? I'm assuming we're keeping Vera out of this for the time being?"

Eloise opened her mouth to reply, but the pub door opened and Hardy appeared, making her almost jump out of her skin. She didn't think she'd ever get used to his super speed, but his lightning-fast response time was rather convenient.

"What's going on?" the vampire asked. "A town meeting this early in the day? Where's Kyne?"

Eloise glanced at the door. "On his way, I hope."

Hardy raised his eyebrows and took the seat next to hers. "You hope?"

"I forget why we're arguing," Blue said, leaning on the bar.

"This is about Rosheen," Eloise told them. "About her lurking, summoning kadaitcha, and putting all of you under a spell."

"A spell?" Hardy snorted. "I'd know if she was messing with me."

"Just because you're a million years old, doesn't mean you know everything," Drew quipped.

"I know a fair bit more than you do, mate."

"Stop it," Eloise interrupted. "That's the whole point of her spell. You *wouldn't* know."

"*Alleged* spell," Wally stated.

Drew let out an annoyed snarl. "She's got you all pussy whipped."

"Pussy whipped?" Hardy asked with a raised eyebrow. "That's a term I haven't heard since the '90s."

"Well, she's pretty and all, but I'm old enough to be the girl's father," Wally stated.

"More like grandfather," Blue said with a laugh.

"*Gross*," Drew muttered, looking at the ceiling. "*Spare us.*"

The door opened again, breaking the awkward conversation. Thankfully, it was Kyne.

"I was just about to go look for you," Eloise said, the tension loosening in her shoulders. "You're a terrible liar, you know."

The elemental grimaced and took off his hat, setting it onto the table.

Her expression faded. "What's wrong?"

"Rosheen, uh... She tried it on," he said sheepishly.

"She *what*?" Eloise exclaimed, standing so abruptly, her chair almost fell over. "When?"

"Just now."

The other men looked scandalised until Drew thumped his fist on the table, making the salt and pepper shakers rattle. "You're jealous? Seriously? It's *magic.*"

Eloise ran her hands through her hair. "Ugh. I wanna hurl."

"I reckon she knows about the seal and the key," Kyne went on. "If it wasn't for Coen and his kangaroo, I'd be back under Rosheen's spell."

Eloise clapped her hands together in triumph. "So I *was* right!"

"Where's Coen now?" Hardy wondered.

"Keeping an eye on the down below," the elemental told him. "As for Rosheen, she took one look at him and hightailed it into the outback. Full-on spirited like her arse was on fire."

"Rosheen is afraid of Coen?" Wally asked, looking worried. "Why?"

"He's special," Drew said, speaking up. "When I shift and look at him, he's... I don't know what it is, but he's got a certain *something* that makes him *super* supernatural. He's connected to the Dreaming in a way that makes me wonder if he *is* the Dreaming."

Eloise sat back down, her mind swirling. Coen *was* the Dreaming? She didn't even understand how that would work.

"It doesn't matter right now," Drew went on. "Is there a way we can break an illusion?" He looked at Eloise. "Your elemental magic is all space and timey, right?"

She made a face "Timey?"

Drew clicked his fingers. "Spirit, or that other thing... What is it?"

"Ether," Hardy told them. "And how do you know we're the ones being manipulated here?"

"Are you serious?" Eloise exclaimed. "You're the one who's been drooling all over her!"

"With all due respect," Blue began, trying to stop their argument before it kicked off, "if we're under some kind of mind-altering spell, we wouldn't know."

"I already said that," Eloise grumbled.

Wally turned to her. "Why aren't you affected?"

"My superpower is literally perception," she stated. "That makes me immune."

"How do you explain Drew?" Blue wondered. "Why isn't he affected?"

The shifter shrugged. "I figured it was some alpha loophole."

"*Whatever*," Eloise declared. "The moment Rosheen comes in here and hears us talking about her, we'll have more problems." She jabbed a finger at the floor. "It's only a matter of time before she makes a bigger play for the you-know-what. Andante warned us about more threats, and Rosheen is a threat."

"Well, if there's an illusion spell altering our perception, then we need to break it," Hardy said.

"There is," Kyne told them, "and it's finite. We don't have time to wait for it to wear off. I'm worried Rosheen's already done something to Vera."

Drew's scowl deepened. "Rosheen has been making her sick. I tried to tell her, but she wouldn't listen."

"I found her standing in the middle of the road," Hardy told them as if he'd just remembered. "Her magic almost undid my daylight spell."

"Eloise?" Kyne prodded.

The Exiles all turned to stare at her, their expectant gazes making her squirm. What did she know about breaking spells and illusions? Nothing. Everything she'd done so far had been one huge fluke. She'd had help this entire time, and none of it had been on her own.

"I have no idea what I'm doing," Eloise complained. "I could do more harm than good. I mean, I used to wipe people's minds not too long ago. That's a thing I don't want to repeat."

"Have you got any other ideas?" Drew asked. "Because we can't go up against Rosheen on our own. We're both as clueless as each other."

He was right. They had no other options.

Eloise stood and flexed her fingers. "Who wants to go first?"

"Me," Kyne said, taking her hands. "Go on, I trust you."

Eloise breathed deeply and felt for her elemental gift. Kyne had said it was second nature to her, that her power had always been with her, regardless if she knew about it or not. Her intent would shape the outcome. That's why she'd changed people's perceptions and memories of her for the worse...because she'd hated herself.

And now? Right now, she wanted to free the man she was falling in love with from the claws of an evil witch intent on destroying them all. Self-love was a work in progress.

*Kyne, come back*, she called. *Come back...*

She expected to feel a surge of magic, but there was nothing. Eloise opened her eyes, almost fearfully, nervous she'd done more harm than good.

"Kyne?" Her heart skipped a beat. Had she done it right or...?

The miner blinked as if he was dazed, then looked up at her. "All good. *Shit...*" He shook his head. "She had us good. You better do the others."

"It...it worked?"

"Don't look so surprised. Were you expecting fireworks?"

She smiled wryly. "It'd help."

"Okay, enough with the mush," Drew declared. "Let's get on with it."

Eloise grasped each of the Exiles, clearing Rosheen's mind-altering magic and returning the equilibrium of Solace to normal.

"Strewth," Wally murmured, his eyes wide.

Blue shook his head in bewilderment, and Hardy just looked mad. The vampire curled his hands into tight fists and ground his teeth.

"I should've known," he hissed. "*I should've known.* Vera was in trouble and I left her with Rosheen. She said she was going to do a cleansing ritual."

"Some cleansing," Drew muttered.

"Now that Coen thwarted her and her illusion was broken on me, she knows we're onto her," Kyne said.

At that moment, Coen appeared inside the pub as if speaking his name had summoned him.

The Exiles all rose to their feet in alarm as they saw who he was carrying in his arms. *Vera.*

"Vera?" Drew exclaimed, rushing to take the unconscious witch from the Indigenous man.

"I was watching the seal," Coen told them as the shifter laid Vera on the table and checked for a pulse. "I found her there. Don't worry, I squashed her."

"Squashed what?" Drew demanded.

"A shadow lives in her," Coen replied. "It speaks with her voice and sees with her eyes. It told her to go to the seal."

"The Nightshade..." Kyne murmured.

"What?" Eloise asked. "She told me about her father's coven, but..."

"The Nightshade legacy," the miner went on. "That's what she called it. The coven had a history with dark magic, but..." His brow furrowed. "She told me once that her father had warned her about her magic, that she was susceptible to something beyond their control. That's why she left Ireland."

"And why Rosheen was so intent on finding her," Hardy murmured. "They want her magic."

"Why didn't you say anything?" Drew demanded.

"Because it's not my place to reveal Vera's secrets,"

Kyne snarled. "Besides, she was adamant that it couldn't use her. She thought her Brinewold magic protected her."

"Stop it," Eloise snapped. "It doesn't matter why. What matters right now is Vera. If you wipe the shit out of your eyes, you'll see her lying on this table in need of our help, not our accusations." She looked around at the men, her eyes narrowed in warning. "We need to get her someplace safe, then we need to find Rosheen and put a stop to whatever plan they've set into motion."

"What about her magic?" Drew asked. "If she's been taken over by this Nightshade thing, she'll just escape again."

"I squished it down," Coen declared, stamping his foot on the ground. "But it will spring back up."

"We need to take her someplace safe," Hardy said. "Somewhere where Rosheen's magic won't find her."

Eloise thought about Andante and her cave. She looked at Coen, who simply shook his head as if he'd read her thoughts. The old woman wouldn't help them. As far as Andante was concerned, she'd done enough when she'd met Eloise in the outback.

"What about my dugout?" Drew asked.

Kyne nodded. "Seems like a good idea. There isn't anywhere else."

"The weather's too hot," Hardy added.

"And it's a full moon tomorrow," Wally reminded them. "Bloody bad timing if you ask me."

"It can't be helped," Kyne said. "We'll figure it out. For now, let's get Vera out of here."

Eloise grasped his hand. "What about Rosheen?"

"I watch," Coen declared with a grin. "Protect."

"I'm going out to scout," Hardy said, standing. "Keep her eyes away until we move Vera." Before anyone could reply, the vampire zoomed out of the pub and into the heat of the day.

"We'll meet again in an hour," Kyne told the rest of them. "We're going to need a plan."

Drew leaned over Vera and placed his palm against her forehead. "I don't care what you do, I'm not leaving her alone again."

Eloise stood beside him and gazed down at Vera. The witch looked serene, her fiery curls splayed out across the table.

"It's going to be okay," she murmured. "We'll figure it out. Vera's strong, Drew. She'll fight the Nightshade."

The shifter sniffed and scooped the witch up in his arms, not replying. His gaze was firmly locked on Vera.

Eloise felt Kyne take her hand and her heart twisted. She hoped she was right...for all their sakes.

---

Drew sat beside a makeshift bed, watching Vera sleep.

The place was pretty much finished, expect for furniture and a lick of paint. Hardy had brought in a blowup mattress—the kind that came with a battery-operated pump—along a pillow and some blankets from his place. Kyne had dragged in an old cinderblock that had been left behind by the old owner of the dugout. For now, it was all they needed.

It was strange to be in his new home, let alone like this. Vera, sick and comatose. Him waiting for her to wake up. Not too long ago, their roles had been reversed. At least now he could start to repay the kindness she'd shown him...more than just taking extra shifts at the *Outpost*.

His scars from his fight with Roth itched as if his memories had stirred something primal. Shifting on the cinderblock, Drew rubbed his side. *Damn, that was annoying.*

Vera stirred. As she opened her eyes, he leaned closer.

"Vera?" Even as he gazed at her, in his heart he knew it wasn't her.

"Where's my magic?" she demanded, bursting into life. "*What have you done with it?*"

She spoke in a voice that didn't sound like her own —deep and rasping, with a darkness wrapped around it. It must be the Nightshade Kyne had told them about.

"Coen squashed it down," Drew told her. "You can't touch it."

Vera slackened, blinked, then focused on him again. "*Drew?*"

*She was fighting.*

He smiled and leaned closer. "I knew you were still in there."

A faint smile pulled at her lips. "I thought you were going to say, 'I told you so'."

"Yeah, nah..." He grinned. "Forget about all that."

"Drew, I... I can't fight it for much longer. Rosheen, she..." Vera grimaced and clutched her head.

Drew looked at her in alarm, his panic threatening to take hold. "What can I do? *Tell me what to do.*"

"My altar," she rasped. "She changed the orientation to trap me..."

"You want me to smash it?"

"*No.* No, it's too late for that." She grasped his hand and tugged him towards her. "You have to stop her, Drew. Through me, she'll..." Her expression twisted in horror. "Oh God, Finn. *Clarke.*"

"What?" Drew asked, tightening his grip on her hand. "What about them?"

"*Oh God. Oh God, oh God...*" Vera sobbed, lost in the Nightshade's fog. "*Please, no...*"

"*Vera,*" he urged, his heartbeat thrumming so loud he could hear the blood whooshing in his ears. "What did you do?"

"I don't know, I..." Vera grimaced as if she was in pain. "You have to tie me up. Trap me. I can't—" Her eyes snapped open and she lunged for Drew with a demonic growl, her fingers raking across his cheek.

Feeling her nails tear into his skin, he stumbled to his feet, but she kept coming for him, lost in a frenzy driven by the furious Nightshade. Her magic sputtered, purple sparks arcing up her arms.

Drew scurried backwards through the door as she advanced, only stopping when his shoulder slammed against the wall in the hallway.

Vera cried out as she hit an invisible barrier, her eyes wild with fury.

"What have you done?" she rasped, her voice ominous. "You *dare* trap me?"

Drew glanced at the talismans he'd placed around the door—emu and eagle feathers, precious rocks, and sprigs of flowers and plants tied into little bunches with dried grass. Coen had given them to him before returning to the seal, promising they were full of magic.

Drew had thought he was mad—like everyone else seemed to—but he'd never underestimate Coen ever again.

"I'm sorry, Vera," he said. "It's for your own good."

"I will gut you, *dog*," she snarled, her pretty features twisting. "You will regret betraying the Nightshade."

"I'll figure out a way to get you back. *I promise*." He took a step backwards, his heart heavy, then turned, striding down the hall.

"But I don't want to come back!" she shouted after him. "You hear me? *I don't want to come back!*"

Drew emerged into the sunlight, his anxiety rising. Right now, he didn't give a flying fruitcake about Solace. What if Vera had killed Finn and Clarke? If they got her back from the Nightshade and she remembered, she'd have to live with their blood on her hands for the rest of her life. Forget about the seal and the cops breathing down their necks. *It'd destroy her.*

Hearing movement on the rise above the dugout, Drew scurried up the side of the ridge. Eloise was arranging more talismans on the ground, working out the perfect pattern with her elemental powers. Directly below lay Vera's temporary prison, and after what he'd just witnessed, he was glad for the extra layer of protection.

"How's it going down there?" she asked.

"She's awake."

The elemental looked up at him and saw the bloody scratch marks on his cheek. She didn't have to say anything. Her expression mirrored what he felt inside—worry, dread, and uncertainty. How the bloody hell were they supposed to free Vera from the hold of a magical entity she was born with?

She stood and dusted her hands on her jeans. "The talismans?"

"They work, but... She..."

"One step at a time," Eloise murmured, laying a hand on his shoulder.

Her touch seemed to rouse him. "Where's Hardy and Kyne?"

"Not far. What's up?"

"We've got a problem."

Eloise let her hand fall away. "What kind of problem?"

He grimaced and nodded towards the town. "C'mon, let's find the others."

Kyne and Hardy were in the yard outside the dugout, leaning over the tray of Kyne's ute.

As they approached, Drew saw they were looking at a worn geological map of Solace, the edges of the paper held down by rocks. Ochre dirt smeared across the white paper as the vampire pointed to a spot.

"We could try there," he said. "She won't come back to town any time soon, and once she knows Vera's compromised, she'll have to retreat someplace."

At the sound of their approach, Kyne looked up and rapped his knuckles on Hardy's arm.

"Vera's awake," Drew told them. "She's done something to Finn and Clarke. She was only lucid for a minute before the Nightshade took over again, so that's all I got."

"Finn?" Eloise's hand flew to her mouth. "What if she's—"

"Don't say it," Kyne interrupted. He looked troubled, but if he was panicking, he didn't show it— which was exactly why he was the leader. "Let's not jump to conclusions just yet."

Hardy sighed. "This is getting complicated."

Kyne didn't hesitate. He flipped into leader mode and began herding them like they were a bunch of wildcats. "We have to split up. Hardy and I will look for

Clarke. If he's still alive, he'll need to be compelled. Wally and Blue can look for Finn. The other fae will be more willing to talk to Blue than any of us, and they need to be warned."

"What about me?" Drew asked. "I can help. I can shift."

"Someone needs to keep an eye on Vera," he replied. "If Rosheen comes back, we need you here. You seem to be immune to her magic for the most part."

"Just the illusions," Drew said. "If she decides to throw me against a wall, I doubt I'd be side-stepping *that*."

"Still, Vera trusts you," Kyne added. "Out of all of us, you're the one she'll want to see what she wakes up."

Drew tensed, his inner dingo stirring. Finally, he nodded his agreement. He was right.

"I'm coming to look for Clarke," Eloise interjected. "I'm not getting left behind."

Kyne shook his head. "No, you're staying here."

"I can teleport people," Eloise argued. "I reckon that's a useful skill to have with a psycho witch on the loose, don't you?"

"I ain't arguing with her," Hardy said, holding up his hands in mock defence. "She's more than capable. I don't want to end up in the Middle East with a pack of dingo shifter bikers."

"Fine," Kyne said with a grimace. "But we go now."

He and Hardy made their way down to Solace, but Eloise lingered.

She looked back at Drew, but he nodded and waved her away. "Go. I'll be fine here."

"Be careful, okay?"

"Always am."

"Yeah, right." She laughed, but the light never reached her eyes.

Drew watched as she broke into a jog to catch up to Kyne and Hardy, the sun hot on his shoulders.

After the way things had gone since he'd found Solace, he wondered if he would've been better off wandering as a lone dingo. It would've been *safer*, and that was saying something. But life in Solace—crazy magic and all—was better than anything he'd been through. *Infinitely* better.

He had a pack, a place to call home, and the love of his friends. It was worth dying to protect.

Drew looked out across Solace one last time before going back inside to watch over Vera.

## CHAPTER 22

Fifteen minutes after speaking with Drew, Kyne followed Hardy into the outback behind Wally's garage, his rifle slung over his shoulder. Eloise brought up the rear, one hand on her hat as a hot wind stirred.

They'd mobilised Blue and Wally, sending them off in search of the fae to the northeast of Solace, with instructions to keep an eye out for Rosheen. So far, the witch hadn't reappeared and Kyne took it as good news. Right now, they needed some.

"We should start with holes in the ground and ditches," Hardy called out. "That kind of thing."

"Aren't we jumping to conclusions? Vera wouldn't kill anyone, let alone Finn or Clarke..." Eloise trailed off, giving away her uncertainty on the matter.

"Technically, but it's not Vera who did these things," Kyne told her.

"I know, but it's *Vera*. She wouldn't let something like this happen, even to Finn."

"It's not a matter of want," Hardy said and turned around. "Even people with the best intentions can be coerced into evil with magic." He should know, he could mind control people with his vampire eyes. How it worked was a mystery to Kyne, who considered 'magic' a lazy explanation.

Kyne placed a reassuring hand on Eloise's shoulder. "You have a good heart, Eloise, but power can do some screwed up stuff to people, especially supernaturals."

Her expression tightened. "So, ditches and holes. Where do we start?"

"This entire area is littered with old mines," Kyne said, gesturing to the flat, scrubby landscape. "There's an old riverbed this way. During the gold rush, the old-timers tried digging for gold there but found nothing, as you already know. There are a couple of opal mines where the river met the ocean long ago."

"All right, so there're stacks of holes to check," she said, taking a deep breath. "Let's go."

Hardy raised his eyebrows at Kyne, who smirked. "You heard the woman. Let's go."

They made their way into the scrub, dodging spiky spinifex grass and trekking towards the ancient riverbed.

"Aren't you afraid it's going to fall out?" Eloise asked from behind.

Kyne glanced over his shoulder. "What?"

"The torch."

He'd picked up the torch from his ute on the way, and it stuck out the back pocket of his jeans.

"Yeah, nah," he replied. "These jeans are tight as a drum."

"I have sensitive hearing you know," Hardy called out from ahead.

Eloise chuckled, although they were currently searching the outback for Finn and a possibly deceased cop. Nothing about their situation was comical, but it eased the tension a little. She wasn't used to their high-stakes antics, though the more trouble they got into, and the more Kyne saw how well she handled it. Eloise Hart was becoming a seasoned pro.

Hardy stilled and turned towards the east. "I smell blood."

"That doesn't sound good," Eloise murmured.

Kyne scanned the horizon. "Where?"

The vampire began walking, leaving him no choice but to follow. Eloise brought up the rear, their boots crunching on the loose dirt and rocks underfoot.

As they trod a familiar path, Kyne's hopes faded, and when they reached the clearing, he shook his head. *Vera, what have you done?*

"It's an old mine," Eloise said, approaching the metal door over the shaft. It was padlocked shut to stop outsiders from interfering, because it'd already happened once with devastating consequences.

"It's Wally's mine," Kyne corrected. "Let's hope he's not down there."

"You don't have the key, do you?" Hardy asked.

"Nope. Wally has the only one," he replied. "For safety reasons."

"Well, he's going to have to get another one." Hardy bent over and snapped the lock open with his vampire super strength. Opening the hatch, he leapt into the shaft and the ladder rattled as he climbed down.

"Wait up here," Kyne said to Eloise. "We won't be long."

She shook her head and scowled. "I'm not staying behind."

He blinked once, then nodded. "Fair enough." Then he threw a leg over the side and followed Hardy down into the mine.

Kyne held the ladder as Eloise climbed down, waiting until she'd put both feet on the ground before he let go.

"He's in here all right," Hardy muttered, sniffing the air. "He's cut himself."

Kyne took out the torch from his back pocket and switched it on, illuminating the tunnel. "Badly?"

The vampire shrugged. "Bad enough that I could smell it above ground, but not bad enough that he's bled out. It's a promising sign."

Eloise glanced at Kyne, her expression uneasy. Hardy's vampiric approach to things could be a little cold and morbid, but it wasn't from spite—death was his reality.

"Sergeant Clarke?" Kyne's voice echoed through the tunnel, bouncing into the darkness.

"He's down there," Hardy said. "I can hear his heartbeat."

Kyne turned the torch down the tunnel. "Let's go."

They moved farther into the darkness, the torch tracking over wolf prints in the dirt.

"Clarke?" he called again. "You in here?"

"We're here to help," Eloise added. "Clarke?"

"He's here." Hardy gestured to Kyne to bring the torch up front.

Clarke held up his arm as the torchlight scanned over his face, and he blinked furiously as his eyes adjusted. He'd scraped both his palms badly at some stage, which accounted for the blood. At least he wasn't haemorrhaging, which was a good start.

"*Get away from me*," he snarled, scurrying back into the darkness. "I'll fight back. *I'm warning you.*"

"He knows…" Eloise said.

Hardy peered at him. "How much, though?"

"Are you going to make me disappear, too?" Clarke demanded as Kyne shone the torch back onto his face.

Eloise's eyebrows rose. "What?"

"I know what you are," he said, backing against the wall. He jabbed a finger at her. "I know what *you* can do."

"Vera told him about Roth," Kyne said with a sigh.

"Vera? She's the one who put me down here!" Clarke exclaimed. "She's a witch!"

Hardy sighed. "Of course, she is."

"And that mechanic is a werewolf!"

"Aw shit," Kyne muttered. Vera, in all her Nightshade craziness, had put Clarke down here so Wally could use him as a chew toy on the next full moon...which was tomorrow night. "Lucky we found you then, mate. Wally's a good bloke, but when he's a wolf...well, he gets a bit carried away."

Clarke's terrified gaze moved back and forth like he didn't know who was going to come for him first—the supernatural standing before him or a crazy werewolf leaping out of the shadows.

"We'd love to explain it all to you, but unfortunately, we don't have time," Hardy said. "You met Dark Vera, so you can understand. We need to hit the reset button among other things."

"Dark Vera?" Kyne asked.

The vampire shrugged. "Simple but fitting."

Clarke's eyes widened in shock. "Y-you're letting me out?"

"We're not the bad guys here," Kyne told him. "No matter what you think about what we did to the Dust Dogs, it was for the greater good."

"We have to get you out of here," Eloise murmured, taking a gentle step towards the sergeant. "It's not safe."

"*No shit!*"

"We don't have time for a therapy session." Hardy

sighed and glanced over his shoulder as if he were listening to something far away. "If you won't come willingly, we have ways of making you."

"Don't come near me!" Clarke edged down the tunnel, out of the ring of torchlight. "I won't let you murder me, too! When I don't report into the station tomorrow, the force will come looking!"

"Oh, for heaven's sake!" Eloise exclaimed. "No one is killing anyone. Hardy's a vampire. He can mind control you."

"He's a *what?*"

"Good going, Eloise," Hardy drawled. "Now his heart is beating so fast, it's a wonder he hasn't burst his left ventricle." He went to grab Clarke.

"*Stop.*" Eloise tugged on his shirt sleeve. "We can trust him."

"How do you figure that?" Hardy asked.

"Because we can't just go around mind controlling people and making them vanish. It isn't right."

The vampire snorted. "Are we really debating ethics right now?"

"We can't solve everything with magic," Eloise went on. "And I have faith in him. What if he's a potential ally?"

Kyne frowned as he watched the back and forth. She was right. Clarke's access would be useful in protecting the seal, but he was leaning towards siding with Hardy on this one. They didn't have time to screw around.

Kyne hissed and grabbed Clarke by the shirt front, deciding to take the middle-road. "If we don't get you out of here now, we're all going to be wolf bait. Vera's not herself, she's being controlled by Rosheen. You remember her?"

Clarke nodded, his eyes wide.

"You're a smart guy—they wouldn't have made you sergeant otherwise—so do us a favour and extend your analytical thinking to include the existence of supernatural beings." Kyne waited a moment for the notion to sink into his human brain. "The Dust Dogs are dingo shifters who threatened our town and tortured and hunted one of our own. We had to settle it the supernatural way, but all the commotion was like sending up a signal flare, and Rosheen came scurrying out of the witchy sewers in search of Vera. Unfortunately for you, you've become collateral damage in all of this. I'd apologise, but right now we have to get you out, unless that damage becomes permanent. You get me?"

Clarke nodded again. "I get you."

"We're not the bad guys here," Hardy said from the shadows. "We're trying to protect more than just our home."

"Protecting what?" The sergeant's gaze moved from Kyne to the others.

"It's need to know," the miner replied. "You're going to have to be satisfied with that for now."

"Step one, out of the hole," Hardy said with a smirk.

Clarke looked between the Exiles as they moved back, creating a path for him.

Kyne shone the torch on the floor, lighting up the uneven surface. "When you're ready."

The sergeant wiped his damp brow and pushed past him, giving Hardy a wide berth as he made for the shaft.

Kyne sighed and followed, tugging on Eloise's hand as he went. Progress at last.

***

Vera glared at the talismans on the other side of the door. The emu feather fluttered as the wind trailed its way down the hallway and into the side of the ridge, the gentle ruffle infuriating her.

She was trapped in here by ancient magic that was cobbled together with nothing but dirt, sticks, and tattered feathers. It was *insulting*.

The dingo was gone. He'd shot off empty promises before running outside with his tail between his legs. She didn't want to be saved...she didn't *need* it.

For the first time in her life, Vera was powerful. There was nothing she couldn't face and conquer. The Nightshade had guided her out of the shadow of her coven's murder and into a new future...and Rosheen had been the one to light the fuse.

Vera narrowed her eyes, glaring at the emu feather. Her sister was out there, pursued by the Exiles—if she hadn't been captured already. She had to get out of here and finish their work. Once they were done with this place, they would return to Ireland and the Ascendants. But first she had to break the power of the talismans.

She reached out with a finger and brushed it against the feather.

"There was a reason I left the Nightshades," he said. "We don't have to do this."

Vera spun on her heel, coming face to face with a man she recognised, and her expression fell. "*Dad?*"

He turned at the sound of her voice, but his gaze moved across her as if she wasn't there.

"I won't," a female voice replied.

Vera gasped as a ghostly figure passed through her and walked to meet her father.

"Ciara, the rest of the coven has already gone into hiding, if they're not dead already. The craglorn have already decimated the Nightshades," he argued. "This baby will become the conduit. People will come looking for it. It will be in danger...and we will be in danger from it."

Vera reached out towards the figure, but her fingers passed through the vision. "Ma?"

"*Her,*" Ciara snapped.

Vera's father hesitated. "It's a girl?"

"I won't kill our daughter before she's even born."

She grasped his face, forcing him to look her in the eye. "Liam, she's not just a Nightshade. She'll be a Brinewold. Whatever happens, *she will have a choice.*"

"Other witches will come looking for her. The fae will look—"

"Let them!" Ciara cried. "I will fight them all if I have to, but I will not murder our child, Liam. Magic is dying and every life is precious. Every single one!"

Liam pursed his lips, his brow creasing. "Ciara... Her life won't be easy."

"We'll be there to protect her."

"You can't guarantee that," he murmured. "You know we can't."

Vera turned towards the door and rushed at the opening, but the talismans held strong. The barrier forced her back and she let out a cry of rage.

It was his magic. *Coen's.* He was trying to remind her of who she was. The weak, pathetic witch who'd run away from the *Gealach Fola* and had forsaken her legacy. This was who she was born to be. The conduit for the Nightshade.

"Get out of my head!" she screeched, fisting her hands into her hair.

The room moved, and she was outside.

Vera ran up the front path towards home, her schoolbag heavy with books. Her uniform was askew, her shirt untucked from her blue and grey pleated skirt. Her tights were torn, her blazer was missing a button, and her tie was stained with blood where she'd wiped her bloodied nose. There'd be hell to pay if her parents found out she'd been fighting again.

Pressing an ear to the front door, she heard nothing and decided the coast was clear. She opened the door and went inside.

"*No*," her current self moaned. "I don't want to see this again. I don't want to see it!"

Stopping in the hall, Vera came to a sudden halt as she saw the scene in the living room.

Death.

Death, blood, and *monsters*.

Twisted creatures bent over her family. Their leathery black hides and razor-sharp claws were the stuff of nightmares. Their humanoid shapes the only clue as to what they'd once been.

*Fae.*

The slaughtered witches were seated within a circle of salt, the candles and crystals they'd arranged in a sigil, scattered. They'd been using magic, the mere flicker of power luring the craglorn to them.

They were dead. Their magic gone, devoured, their bodies...

A dark voice stirred within her. *Kill them all, kill them all. Kill. Them. All.*

Vera dropped her schoolbag, the sound drawing the attention of the craglorn. As their black, starved eyes turned on her, she let go of her magic.

Her mouth opened, letting out a shrill scream and indigo fire exploded around her, the shock wave pulsing through the room. The blast shattered the windows, splintered the furniture, and tore through the craglorn, pulling their twisted bodies apart.

*Remember*, the Nightshade whispered to her. *Remember the midnight fae.*

"Finn," she whispered. Her lips pulled into a twisted grin as she separated herself from the vision.

Looking towards the talismans outside the door, Vera drew on her connection to the seal and stepped across the threshold of her prison.

"Game on, bitches," she drawled, walking towards the light. "Game. *On.*"

## CHAPTER 23

Drew looked out over Solace, his thoughts troubled.

Finn was missing, Rosheen was on the loose, Vera was possessed by a screwed up hereditary magical entity, and a cop was in mortal danger. Things had been bad when he was running from the Dust Dogs, but this...? This was worse.

He scuffed the toe of his boot in the ochre dirt, cursing under his breath. Right now, he wished he could do more than just shapeshift into a dingo.

Footsteps echoed in the dugout behind him and he rose sharply, his breath catching when he saw Vera emerge through the front door. How the hell did she get out? Coen's talismans should've kept her inside. *Bloody hell.*

He stepped in front of her. "I can't let you leave."

Vera swept her arm through the air and an invisible force knocked him clean off his feet.

He flew backwards across the clearing and slammed into a tree. He fell flat on his face, pain stabbing through the jagged scars on his chest and back.

She said nothing as she strode by, her mind set on some unknown purpose.

"Vera!" he shouted, pushing to his hands and knees.

She didn't turn around.

He spat dirt onto the ground and cried, "Stop!"

"Don't follow me, Drew," Vera called, the Nightshade speaking through her. "I will kill you if you do."

*Stuff that.* He got to his feet and ran.

Vera turned, her eyes black, and held up her hand. Magic slammed into him, forcing him to such a sudden stop, his head snapped back.

"I won't warn you again."

"And I won't stop trying."

"Stay away, Drew."

"You won't kill me, Vera. If you really meant it, you would've already gutted me." He pushed against her magic, but it held steady. "That's how I know you're still in there. *Fight it.* You have a choice."

Vera sneered and waved a hand in the air, flicking her wrist like she was swatting at an annoying fly.

Drew blinked as his vision slipped and everything went dark.

"Drew?" A hand slapped his face. "Drew, *wake up.*"

Drew blinked, his vision clearing. A pair of old grisly faces peered down at him and he coughed, sitting bolt upright. He was still in the yard outside his dugout, but Vera was nowhere in sight. How long had he been out? It couldn't have been long...

"Careful," Wally said, brushing rust-coloured dirt off Drew's shoulders. "Don't rush yourself."

"Vera," he rasped. "She got out."

"Strewth," Blue said, glancing at Wally. "That's a problem."

"I'll say," the werewolf replied.

The wind stirred around them, and Drew rubbed the dirt from his eyes. "Where did she go? Have you seen her?" The Exiles helped the shifter to his feet. "We have to go after her."

"It's been quiet," Blue said. "A little *too* quiet."

"No sign of Rosheen, either," Wally confirmed.

Drew's brow creased as he looked to the sky. The sapphire blue was gone, replaced with a dirty orange haze.

"There's a dust storm coming," Blue said, the tips of his handlebar moustache swaying in the breeze.

"It doesn't feel like a natural storm to me," Wally muttered.

Drew's heartbeat faltered as he sniffed the air. It carried the metallic tang of magic. He knew Vera was cutting off Solace from the outside world, using the storm as a natural barrier. She was making a play for the seal...she had to be.

"Where's Finn?" he asked. They could really use some extra magical firepower right about now.

"We couldn't find him," Wally replied. "The fae camp was unreachable. Finn must've put some kind of barrier around it."

Drew grimaced as the wind picked up speed. Maybe it was a good thing, considering the bad blood between them and the witches. They'd be safe hidden in the outback.

"We need to find Vera right now," he said, grasping Wally's arm. "This is her."

Blue's eyes widened. "The storm?"

"If she can get past Coen's magic, then there's no telling what she could do." Before the two old-timers could reply, he took off down the hill towards the highway.

He had no idea how he was going to stop Vera—knock her out, perform an exorcism, douse her with holy water—but he was going to at least *try*. He owed her that much.

Skirting around the back of Hardy's opal shop, Drew pressed his back against the wall. As he peered around the corner, he caught sight of Vera.

She stood in the centre of the highway, alone, her arms stretched towards the sky—the eye of the storm.

Wally came to a halt beside him, finally catching up. "Is she...?" the old wolf got out between breathless gasps.

"Standing right over the seal," Drew muttered, the dread clear in his voice.

"Shit," Blue hissed, announcing his arrival. "We've got to stop her before she cracks it open."

"She's still in there," Drew murmured. "I can get through to her. I know I can."

"Drew, *wait*." Wally tried to grab his arm, but the shifter was too determined to stop and listen.

He jogged towards Vera, the wind whipping through his sandy blond hair. Stopping on the side of the highway, he glanced at Clarke's police 4WD that was still parked outside the *Outpost*.

The Vera he knew would never hurt anyone, least of all Clarke. Despite what the cop had done, the guy cared about her. Drew saw it now, though he didn't want to believe it. Vera would never be his, not like that, but she deserved happiness...no matter where it came from.

"Vera, stop," Drew called, stepping onto the highway. "Come *home*."

The witch lowered her arms and turned, the wind tugging her fiery curls across her face. Her gaze met his and his expression froze. Her eyes were completely black—the Nightshade had sunk its claws deep—but he could still see a familiar light burning inside her heart.

"Fight it," he murmured. "Come home, Vera." He held out his hand. "*I'm here...*"

Drew almost believed he was getting through to

her for a moment, but Vera's features contorted and magic grew around her, the air shimmering indigo as it crackled with building electricity.

"I warned you, Drew," she said. "*I warned you.*"

---

When Eloise emerged from Wally's mine, it was to a changed world.

The blue summer sky had turned an eerie shade of burnt orange that reminded her of the thick bushfire smoke that had coated much of the state the year before.

Eloise stared at the sky and held her hat as the wind buffeted the brim. The wind had risen and seemed to be picking up speed by the second.

She stood beside Kyne, Hardy, and Clarke, who looked just as baffled. "What's going on?"

"A dust storm," Hardy said, following her gaze. "An unnatural one by the smell of it."

Clarke stared up at the swirling mass of dust in disbelief and balked as a writhing mass of shadowy figures swirled through the air currents. "What the hell?"

Eloise swallowed hard. "Are those...?"

"Kadaitcha," Hardy confirmed.

Kyne let out a frustrated groan. "I think it's safe to say that Vera has escaped."

"Maybe it's Rosheen," Eloise said hopefully.

"Not likely," Kyne told her. "This is serious magic. Rosheen doesn't have the strength to pull off something like this. This is the work of the Nightshade."

Clarke turned to the Exiles. "What's wrong with Vera?"

"Her witch legacy comes with an evil hitchhiker," the vampire replied. "Unfortunately."

"This Nightshade thing... It's taken control of her?"

"You can't fight this," Kyne told him, picking up on the cop's train of thought.

"But—"

"This is supernatural, sergeant," Hardy interrupted. "It's no place for a human being."

Clarke's brow creased. "What about Vera? You can't just leave her."

"Wait." Eloise placed her hand on Hardy's chest and peered at the cop. "You really care about her, don't you?"

"I had plenty of time to think while I was trapped in that mine waiting for a werewolf to tear me apart," Clarke scoffed and shook his head. "A bloody *werewolf*."

She snapped her fingers. "*Focus*."

"She's been through so much with her family," Clarke went on, "but there's something about her...a light, a passion I've never—"

"We don't have time for heart to hearts," Hardy

interrupted. "You need to stay outside of the storm and don't come into town for *anything*. You hear me?"

"If Vera's in trouble, then I'm coming with you," Clarke argued.

"Now he grows a pair," Kyne drawled. "God help us."

"This isn't a police matter, Clarke," Hardy told him. "You can't pull out your badge and threaten arrest."

"*I won't leave her.*"

Hardy sighed and grabbed the sergeant's shoulders. "Listen to me," he began.

As Clarke's expression slackened and his protests stopped, Eloise realised the vampire was compelling him.

"You're wiping *all* his memories?" she asked. "Even of Vera?"

"I have to," Hardy replied. "This isn't about us, Eloise. We've got bigger things to protect here. I'm sorry, but Vera's heart has to sit this one out."

"He's right," Kyne said, laying a hand on her arm. "It sucks, but it's the reality of being an Exile."

Her throat tightened. "The seal before *everything*?"

"This time, yes." Hardy grasped Clarke's shoulders and resumed his compulsion. "You will leave Solace and go back to Lightning Ridge. You'll forget about everything that happened here. You won't remember any of us, especially not Vera Walsh. Solace is just a simple opal mining town on the edge of nothing. There's nothing to see here. Nothing at all."

"What about his car?" Kyne asked. "It's sitting out the front of the *Outpost*."

"I'll return it as soon as we're done here," the vampire replied before he turned back to Clarke. "For now, you can take Wally's ute. It's parked out the back of the garage. The keys are in the glovebox." Clarke blinked as the compulsion took hold. "Got me?"

The sergeant nodded. "I got you."

"Off you go then." Hardy gave him a push towards the garage and he stumbled forwards, vanishing through the scrub.

"Let's get back to town," Kyne said, striding away, his rifle still slung over his shoulder.

"You're not going use that, are you?" Eloise asked, following the men.

"We have to do whatever it takes," he replied. "If you're coming, you have to—"

"I'll do what I have to," Eloise snapped. "But I'll always try to save people before I resort to shooting them."

"Good," Kyne declared, not turning. "We're all on the same wavelength."

They reached the garage just as they saw Wally's old ute tear across the yard and fishtail onto the highway, headed south.

Eloise took off her hat and flung it inside just as the swirling tornado consumed them...and continued to grow until it'd encircled the entire town.

Kyne grabbed her hand just as a shadow figure soared past them, its fingers stretching towards the three Exiles.

"Kadaitcha," Hardy shouted over the roar. "Be careful."

As they reached the highway, their dire situation became all too clear. Eloise saw Vera standing in the centre of the storm, directly over the seal. The Nightshade was in full control now, and it was clear it wasn't leaving Solace until it cracked open the bluestone and unleashed more horror onto the world.

Drew stood before Vera, trying to talk her down, but she raised her hand, her expression twisting as purple magic crackled around her. She said something, but the wind tore the sound away from her lips.

"Oh my God," Eloise cried. "She's going to—" But Hardy sprang into life before she could finish her thought.

The vampire tore across the yard and onto the highway in less than a second, but it wasn't fast enough. Vera swept her arm through the air, tossing both Hardy and Drew backwards like they were nothing.

"I warned you!" she shouted. "Try to stop me again and I won't be so kind. *Don't stand in my way.*" Vera's black gaze locked onto Wally and her head tilted to the side.

The mechanic fell to his knees with a roar and the Exiles staggered as his bones snapped.

"She—" The mechanic howled in pain as his hips snapped and his back arched. His eyes flew open and Eloise grasped Kyne's arm.

"He's turning," Blue said. "*Vera made him turn.*"

"I can't stop it," Wally rasped, his chest heaving as he sucked in breath after breath. "You have to run."

Eloise fell to her knees before him and grasped his face. "*I'm not leaving you.*"

He stared back at her with glowing amber eyes and shook his head. "Get out of here, Eloise. You have to—" He cried out in anguish as his left arm snapped.

Kyne grabbed her under the arms and dragged her away. "Eloise, we have to fall back."

"But the seal!"

"Coen is the only one with enough power to stand against the Nightshade now," he murmured. "We have to trust him."

Eloise nodded, casting one last look back at Wally, who now looked more like a wolf than a man. His clothes were shredded, his skin had sprouted grey tufts of fur, and his face—

"*Eloise!*" Kyne shouted.

She snapped to attention and fled, tearing away from Vera and the unfolding scene on the highway, and took the side road out of Solace. As she ran, her power flared, carving a path through the writhing mass of shadows, parting them like a certain dude did to the Red Sea.

She hadn't gone far before she realised she was alone. Kyne wasn't behind her, and there was no telling where the others had gone. The last time she'd seen Drew, he was lying on the highway. Hardy, she wasn't sure. Blue would go to the pub, and Kyne... *Damn it!*

The last time she'd run from Wally had ended in disaster, and as soon as she realised she was doing it again, Eloise skidded to a stop and turned towards Solace. She wouldn't make the same mistake twice.

Eloise listened, squinting her eyes as dust swirled around her, the grit hitting her exposed face like a wad of sandpaper. The kadaitcha rushed towards her, but she lifted her hand and willed them away, her elemental power manifesting enough to keep them at bay.

*About time I figured that out.*

"There you are," an ominous voice echoed behind her.

Eloise spun, her breath catching as her gaze met the last person she wanted to see.

*Rosheen.*

"I've been looking for you," the witch snarled... then she struck, colliding with Eloise and dragging her into the tornado.

She fought the witch, thrashing and striking out as they fell headlong through the storm, the kadaitcha tearing at them with ghostly black fingers.

Rosheen laughed, cackling in glee as she clutched onto Eloise. The shadows screamed and wailed, pulling at her hair, their icy touch searing her flesh down to the bone. Then they broke free of the storm and the kadaitcha shrieked in despair at losing their prey.

They spun across the ground, bashing against rocks, trees, and spinifex, only coming to a halt when Rosheen wrapped her hand around Eloise's neck.

The wind had died down and above them, the sky was a brilliant shade of dreamy blue without the slightest whisper of white cloud to be seen.

Eloise gasped as Rosheen dragged her to her feet, the witch's fingers biting into her neck.

"Where is it?" she demanded.

"Where's what?" Eloise rasped. She glared at Rosheen, who was silhouetted by the raging dust storm that still surrounded Solace.

"The key. *The coral key.* Only an elemental can retrieve it."

"Oh, I see," Eloise said, grasping at Rosheen's hand. "You couldn't get to Kyne, so you came for me. Well... only he knows, and he's smart enough not to tell anyone, *not even me.*"

Rosheen's hand tightened around her neck and she called on her elemental powers. Anything to make the witch let go.

Eloise tried to drill into her mind, to give her a taste of her own medicine, but nothing happened.

"Your pathetic attempts at using your magic won't work on me," Rosheen drawled. "And, unfortunately for you, I don't believe a word you're saying. Luckily, I have painful ways of dragging the truth out of you. Do you know what *Gealach Fola* means?"

"It's Gaelic..."

"*For?*"

"Blood...moon."

Eloise screamed as Rosheen forced her blood magic into her brain and began to sift through her memories.

"Poor little Eloise Hart," the witch snarled. "You made everyone you loved into hateful beasts. They turned on you, despised you, ran you out of town. They were only a reflection of all the self-loathing you held in your pathetic heart. You think Kyne loves you for who you are? He only wants another elemental so he doesn't feel as alone as you do. He will ruin you, Eloise, just like this stupid pact to protect the seal will ruin your *entire life*. If you give me the key now, then you will be *free*."

Eloise grimaced as she tasted blood in her mouth. "I...will...*not*..." She lunged, grabbing Rosheen's face, and screamed as her elemental power rushed forth in a consuming tidal wave.

The witch gasped as they fell through the earth and tumbled into the blackness of space. Stars rushed past them so fast, they elongated into long strips of white before they broke through the colourful cloud of a nebula, only to land in the middle of a patched landscape of green and black.

The black mountain towered over them, piercing through the green canopy, and reached high into the aquamarine sky. The air hummed with a low sound Eloise couldn't quite make out. A whisper, a chant, a warning, a *promise...*

"What is it?" Rosheen whispered. "What sleeps in the mountain?" She tugged at her hair, her eyes wide as if she was staring into the maw of eternity and was terrified of it. "Where is it? *Who are you?*"

Eloise jerked back, tearing free of Rosheen's hold. As the landscape around Solace shimmered back into existence, the witch stumbled, her eyes still full of the haze of their vision.

Eloise only had a split-second to react, so she did the only thing she could think of. She hurled her fist at the witch, striking her in the temple. The blow jarred up her arm, and she leapt back as Rosheen collapsed, falling to the ground like a sack of potatoes.

*Damn, that felt satisfying.*

As Kyne and Eloise fled into the storm behind him, Hardy did the opposite.

Wally howled, his wolf form taking control, and Vera turned her back on them, continuing whatever spell she was using to control the flow of magic from the seal.

She was channeling a tremendous amount of power, but even Hardy understood there was a limit to how much she could handle...unless she had a way to buffer it. But how could she even access the ebb of power that always emanated from the seal?

Hardy's expression fell as he realised what she'd done. *Finn.* She was using Finn as a conduit.

Vera had access to endless amounts of magic without even opening the seal. If he didn't stop the Nightshade now, it was all over.

Wally leapt towards him, his fangs bared. Hardy sprung into the air, colliding with the wolf, and they tumbled over and over, wrestling for dominance.

Neither of them could get the upper hand, and they broke apart somewhere south of where Vera stood. The wolf prowled before Hardy, growling and snapping.

"You have to fight it, old man," the vampire murmured. "I know you can."

Wally edged closer.

"You need to distract her for me," he went on. "Just long enough for me to get to her." He held up his arms as the wolf snapped viciously. "As soon as I knock her out, her hold over you will be broken. You'll be able to shift back."

Wally lowered his head but his burning amber eyes never left the vampire.

"There's still time to stop this. Wally, *please.*"

The wolf growled and snapped, shaking its head as if it were trying to fight. It pawed at the air and howled in torment, its eyes burning with supernatural fire.

"That's it," Hardy urged. "Keep fighting. *You're doing it.*"

Finally, Wally let out one last mournful howl and took off into the storm, following the highway north.

Hardy wasted no time running after him. Fighting past the dust and shadows, he was just in time to see the wolf leap through the air towards Vera.

The witch spun, her eyes wide as she saw the mass of grey fur and fangs rush at her. Her magic sparked, and the blow slammed into Wally, knocking him off course.

He tumbled across the road as Hardy rushed at her, the vampire emerging out of the swirling dust like lightning and struck her from behind.

The blow had the desired effect. Vera slumped, falling into the vampire's waiting arms, and the wind came to a sudden, screeching halt.

The kadaitcha dissolved as the ochre dust fell back to Earth, the dirt coating everything and everyone in a fine layer of grit.

The vampire huddled with the unconscious Vera in the middle of the dusty road, his cold, dead heart beating faster than it had in a century. The summer sun burned down on them from its place high in the sapphire sky, the wind and wailing spirits now eerily silent.

Wally looked up, his human eyes blinking furiously.

"*Crikey*," the old wolf rasped. "I'm going to have to crack out the leaf blower."

## CHAPTER 24

Kyne leaned against the tray of his ute, his arms crossed over his chest.

In all his years living in Solace, a tornado infested with angry shadow spirits was pretty much the craziest thing he'd ever seen—and considering he was an elemental who could shape rock with his hands, that was saying something.

The entire town was coated in a thick layer of rust-coloured dirt but cleaning up was the least of their problems. They still had the Nightshade to contend with.

Eloise wrapped her arm around his waist and leaned her head on his shoulder.

"I can't believe you punched out Rosheen," Kyne said. "I wish I was there to see it."

She laughed. "Yeah, well, my hand hurts, so I'm not keen to repeat it. I'm just glad Hardy was able to stop Vera before she cracked open the seal."

"Who knows if it would have opened," Kyne mused. "Without the key, it's just a big rock."

"Allegedly." She looked down at Solace. "Where's Blue and Wally?"

"Out looking for Finn. Did Drew take care of the altar?"

"Yeah." Eloise handed him a shard of broken quartz. "He smashed it good. Dragged all the bits outside. Vera told him it was too late, but any little bit helps, I guess."

Holding the jagged slice of crystal, Kyne shuddered as he felt the slimy residue of Rosheen's magic inside it. Whatever she'd done had changed the energy into something twisted. It must have been how she'd summoned the Nightshade. With the spell shattered, maybe it would help Vera regain control.

"I've got to go in there and question our houseguest," he said, pocketing the quartz. "You wanna come?"

"Yeah, nah. I'm going to help Drew watch over Vera," Eloise said. "I've had enough of Rosheen and her shenanigans. If I hang around, I might smack her again."

"Hey," he murmured. "What's wrong?"

"When she grabbed me, she had a vision…" Her gaze lowered. "It was the black mountain."

"That mountain again?"

Eloise shrugged. "Whatever. It's just a lump of rock."

Kyne didn't think so, but they didn't have time to ponder the meaning.

"You'll be okay in there on your own?" she added.

"Yep. It's all good. The talismans have been replaced."

"Good. I'll come and check on you later."

Once Eloise had gone, Kyne went inside. Drew's dugout was pretty much done, except for another coat of paint and some furniture, but after this...someone would have to come in here and do a serious cleansing on the place.

Rosheen was in the back bedroom. She'd been tied to a chair, but the rope was just for show. Hardy had rearranged Coen's talismans around the door and on the ridge above so the witch was well and truly contained. But this time, a bunch of sticks, feathers, and leaves were hanging from the roof directly above her head. There'd be no arcane misadventure in this room today.

Rosheen's gaze moved to the emu feather dangling above her, and Kyne was sure he saw a flicker of fear pass through her eyes. She was afraid of Coen, that much was clear when she ran from him earlier.

"Where's Finn?" he demanded. "We know you've done something to him."

She sneered and jutted out her chin in open defiance.

"You're not helping yourself here, Rosheen," Kyne went on. "We have all the power here."

"You really think a bunch of feathers and twigs can keep either of us trapped?" the witch scoffed. "It's only a matter of time before our magic overwhelms those pathetic talismans. It's already happened once."

"You're wrong, Rosheen."

"*And you're naïve.*"

Kyne shook his head. "We're family and we trust one another implicitly. All of us. I've known Vera a long time, and she's confided a great deal in me and the other Exiles about her magic and family, so I know without your influence over her that Vera will have enough strength to fight back against the Nightshade."

Rosheen snorted. "You think you have all the answers, but you'll be sorry. The Vera you know is *gone.*"

Kyne rolled his eyes. "You're stuck so far up your own arsehole that you haven't been listening, Rosheen." He reached into his pocket and took out the shattered quartz crystal. The moment her gaze touched the cloudy white stone, her expression fell. "Your hold over Vera is broken. Coen's talismans will hold you because you only have a fraction of the magic Vera holds in her little finger. Now is the time to start talking."

"I have nothing to say to you."

"Of course, you don't," he murmured. "Tell me... Can you say that trust is something you've ever had with your coven?" She stared at him, her lips pursed. "I don't think so. Otherwise you wouldn't be here trying to prove yourself. You're a pawn."

She grinned up at him, her eyes narrowing.

"You came here for Vera and the Nightshade. Why?"

She said nothing. Her smile twisted into an almost manic looking grin.

"Power," he answered for her. "It's always power with people like you. You think having it will solve all your problems. That's why your coven took her in after her family died. What kind of problems do blood moon witches have?"

"The *Gealach Fola* are *weak*," Rosheen hissed.

*Interesting*, he thought. *That got a bite.* "And who's stronger? Who could stand up to the Crescents and the fae and live to rule another day?" Her eyes widened slightly. "Give me some credit, Rosheen. I'm not just some stupid miner scratching around in the dirt. I did tell you us Exiles are family."

"When the Nightshade breaks free, we will kill you first," she hissed, struggling against the hold of Coen's talismans.

"Sounds like a party."

"The Ascendants will rise and squash your pathetic town and open the seal. You will all d—"

"Who are the Ascendants?" he interrupted, already over her ranting and raving.

Rosheen gritted her teeth. "A coalition of witches who are unsatisfied with how things are run...and who they align themselves with. The old ways are folly. There will be a new order."

Kyne sighed. She was a member of a terrorist organisation who hated the fae and wanted to dominate the witches. Where had he heard that before? Wars had been fought over that kind of oppression, so who was he to think that the supernatural were immune from their own racial power struggles?

"So, which is it?" he asked. "Cult or terrorism?"

Her scowl deepened. "You can never understand."

"Racism and oppression are all the same no matter what name you put on it or what parallel world it occurs in. I know Finn is innocent. He may be a smartarse with an attitude problem, but he's been living here in peace, never lifting a finger to harm anyone...especially not Vera." He leaned closer. "I'll ask you once more time. *Where is Finn?*"

"Why would you suffer a creature like him? He's a parasite, feeding on the very magic you're trying to keep locked away. *They don't belong in our world.*"

Kyne didn't react, he simply said, "He is a member of our family."

He was sure they'd done something horrible to him, but he hoped it wasn't too late. They needed him alive so they could tap into the magic bleeding from the seal. Rosheen hated him, but he was useful. That was the one thing that'd saved his life so far.

"If you could see what they've done," she began, her face reddening.

"Whatever," Kyne said. He stood and walked towards the door.

"That's it?" Rosheen asked. "That's all you've got?"

He lingered in the door and glanced back at her. "We're not monsters," he murmured, "which is more than I can say for you."

She shrieked as he walked down the hall, calling him foul names, the sound echoing off the rock and giving him a headache. By the time he got outside, he'd learned three new Irish slang words and the Gaelic word for bastard.

"She's a spirited one," Hardy said as Kyne stood next to him.

Outside, the sun had lowered from its summer apex, but the day was far from over.

"She's not talking," he murmured. "At least not about Finn."

Hardy narrowed his eyes. "I can't compel her, either."

"We're just going to have to keep searching and wait for Vera to..." he trailed off, his brow creasing.

The vampire put a chilly hand on Kyne's shoulder. "She'll win. It's Vera we're talking about here. If anyone can beat the Nightshade, it's her."

"I know."

"What else did she say?"

Kyne told him about Rosheen's affiliation with the

Ascendants and the real reason she'd come to Solace—power, dominance, revenge…it was all the same. The only difference in the witch's eyes was that the seal was a happy accident—a bonus prize to deliver to her extremist masters.

"I've known a lot of men who claim to be messiahs," Hardy said thoughtfully. "They spew out their hot air manifestos, but they're all the same in the end. They're inflicted with the curse of power and anger, humanity's worst and most dominant qualities." He glanced back at the dugout. "Power over the minds of their followers… It's true what they say about truth being in the eye of the beholder. Rosheen is a pawn in a game she likely doesn't understand, but if she does…"

"That's a problem for tomorrow," Kyne told him. "For now, we do what we can to help Vera and Finn."

"Speaking of, now that things are settled and we're not going to be murdered by crazed witch spirits, I'm going to head out and resume searching for Finn. He's got to be somewhere close." The vampire squinted at the horizon and took off his hat. "You should talk to the fae. They like you more than you realise."

Kyne grunted. "A resigned acknowledgement that I speak for Solace, nothing more."

"You sell yourself short, mate." Hardy clapped him on the shoulder. "I'm off. Take care of my hat for me. Can't wear it on the run, it just blows off. I've lost so many in the outback I've lost count…and I can't be bothered replacing any more."

Hardy was gone before Kyne could reply.

Shaking his head, he tossed the vampire's hat into the tray of his ute, then set off north along the trail in search of the fae camp.

He had to trust that Vera had the power to fight her demons, but he knew that if anyone could stand up to darkness and win, it was Vera Walsh.

---

Vera gasped for air, her eyes snapping open.

"Hey, it's okay," a familiar voice murmured. "You're safe."

"Drew?" She sat up, swatting away the shifter's hands.

"Vera?" Eloise asked, coming into view beside him. "Is that you?"

"I, uh..." She ran her hands over her body and shivered. She crackled with the afterglow of some serious magic, and her hair felt like it was full of grit. What in the world had she been up to?

She'd won the struggle for control—not that she remembered it—but the Nightshade still surged inside her, just below the surface.

"Where's Clarke?" she blurted. "It put him down a hole somewhere. I... *Oh God.*"

"We found him," Eloise reassured her. "He's fine. Hardy compelled him, and he's gone back to Lightning Ridge."

Vera squeezed her eyes shut. *Compelled?* He would've forgotten all about Solace, the seal...*her*. Not just what she'd done under the Nightshade's influence, but their date...his feelings. Problem was, *she'd* never forget.

Vera blinked, shoving her feelings aside. "Finn?"

Eloise and Drew glanced at one another.

She took a deep breath. "He's still missing, isn't he?"

"Do you remember what happened?" the elemental asked.

Vera scowled, wracking her misty thoughts for some kind of clarity, but found none. "No. I..." The Nightshade was hiding it from her.

"I smashed your altar," Drew said. "I know you said it was too late, but... It's all gone now. I got it out of the house."

Vera wasn't really listening. The altar was ruined anyway, so it was a good thing it was gone. Tossing the pile of junk would've been the first thing she did when she was strong enough. She'd have to build another one, or maybe she could do without.

"Rosheen," she murmured. "Where is she?"

"We've got her in my dugout," Drew replied. "Coen gave us a bunch of talismans to keep her magic bound. She's not getting out."

Vera threaded her fingers through her hair and massaged her scalp. Anything to soothe her headache.

There was a chance Rosheen wasn't acting of her

own volition. Vera had heard a lot of stories about the Ascendants, some of which chilled her to the bone. Some of it was likely overblown, but there had to be some truth rooted in the now-urban legends. Stories of brainwashing, parasitic control, dark rituals, and spirit attachments. As a blood-born member of the *Gealach Fola*—a coven who used blood in their rituals—Rosheen was susceptible to the Ascendants chosen form of doctrine. *That meant she could be saved.*

"I have to face her," Vera said, lifting her head. "I can enter the astral plain and confront her on equal footing. There's nowhere to hide there. Rosheen will be exposed, I can get the truth, find where Finn is, and sever the Nightshade from my Brinewold legacy."

Eloise frowned and glanced at Drew. "Is that wise?" she asked. "I mean, we destroyed your altar, but Rosheen was the one who triggered the Nightshade to take over..."

"Without the altar clouding my mind, I can hold back the Nightshade," Vera explained. "It's still there, but I can do this. *I have to.*"

"You said sever," Drew said.

She nodded. "I'm going to get rid of it once and for all."

"You can do that?"

"Theoretically."

Vera mulled over her options. There were other members of the Nightshade coven out there—though they'd been long stripped of their magic by the

Crescents—but only one who could channel the *actual* Nightshade legacy at any one time. If she severed herself from it, the spirit would return to the void and never bother them again.

There was only one problem with her plan. No one had ever tried, and even if they had, they'd probably hadn't lived to tell anyone about it—or the spirit had simply jumped to the next eligible coven member.

"Theoretically is not good enough," Drew exclaimed. "We haven't come this far to lose you."

"Too bad. I have to go now before…" She glanced at Eloise. "Do you understand?"

The elemental nodded, her expression grave. "One last battle, right?"

She laid back down and stared at the ceiling. "One last battle."

"You're going right here?" Drew cried. "Vera—"

Eloise grasped his arm and pulled him back. "Trust her," Vera heard her say as her eyes fluttered closed. "She knows what she's—"

The world faded round her, her mind separating from her physical body and floating beyond. She fell through nothingness, a place where no light touched, then soared amongst the dust of the universe—stars, comets, and the dark places in between.

Finally, her feet settled on the ground as her astral form took shape.

"Rosheen?" Vera called, her voice echoing amongst the stars.

The Nightshade was the thing she wanted the most. She'd come.

"Rosheen? I know you can hear me."

Silence.

Vera looked around, sensing someone else lingering. "Coen? Let her through, would you?"

The landscape changed, the light tinting the astral plain red as a blood moon rose, the crimson orb shimmering through a mirage of stardust.

Rosheen prowled out of the shadows, grinning as they met. Here, beyond the laws of the physical world, they were equal, or so the witch believed.

"A bold choice," Rosheen purred, channelling the manifestation of her magical legacy. "Meeting on the astral plain, beyond the control of the elements. Yes, bold indeed."

"It's past time we settle things between us," Vera said.

Rosheen prowled closer, the blood moon growing larger. "Legends say the Nightshade shows the vessel visions of their past as it wrestles for control." Her smile widened. "What did you see, Vera?"

Vera gritted her teeth, forcing the memory of the craglorn tearing apart her family as far away as she could.

"Oh, dear." Rosheen feigned shocked surprise. "You saw your them die again, didn't you?"

"It wasn't about their death. Why were they

casting?" she demanded. "Why were they using magic the day they died?"

"They were trying to hide you," Rosheen replied with a smirk. "At any cost. But it seems the price was too high even for the mighty Brinewold."

"Hide me? From whom?"

"From the Ascendants, of course."

Vera's expression faded. It seemed everything had come full circle...and it was up to her to end the cycle once and for all.

But what about Rosheen? If she went back with the Nightshade, they'd push her aside without reward—she was a means to an end. But if she went back empty-handed, they'd kill her.

"They're controlling you, Rosheen," Vera said. "Can't you see? They've cursed everything that's good about you and twisted your hatred of your coven for their gain. They're using you. They don't care, Rosh."

"I do this for the greater good, Vera. My life is a small price to pay for returning with the Nightshade."

"Rosheen, *no*. The Nightshade can never be tamed. It does what it wants. It has no master. If the Ascendants unleash it on the world, there will be more hell to pay than their single-minded struggle for power. I can't let that happen, Rosh. I will do whatever it takes to stop it from rising."

"You would sacrifice your life?" the witch scoffed. "What a *waste*."

"And you would sacrifice yours?" She threw her

hands into the air. "For what? Revenge is a fool's game. So is fuelling the flames of a pointless war that ended centuries ago. You won't die a hero or a martyr. You'll die for nothing."

"And what would you die for? You ran away from your own people!"

"The Ascendants have twisted you, Rosh. They have twisted you into something dark and awful, but I'm going to save you. The Brinewold will bring you home."

"The Brinewold is *nothing* while the Nightshade lives."

Vera readied herself. "That's why I'm going to start with this." She plunged her hand into her astral form and grasped the purplish-black shadow writhing inside her...and tore it from her body.

She stumbled, pain searing through her mind and into her physical body back in Solace.

"No!" Rosheen shouted, lunging for the swirling shadow as it dissipated. "It's not possible! *You can't—*"

"I just did," Vera interrupted, her mind sharpening. As she breathed in, she felt her lungs fill with the magic of the Brinewold—clean, clear, crisp, cleansing water. Her legacy rose like a tsunami, filling the dark spaces inside her, healing the deep scars the spirit had left in its frenzy to claim her soul.

Just like that, the Nightshade was gone. The Brinewold had healed her.

"No," Rosheen cried. "No!"

Vera reached towards her sister, guiding the waves towards her. "It's time to come home. Be free of the darkness. Let the water wash it all away."

The witch stared at her, dazed.

"I know your true self can hear me," she said. "Come home, Rosh. Let me show you the way."

Finally, she reached out for Vera's hand and took it. Their fingers entwined and magic flowed all around them, bringing them together. Above, the blood moon shattered, splintering into a million shards of shimmering crystal.

"Vera?" Rosheen blinked as if she was stepping out of the darkness and into the light for the first time in her entire life. "Vera, is that you?"

"You're free now," she murmured. "The Ascendants' hold over you is gone."

The witch tried to speak, but no words came from her lips. Reconciliation with her own heart would take time.

"The fae," Rosheen rasped. "He's in the water tank. He's…"

"Thank you."

"Tell him, I'm sorry. I…"

"It's time to go home," Vera murmured, placing her hand on her sister's cheek. "Go home to Ireland. The Crescents need to know about the Ascendants' plan. They need to know the Nightshade is finally gone. Warn them. They'll keep you safe."

Rosheen threw her arms around Vera. She held her

tightly and sobbed. "I'm sorry. *I'm so sorry.*"

"I have to make you forget me, Rosh," she said. "You know that, right?"

"Yeah." She sniffed as she drew back and wiped at her tears. "Even without the Nightshade, you're one of the most powerful witches Ireland has ever seen. Maybe even as powerful as the Crescents. They'd just try to corrupt you like they did to me."

"I'd come home, but—"

"You have a war of your own brewing." The astral plain shimmered around them. "Whatever the seal is holding down there, it's powerful. It needs to be protected."

They stood together for a moment, neither knowing what to say. Vera didn't know if there were any words to describe how she felt. She'd have to say goodbye to Rosheen forever, but maybe there was hope they'd see each other again one day. Perhaps.

The astral plain shimmered again, as if it was giving them a reminder.

"It's time," she murmured.

"I wish we had more than a minute or two."

"Maybe one day..."

"Go on then," Rosheen told her. "I've got a long drive ahead of me and you've got a fae to rescue."

"Goodbye, Rosheen," she whispered.

"*Slán...go fóill,* Vera." *Goodbye...for now.*

Vera placed her hands on her sister's face and let her turquoise magic do the work.

## CHAPTER 25

Eloise sprinted across the highway, her heart beating a million miles an hour. Drew followed close behind, his boots thudding on the ground like booming thunder.

The windmill and water tank sat beside the road as it always had—rusted, dilapidated, and a relic of another time. Abandoned, dilapidated... Why hadn't they thought of looking there in the first place?

Eloise scurried up the ladder, forgetting her fear of spiders and creepy crawlies. Wally had said it'd looked like something was living in there, but she'd thought he was joking. Maybe it was an omen. There'd been plenty of those over the last few weeks.

"Eloise, wait!" Drew called from below.

She didn't stop until she'd reached the top and found the hatch.

Wrapping her hands around the rusted handle, she heaved, pouring her elemental magic into the metal.

The rust flaked and fell away from the hinges, then metal scraped against metal.

The hatch opened and Eloise pushed her shoulder underneath and heaved with all her might, sending it flying over. It slammed against the top of the tank with a deafening bang, but she was falling to her knees, peering into the darkness.

"Finn?" she cried. "*Finn?*"

Light poured inside the tank, illuminating a hunched over body in the corner. Finn looked up, blinking furiously, his face grey and withered.

Eloise faltered, then shouted to Drew, "He's here! Finn's here!"

The fae seemed to focus on her and attempted a smile. "About time, desert pea."

---

The dawn of a new day saw Solace rise into the heat of the blistering summer, the dry season kicking off with a scorcher.

Vera stood outside the *Outpost,* the shade of the verandah shielding her pasty Irish skin from the excessive UV exposure.

Hardy had gone to Lightning Ridge to return Clarke's 4WD, Eloise was helping Finn recover, Drew was cleaning talismans and negative energy out of his dugout, Wally was recovering from last night's full moon, and Blue was tending the grill inside the pub. And Coen... Well, Coen was wherever Coen was.

That left Vera and Kyne to see off Rosheen. She wasn't offended that the others weren't here. It was probably for the best. The less the witch remembered of her time in Solace, the better.

"You've built yourself a hell of a life here, V," Rosheen said, embracing her. "Even though it's dusty and hot, I can see why you like it."

"Yeah?" she asked, drawing back. "And why's that?"

"It's a magical place." She glanced over her shoulder. "The sky, the land...the absence of people. All our business in Ireland is so far away. I can understand why you'd want to live in a place like this." Her gaze met Kyne's. "All of you."

The elemental nodded and hung back, letting the women say their goodbyes.

"I know I'll forget all about this place the moment I leave," Rosheen murmured. "I understand why, even though the Nightshade is long gone."

"I'm sorry I can't come with you."

The witch nodded and reached for her sunglasses. "You've been gone a long time. If the Ascendants knew where you were, they'd come. The last Brinewold is still a valuable prize."

She rolled her eyes and laughed. "Lucky me."

"Thank you." She glanced at Kyne, but he'd taken a few steps away and lowered the brim of his hat. "I don't know where I would've ended up if it wasn't for you."

"You don't need to thank me."

"I do, Vera. And I need to apologise. Not just for what happened here, but for the way the *Gealach Fola* treated you. For how I treated you. I was so jealous..."

"That was a long time ago, Rosh. We've both grown up since then."

Rosheen smiled and slipped on her sunglasses. "I don't think I ever did, but," she hugged Vera one last time, "now I have the chance to because of you." The witch hopped down off the verandah. "Oh, before I forget... The mountain from Eloise's vision. It spoke to me."

Vera glanced at Kyne.

"I can't remember what it said, only that it was something important," Rosheen went on. "Be careful, okay? I have a feeling it's not done with this place just yet."

"Thanks," Vera told her. "We will."

Rosheen nodded and got into the silver rental car. She started the engine and fiddled with the air conditioning, positioning the vents, then waved.

Vera lifted her hand as Rosheen reversed the car onto the highway, then took off south towards Lightning Ridge, where Kyne had helped her book a small chartered Regional Express flight to Sydney. From there, it was a thirty-hour marathon of airports and 747s back to Dublin.

Kyne waited with Vera as she watched Rosheen's car disappear over the horizon, shimmering through the mirage wavering on the highway. By now, her memory of Solace would be fading and soon, it would be gone entirely, never to return.

"What do you think that mountain thing is all about?" Kyne asked.

"No idea, but knowing our luck, it has something to do with the seal."

Kyne sighed and looked down the highway. "What will she do now?"

"She's going home to Ireland," Vera replied.

"What about the Ascendants? Won't they expect her to go back?"

"I've asked her to go to see the Crescents," she explained. "They're the reigning coven and what they say goes. They need to be warned. Their matriarch will know what to do."

Kyne grunted but said nothing.

"What?" She turned to face him. "You don't agree?"

"It's witch business, Vera," he told her. "I don't assume to understand any of it, but I trust you. Always have, always will."

She smiled, her exhausted heart fluttering a little.

"Wally sends his regards," he went on. "He's still recovering from last night's full moon."

"Another thing I need to apologise for," she murmured. She'd forced him to turn, but in doing so, had made his usual transformation all the more painful. Going from once a month to twice in as many days was a terrible drain on his strength...and Wally wasn't a young wolf anymore.

"He understands," Kyne told her. "He doesn't blame you. It was the Nightshade."

"For as long as I live, I hope I never hear that word again."

The elemental looked at her and smiled, placing a hand on her shoulder. "Me, too."

---

Vera walked, leaving Solace behind.

She moved towards the outback, her tired mind clearing from all the dust she'd stirred up. Before long, she had wandered all the way to the site of the ritual that'd forewarned her to the coming mess. A warning she'd chosen to ignore.

The site sat silently in the scrub. Not even the wind stirred the branches, as if it knew to leave this place alone and untouched, but even as Vera stood there, she knew it'd changed. The full moon had cleansed the land and the remnants of her magic were long gone.

Standing at the foot of the clearing, she saw a carved totem sitting in the centre. It leaned to one side, knocked askew by the tornado the Nightshade had risen in the town.

She squatted before the carved block of wood and studied the length of it. It had a little roof with an opening and holes along the length that were big enough for tea light candles to sit inside. It was an offering, one carved by an expert hand, but she hadn't left it.

"It's a *lor'ashlar*."

Vera looked up as Finn emerged from the scrub. He looked much better, though his skin was still a little blueish.

"I've heard of them before," she told him as she rose. "They're shrines to commemorate the dead, right?"

He nodded. "The dead are sacred to the fae. They demand respect always."

"I, um... I..." She couldn't meet his gaze. "I'm sorry about your snake. I, uh... I know how much she meant to you."

"*Ashlar an lor*," he murmured. "Honour the dead—"

"*Shride lei an val'ash*," she finished. "For they give us life."

"I was..." He hesitated and looked at the *lor'ashlar*. "I just wanted to pay my respects."

"I know." Vera smiled. "Taken out of context, your prayer could be offensive to a witch. That's what you're worried about, right?"

He nodded. "When I was trapped here—"

"You don't owe me an explanation, Finn," she interrupted. "I will never understand, but I know who you are."

"You do?" He blinked, lost for words in what she expected was the first time in his long life.

"Supernaturals come to Solace to start over," she said. "To leave behind the mistakes of their past and make peace with them. We all have secrets, Finn, but it's what we do today that matters."

Vera held up her hand and allowed her magic to gather on her palm. Turquoise pooled, the surface shimmering opalescent like oil on water. It grew and formed the outline of a snake—a death adder. A memory. An homage. *An apology.*

The fae's eyes widened. "Your magic..."

"I bring the water to this sunburnt country now," she murmured. "It extinguished the flame of the Nightshade. The curse is gone and now..."

"The land can flourish." Finn covered her hand with his, his own magic reaching out towards hers. *"A'ladrei,* Vera Walsh."

## CHAPTER 26

Eloise opened the door of the pub and stepped inside, escaping the searing rays of the sun.

Cool air blew against her flushed cheeks and she sighed blissfully. Air-conditioning. Blessed *air-conditioning.*

Kyne was right. Her van would be boiling over the summer, even with air-con. Actually, it already was. Maybe she should take him up on his offer of building them a dugout...and move in with him.

Spotting Finn sitting on his usual stool at the end of the bar, she went over to join him.

He looked up at her arrival, his silver gaze finding hers. "Well, if it isn't our little desert pea."

"You're looking much better," she said, sliding onto the stool beside his.

"Anything's better than being a withered, magic-starved husk," the fae drawled.

"How are you feeling?"

"Delightful."

"I'll take that as a positive."

"You know me so well." He said it in his typical dry fashion, but Eloise noticed the tiny smile tug at the corner of his mouth. "Are you still going to paint a mural on that tank? Can I recommend some jail bars?"

Eloise grimaced. "I think we should shelve that project. At least for now, hey?"

"Here you go," Blue said, setting a bowl before the fae. "I say you've earned 'em."

Finn wrapped his arm around the bowl of hot chips and drew it towards him. "Thanks."

"Strewth," the publican exclaimed. "I think that's the first time I've ever heard you say that."

Eloise laughed and spun around on her stool as the door opened, announcing the arrival of Kyne and Vera.

"Hey," she said, reaching out for the elemental, who kissed her on the lips. "How did it go?"

"Good," the miner replied. "The place is all cleaned out and cleansed."

"I went through my entire stash of sage," Vera stated, sitting at their usual table. "But all traces of the Ascendants and the *you-know-what* are gone."

"Good," Finn said, his voice muffled by a mouthful of potato.

The witch smiled, trying her best not to aim it at the fae, and thanked Blue as he put a jug of beer on the table.

Vera was just a Brinewold now, though Eloise felt a

little bittersweet on her friend's behalf. She'd had to give up her father's legacy in order to remove the Nightshade, and that couldn't have been easy for her.

"Drink up," Blue said, fetching a stack of glasses. "We need a celebration today."

Kyne handed Eloise a glass and began to pour. "I don't know about celebrating, but maybe we can raise a glass or ten."

"Where's the dog?" Finn asked. "He should be here."

There was a moment of stunned silence, then Kyne said, "He won't be far. He went over to collect Wally."

"Poor bloke's got sore bones after turning twice in two days," Blue said as he refilled the jug of beer. "Give 'em five."

The two men arrived not long after, Wally shuffling in with Drew propping him up so he wouldn't seize.

"Oh my goodness, *Wally*." Vera stood, her cheeks reddening.

"Don't worry yourself, love," he said, dismissing her with a wave as he sat. "My bones are a bit buggered right now, but I'll be right as rain tomorrow. I may be an old wolf, but I'm still a wolf. I heal fast...*ish*." He reached for the beer, but Drew knocked his hand away and poured him a glass.

The shifter had just sat down when Hardy appeared out of thin air, the pub door swinging closed.

"How did your trip down to the Ridge go?" Kyne asked the vampire. "No problems?"

"Smooth as a baby's bum," Hardy replied. "I learned something interesting, too."

"Don't leave us in suspense," Vera said a little thinly, but Eloise knew she was disappointed about having to let Sergeant Clarke go.

"The Dust Dog investigation in Solace is officially closed," he went on. "They found nothing of note up at the squat and have turned their attention elsewhere."

"I wonder how that happened," Kyne drawled, leaning back in his chair.

"*Magic*." The vampire grinned and poured himself a beer from the jug.

"So, there's one thing I don't understand," Wally began. "Who were the witches who controlled Rosheen?"

"The Ascendants are an ancient cult hellbent on the destruction of the fae," Vera explained. "They are the disciples of an evil witch whose racist manifestos triggered the closing the portals that trapped the fae here, leading to the creation of the craglorn."

"Craglorn?"

"Magic-starved fae," Finn told them. "Without a link to magic, we, uh...devolved." He glanced nervously at Eloise.

She gave him a small smile and nodded, letting him know she understood. She'd seen his face when she'd opened the tank.

"Are the Ascendants still out there?" Hardy asked.

Vera nodded. "They are, but after what I did to

Rosheen, they won't be bothering us. We've got enough to worry about without inserting ourselves in a war happening on the other side of the world. That's another story entirely."

"What happened to the evil witch?" Drew asked.

Vera's smile faded a little. "She got what was coming to her...even if it was a little too late for my family."

Drew leaned towards her, his brow creased. "What do you mean?"

Vera's cheeks flushed and she curled her hand around her glass. "They were trying to hide the Nightshade. I was the vessel..."

"They did it to protect you," Eloise murmured. "It wasn't anyone's fault."

"I know," Vera replied. "I wish they would've been honest with me about the Nightshade legacy and what they were doing to protect me from it...Maybe then I wouldn't have been such a little gobshite and helped them." She sighed. "But hindsight is twenty-twenty, right?"

"We're all safe," Hardy said. "And you're safe, Vera. That's all that matters."

"And so is the seal," the witch added.

"Maybe now we'll get some time to rest," Wally declared.

"Don't jinx it!" Eloise cried, making the Exiles laugh. "Quick!" She thrust out her hand, holding out her little finger. "Someone pinky swear!"

"She's gone mad," Finn said, staring at her in bewilderment. "What's a pinky swear?"

Kyne shook his head and hooked his little finger around hers.

"That was a close call," Eloise said, smiling up at the miner. "*Too close.*"

***

Vera strolled along the footpath, her dress swirling around her legs as she walked.

Lightning Ridge wasn't exactly the largest or the liveliest of towns, but it was virtually a metropolis compared to Solace.

They had everything a person could need, including the local battalion of opal miners. It boasted three caravan parks, a petrol station, a hardware store, bank, post office, supermarket, cafés, an art gallery, schools, a bowls club, a small airstrip, and more besides. It wouldn't be a terrible place to live, except she'd become used to Solace and her monopoly as the only local general store for two hundred-ish kilometres.

Approaching the bank, she lingered outside, pretending to sort through her purse.

The door opened and a tall man strode out, his police uniform blue and crisp, his hat shading his handsome eyes from the harsh summer sun.

*Right on time.*

She stepped forwards, colliding with the police officer, and let go of her purse so it tumbled spectacularly to the ground.

"*Oh no,*" she cried, dropping to her knees to scoop up the cards and coins that had scattered over the footpath.

"Bloody hell, I'm sorry." The police officer knelt in front of her, helping catch the small change that had rolled over the concrete. "Are you all right?"

"Don't worry, it was an accident." Vera smiled up at Sergeant Andrew Clarke, her heart fluttering. "I should've been watching where I was going."

The sergeant hesitated as his gaze met hers. "Pardon me, Miss...?"

"Walsh," she replied, holding out her hand. "Vera Walsh."

## DESERT FLAME
### *Australian Supernatural - Book Three*

**Vampires, convicts, and revenge plots. Who knew small town living could be so complicated?**

The Australian Outback is a vast landscape rich with natural resources, but it's an ancient land imbued with magic — some forgotten, and some just simmering underneath the surface.

Solace, the small opal mining town in outback New South Wales, has both.

But when big time mining company *EarthBore* sets up camp north of town, the Exiles are worried. There's no telling what kind of impact it will have on the seal they're protecting...and if it fractures, it could unleash a devastating power onto the world, leaving it in ruin.

The moment resident opal buyer and vampire Hardy looks into their new neighbours, he runs into an old acquaintance who makes one thing clear — their arrival is no coincidence. Solace has something they want, but the problem is, *Solace ain't selling*.

Hardy's painful convict past collides with the Exile's future in spectacular fashion, and as the threat grows, they will have to make their most difficult choice yet.

Stay protectors...or go to war.

# ABOUT NICOLE

**Nicole R. Taylor** is an Australian Urban Fantasy author.

She lives in the western suburbs of Melbourne dreaming up nail biting stories featuring sassy witches, duplicitous vampires, hunky shapeshifters, and devious monsters.

She likes chocolate, cat memes, and video games.

When she's not writing, she likes to think of what she's writing next.

## Follow Nicole Online:

*Website*: www.nicolertaylorwrites.com
*Facebook:* facebook.com/nrtaylorwrites
*Newsletter:* www.nicolertaylorwrites.com/newsletter
**Email:** nicole.this.is@gmail.com